NO RULES OF ENGAGEMENT

F
Richardson, Tracey.
No rules of engagement

DEC. 1 8 2009

MID-CONTINENT PUBLIC LIBRARY
Smithville Branch
205 Richardson
Smithville, MO 64089   **SM**

WITHDRAWN
FROM THE RECORDS OF THE
MID-CONTINENT PUBLIC LIBRARY

Tracey Richardson

Bella
BOOKS

2009

Copyright© 2009 Tracey Richardson

Bella Books, Inc.
P.O. Box 10543
Tallahassee, FL 32302

All rights reserved. No part of this book may be reproduced or transmitted in any form or by any means, electronic or mechanical, including photocopying, without permission in writing from the publisher.

Printed in the United States of America on acid-free paper
First Edition

Editor: Medora MacDougall
Cover Designer: Linda Callaghan

ISBN 10: 1-59493-159-3
ISBN 13:978-1-59493-159-8

To the unfinished journey.

MID-CONTINENT PUBLIC LIBRARY

3 0000 13157181 6

MID-CONTINENT PUBLIC LIBRARY
Smithville Branch
205 Richardson
Smithville, MO 64089

SM

Acknowledgments

Thank you to my wonderful support network of loved ones, whose love, patience and support make it all possible. Foremost I want to thank Cris for her selfless dedication, support and for pushing me further into new and fulfilling territory. This book would not have happened without her. Brenda and Stacey for telling me like it is and offering helpful suggestions. Maryann and Sue were there for me. Sandra, thanks for encouraging me to do all this way back when. A big hug to the Bella family for all their tireless work and support, in particular Karin Kallmaker. My editor, Medora MacDougall, thank you for sharpening my focus and my sentence structure! My hat is also off to the great cover art. Last but certainly not least, thank you so much to the women who read my books. *You* are my inspiration and motivation!

About the Author

Tracey Richardson is the author of *The Candidate* (*a Golden Crown Literary Society Award Finalist for Best Contemporary Romance*) and *Side Order of Love*. She grew up near the border city of Windsor, Ontario, Canada. Her day job is working as an editor at a daily newspaper, but she longs for the day when she can write full time. Visit www.traceyrichardson.net.

CHAPTER ONE

PART ONE
Kandahar, Afghanistan

Jesus, don't tell me I'm going to die before I even get there!
The irony and terribleness of the thought both horrified and amused Jillian Knight. It would be just her bad luck, she thought with surprising detachment, to die in a plane crash before her first experience with war and the people who called themselves warriors. To be killed before learning their stories and training her camera on them, her portfolio forever lacking the one thing any award-winning photojournalist craved—a stint in a war zone.

The descent was so steep and sharp, she had the sensation of her lips being pulled back to her ears. The skin of her cheeks hurt from the force of such unforgiving gravity. The plane, a no-frills, cold and noisy military transport, rattled in perfect synchronization with every bone in her body as it pitched forward—a seeming nosedive straight into the desert. There was no emotional detachment now as she prayed hard for the rivets to hold just a little longer.

The young corporal beside her laughed like it was a joke, and she wanted to pound him with her fists.

"This is nothing," he said, his nose twitching as though he could smell her fear. But his words weren't really meant to comfort. Her agitation was just another opportunity for him to mock her. "You should have seen how sharp the landings were before we realized the Taliban don't have proper surface-to-air missiles." His laugh was evil. "Christ, your balls would be around your ears."

She tried to scowl in his direction, but the bump of the landing gave her a final, hard jolt. They'd made it.

"Welcome to Kandahar Air Field," he mumbled sarcastically as they unbuckled. She had already introduced herself to him as a photojournalist—her first mistake—and from that moment on, he had tormented her with his stories and bluster. "Just remember what I said. If you hear the high-pitched whine of a rocket, hit the deck."

"Thanks, but I'm not sure how much I'll even be going off base," she answered, purposely vague. She would have to negotiate any forays off base, and the prospect of venturing into unpredictably dangerous territory alternately terrified and thrilled her.

"It's called 'outside the wire.' And it doesn't matter." He winked, and with his words her stomach dropped as if the plane were still in the air.

The heat, when she finally exited the plane, hit her like a wall. It sucked out her breath along with every drop of moisture in her body. She would have cursed except she couldn't muster the breath to do it. And then she wanted to curse again at how unaffected the other dozen or so civilians on the tarmac looked. Mark Kennedy, Jillian's best friend from her earliest memories and her trusted assistant, loosely slung his arm around her shoulders. There was not a single concern showing on his handsome, unshaven face, and for a moment it was as though they were back in high school in Michigan, dissecting one of Mark's football games, him cocky and totally unconcerned, her fretting over the score or a missed play. It was astonishing how little they'd changed in twenty years.

"Relax," he said indifferently. "We made it."

"Yeah, but will we make it out?" Jillian brooded quietly. Being in Afghanistan was a tremendous opportunity for her career. She just hoped like hell it wouldn't be her last.

"C'mon. It's only two weeks, Jill." He flashed her that toothy, boyish smile that still made women swoon. Luckily, she was immune. "Besides, we're going to shoot the best damn photo essay on war doctors that anyone's ever done before. Period."

"Yeah." She nodded confidently. "We are." He was right. There no longer existed the mobile hospital units that had become popular in Korea and World War II, where rough surgeries were performed practically right on the battlefield. War was different now. Permanent base hospitals, with their elaborate equipment and well-trained staff, provided the primary treatment. Improved evacuation methods and the fact that there were seldom "battlefronts" anymore had also changed the work of military doctors. Jillian's photo spread, she hoped, would show how much more advanced war medicine had become and, by extension, how many more lives were being saved because of it. She also hoped her photos would reveal something of the true personalities of the doctors and nurses who were sacrificing so much. They were among the unheralded heroes of war, and it was time to shine a light on them.

A lieutenant was handing out flak jackets and Kevlar helmets to the group, along with a stern lecture to wear them—often. As in all the time. Which was probably good advice, she had to admit as she surveyed her surroundings. The dusty steel, plywood and even canvas facilities looked anything but protective. Everything looked flimsy, transient, hastily constructed and extremely grimy. Her Gucci ankle boots were already well coated in fine brown dust, which was not unexpected but did annoy the hell out of her. Somewhere between London and Dubai her heavy work boots had disappeared into the vortex of lost luggage.

"C'mon," she said to Mark and fell in with the group. The lieutenant, a stony-faced middle-aged man, shepherded them toward a large metal hangar.

Conversing quietly among themselves, the new arrivals went where they were told. The hangar, hollow and battle-scarred, echoed with their footsteps and excited whispers. There were twisted bits of sheet metal every few yards, and bullet holes pockmarked the walls like Swiss cheese. Jillian wasn't scared. Not really, and in fact she couldn't wait to start taking photos of her surroundings. Her photography had taken her to many interesting corners of the world and had thrown her into some dicey situations—a week with the leader of a drug cartel in Colombia; a few days at one of Florida's hard-bitten women's prisons for a photo essay on women behind bars; her award-winning piece on a refugee camp in Darfur. It was the unexpected randomness of war, however, that gave her a slightly sick feeling in the pit of her stomach. Suicide bombers, improvised explosive devices, land mines, rocket-propelled grenade attacks, snipers. An enemy you couldn't see before it was too late. You could be dead before you even knew what hit you. *That* was some scary shit.

The lieutenant approached them. "I've got someone taking your equipment to the hospital." He glanced around, growing irritable. "Shit. I thought someone was supposed to meet you here."

Jill hadn't been given many advance details of what to expect, other than that she had pretty much been given wide-ranging permission to interview and photograph the medical staff at the Multinational Medical Unit, or "Role 3" hospital at the base. Anything beyond that, she would have to negotiate herself.

The lieutenant briskly strode to a wall phone and barked into it. She hoped the official welcome wagon was friendlier.

"Someone from the hospital will be along to get you," he said shortly. "You can wait here."

The others began to drift away with their soldier escorts. They were new civilian workers, a handful of print and television journalists, a couple of government types. They were easy to figure out. The civilian workers looked anxious, like they were starting their first day of school. The journalists were trying to look cool, as though they weren't worried about anything, while the bureaucrats looked a little jumpy and…soft. They'd been sitting behind desks too long, if the size of their guts was any indication.

She wondered how she and Mark must appear to the others—probably like an odd couple. Mark, the handsome, aging athlete, sandy-haired with the slightly unkempt look and quick grin of a surfer and the air of someone heading to the beach for the day. She, a little exotic looking, a little tense and much too sophisticated for all this dust and the detritus of war.

She thought of the old Chinese curse, "May you live in interesting times." This, for sure, would qualify. She couldn't honestly say at the moment whether such a fate was a blessing or a curse, but she had a funny feeling the answer would become clear soon enough.

Colonel Ron Patterson sat back in his chair with his hands clasped behind his head. He had the presumptuous look of someone who expected nothing less than full capitulation, which, of course, he had every right to expect. "It's your lucky day, Major Sharp."

Logan Sharp, one of a dozen doctors attached to the hospital of the MMU, had the distinct feeling it would be anything but. "Sir?"

The colonel looked from her to Captain Meg Atwood, one of the hospital's best nurses and also Logan's best friend. They'd arrived at KAF within days of each other ten months ago, and the warm connection had been immediate.

"You, too, Captain Atwood," he added with a trace of sarcasm.

Oh, shit, thought Logan.

"Two weeks leave, sir?" Meg shot back. She was lucky she'd made it to captain and would be even luckier if she held onto her rank. She constantly courted the threat of demotion with her sassy comebacks and her risky sexual exploits. She played dumb or careless about it, but Logan cringed every time Meg brought negative attention to herself.

The colonel's frown was so deep, Logan feared it might become permanent. "Hardly," he growled at Meg before his unwelcome attention shifted back to Logan. "There's a special photographer arriving later today. You may have heard the rumors."

Logan had, but she'd learned to discount rumors—particularly on a military base of ten thousand people—until they became fact. "What's this about, sir?"

"She's doing a photo spread on us for *National Geographic*. She and her assistant will be here for two weeks, and I've elected you...and by extension you"—he flicked a glance at Meg— "to keep them in your pocket the entire time. They'll be embedded with us."

"Sir?" Great, Logan thought irritably, conjuring for herself a mental image of someone constantly cramming a camera in her face and following her every move like some eager and obnoxious puppy. "Are you serious?"

"Of course I'm serious." His thick hands dropped heavily to his metal desktop. "Do you think you'd be here if I wasn't?"

"No, sir." She wanted to roll her eyes but knew Patterson would have her head if she did. Not only was he in charge of running the hospital, he was the only neurosurgeon on staff. Working with him was already difficult at times. Pissing him off would make it just about impossible. "What exactly would you like me to do, sir?"

"Babysit, for one thing. Work some public relations magic for another. Christ, Major Sharp, make them feel important. Welcome. *National Geographic* is great exposure for our unit, but I also want to make sure they don't get in our way, so you'll need to manage them."

Fuck. She went through med school and residency and had spent more than three years in the military so she could *babysit*?

Logan tried to rein in her exasperation. She cleared her throat and said with all the neutrality she could muster, "Wouldn't you rather have Newman or Brown front and center? Or even Thorson?" They were surgeons, while she, Logan, was much lower on the food chain as an ER physician. Surgeons would seem much more exotic, more exciting to an accomplished photographer. And if it would get these pests out of her hair...

Patterson put a quick end to her diversion tactics. "Major Newman is as cranky as a bear with a sore ass even on one of his good days."

Meg let out a snort.

"Major Brown is absolutely phobic about any attention, and Captain Thorson is too new here. So that brings me to you, Major Sharp."

The handful of other doctors on base were all civilians, which meant she was most definitely stuck. The chain of command would want someone in the Forces keeping a close eye on any embedded journalists. Logan bit her bottom lip until it stung, and she stole a glance at Meg, who seemed far too happy about it all. Meg was the one who should be squirming on the hot seat, not Logan. *Must be nice to have such a short memory, Meg.*

"We want to put our best face forward with this. I don't have to remind you that support for the mission is flagging back home. I want someone for this assignment who's competent. And nice. Someone who won't embarrass us or make us look bad. And you, Major, are *nice.*"

He said it almost as if it were a bad thing, but she knew her superior had a quiet, if unspoken, respect for her.

"What about me?" Meg interrupted haughtily. Logan nearly fell off her chair at Meg's brazenness—or stupidity.

The colonel scowled at her, which, of course, had zero effect on Meg. "Don't push your luck, Captain Atwood. Consider this assignment a little test. You'll be Major Sharp's backup in the hand-holding department, and this time you're going to be a perfect angel." He leaned menacingly over his desk. "You fuck up and you'll be cleaning bed pans for the rest of your mission."

Meg tried to look chastened, which was laughable to Logan. She knew Meg wasn't the least bit concerned. The military was Meg's career, but she was cocky because she knew there was always a shortage of nurses in the regs.

"Look," Patterson directed his words at Logan, softening his tone. "What we do here is not just about the surgeries and all the glory stuff. They want a full picture of the base hospital. I want you to give them that, including taking them out to that polio clinic you've set up for tomorrow. It'll make for some great PR."

"I can take them off the base, sir?" Logan was a little surprised. She knew the dangers well.

"At your discretion, Major."

"Yes, sir. Anything else?"

Patterson stood. "Go ahead and make their lodging arrangements and collect their security passes. Then you can go and collect *them*. They should be arriving any minute." He pushed a few pages across the desk toward her. "Here's a debriefing on what they're trying to accomplish here, as well as what *we* want them to accomplish. As far as I can see, they're pretty much the same. Just make sure they stick to making us look like saints."

Logan stood too. "Yes, sir." *Saints?* Okay, he was definitely kidding.

Meg slipped out the door, but the colonel held Logan back with his hand on her arm.

"Major, a word?"

"Of course." Logan closed the door. They both remained standing, signaling the discussion would be brief.

"It's about Captain Atwood." The colonel spoke in low tones, as though Meg might have her ear glued to the other side of the door, which Logan actually wouldn't put past her. "I don't need to remind you what happened the last time Atwood was assigned a civilian to keep under her wing."

Logan stilled herself, remaining calm. Goddammit, why did *she* have to get swept into Meg's messes? Logan swallowed, wishing not to remember the minor calamity Meg had brought on herself by getting caught having sex with a visiting Associated

Press news reporter. "Yes, sir," she said plainly.

Patterson's eyes were grave. "This is a little test for her—and for you, too. Consider yourself not only the keeper of this photographer, but Captain Atwood's keeper as well. We're a team in this hospital. And we're professionals. We cannot have Atwood continue to be a blight on us, particularly where outsiders are concerned. You are to ensure that doesn't happen. Is that understood?"

Great, Logan thought. She'd tried to be a big sister to Meg or at least the voice of reason to her reckless, often cavalier friend. Now she was officially responsible for her for the remaining two months of their tour.

Logan nodded curtly, saluted and nearly collided with Meg in the hall. She frowned at Meg, still feeling pissy about her dual assignment, and removed the green dress beret of the Canadian Army, tucking it safely under her arm.

She'd put on her pale green, starched dress shirt and pressed forest green slacks for the meeting with the colonel. Meg, as usual, was wearing scrubs, but Logan was a stickler for protocol. Another obvious difference between them.

"So, were you getting a pep talk from Patterson? Some secret assignment I'm not ranked enough for?" Meg was grinning, but fishing nevertheless. "Let me guess, I'm up for nurse of the month!"

Logan frowned, shook her head. She wanted to laugh but didn't dare. "Behave yourself, Atwood, and that's an order." *Boy, is it ever.* Logan felt like adding "please" but didn't. She didn't want to be the heavy with Meg and hoped it didn't have to come to that.

"Anyway, I know I'm not as *nice* as you," Meg said, thankfully moving the conversation along. "But do you want me to pick these two up and give them the ten-cent tour of the base?"

"I'll do it," Logan answered wearily, the thin sheaf of papers from the colonel in her hand.

"Oh, come on, ya grouch." Meg slapped her lightly on the shoulder. "It's kind of exciting, don't you think? And it's your big

9

chance to get famous, after all."

Logan tried for a withering look. "I'm not looking to be famous. And neither should you."

Meg grinned as they walked toward the staff lounge. "Being famous could have its upside. Think of all the women after you."

Logan raised her head and gave her friend another scorching look. The woman was incorrigible. "I'm not looking for that, either."

"Your loss."

Meg was always on the lookout for love—or its facsimile. A career military nurse, she had been in a long-term relationship that broke up just before she shipped out, and now she appeared to be making up for lost time. She'd take it wherever and whenever she could, and not always discreetly, even though she claimed she tried to be. By law, the Canadian military wasn't allowed to discriminate against gays any longer. There was no "don't ask, don't tell" policy. As a government branch, the military was not allowed to deny gays and lesbians entry, nor deny them promotions or any other rights on the job. In fact, they had to pay benefits and pensions to their same-sex partners now, but it didn't mean they were about to throw them a tea dance. Meg flaunted her sexuality, or maybe she just didn't care, since it was her God-given right, but the military was still a conservative, old-boys institution. Logan was sensitive to that, along with the strict rules against fraternizing with people below your rank. Following the written and unwritten rules was her handy excuse to rebuff Meg's offers of double dates. That was easier than explaining that she just could not bring herself to get involved in meaningless or transient relationships. She was content with her life of celibacy, but explaining that to Meg would be like speaking to her in a foreign language.

Logan thrust the papers at Meg. "Why don't you read these to me while I get ready."

Meg sighed unhappily but obeyed. The point of the photo essay, the brief summary said, was to show the work of medical staff at a military base in a combat zone. The photographer and her assistant had been given carte blanche permission to stay at KAF for two weeks and to photograph and write whatever they wanted. There was some fine print, of course, about protecting the privacy of patients if they were NATO troops—they would have to blur or crop their faces out if there was anything graphic—and they had to obey the staff. "Hmm, the obeying part I like," Meg quipped.

Logan dialed in the combination of her locker and reached for her sidearm. She didn't wear it at the hospital, but the base rules dictated that all soldiers must carry a weapon on base, and so she did whenever she left the hospital, even if it was for a cup of coffee. Although she was a physician by profession, to the military she was a soldier first. "Anything else?"

"The photographer sounds interesting." Meg, a few inches shorter, leered up at Logan, who was snapping her holster onto her belt. "Jillian Knight. She's thirty-six, from Michigan. Graduated from Columbia University. She won a Pulitzer Prize for a photo essay in Darfur three years ago. It was for *Newsweek*."

Meg whistled. "She sounds impressive."

Logan attached her pager to her belt as well. "The name or her credentials don't mean squat to me." She hadn't expected them to. She paid little attention to photo essays in glossy magazines. She read newspapers and books religiously, as well as the never-ending pile of medical journals that crammed her mail every week. If she had ever happened to notice a really good photo, she couldn't remember ever looking to see who'd taken it.

Meg's eyebrows shot up suggestively. "Well, with luck, she'll be good looking at least."

"Atwood, you're impossible." Logan sighed, full of pretend contempt. She wasn't truly annoyed; she found Meg amusing and refreshing. They were opposites in so many ways—Meg the extrovert with a devil-may-care attitude and a biting wit, Logan much more careful and reserved. Meg was extremely loyal, though, and a damned good nurse. Logan was grateful for their friendship. If only Meg would behave for the rest of their tour, it would make life easier for both of them. She would need to have a serious chat with Meg—again. She couldn't begin to count the friendly warnings and advice she'd already given her to be more careful, to not draw such attention to herself, but this time she would need to put more weight behind it. There was just no time to do it right now.

Logan closed her locker before claiming a set of keys for one of the Jeeps at their disposal. "I could care less what she looks like, as long as she doesn't drive us all nuts."

"You don't fool me, Major Perfect. You can't tell me you don't want someone good to look at around here—besides me, of course. Fresh eye candy would be a godsend right about now."

Logan shook her head, but a smile inevitably escaped. "I'd be immune to it anyway."

"I know. You'd do well to take a page out of my book once in a while."

"Or not. So what's the assistant's name? Let's not leave him out of the admiration society."

"Oh, Logan." Meg pinched her cheek affectionately. "You are so damned *nice*. Always thinking about others. Were you class president or something?"

"Shut up, Atwood."

Meg laughed, calling out as Logan strode off, "Mark Kennedy is his name."

Logan waved without turning around. "Go pick up their security passes for me, would you?"

With one look, Jillian knew the young officer was a major. There were three bars on her epaulets—the two outside ones wide, the middle one narrow. Jillian had memorized the rank insignia of both American and Canadian military personnel, since the base was filled with both, with a smattering of Dutch, Australian and British troops thrown in. The Canadians actually ran the hospital, and so she noticed right away the small red maple leaf embroidered on the shoulders of the major's crisp dress shirt.

The major leapt out of the open Jeep and strode briskly to them, looking neat and fresh, a miracle in this heat. She stuck out her hand after succinctly introducing herself as Major Logan Sharp. She handed them their security passes and a little handbook that probably spelled out the house rules in agonizing detail.

"We get a major as our tour guide?" Mark blurted out. "Cool."

A tiny frown was there and gone in an instant. The major's face was unreadable as she replied, "Tour guide, assistant and keeper, all in one. I'm also one of the physicians at the hospital here."

Relief swept through Jillian. She was glad they hadn't been stuck with a low ranker—someone with no influence or power and whose head she would have to constantly go over if she wanted something. Having a senior officer assigned to her meant the powers-that-be had taken her assignment seriously. "It's a pleasure, Major Sharp. I'm Jillian Knight and this is Mark Kennedy. By the way, do we refer to you as Doctor or Major?"

Major Sharp smiled dutifully. She certainly had politeness down to a science. "My pleasure as well, Ms. Knight. The protocol goes either way, Major or Doctor." She studied Jillian and Mark, her expression still perfectly blank, and it occurred to Jillian just how good these military types were at masking emotion. "By the end of your stay you might even be calling me Logan. We'll see how it goes." She narrowed her eyes a little, and Jillian guessed it was an attempt to be a little playful, but she couldn't be sure. Perhaps she was even daring them to ingratiate themselves. *We'll see about that, Major Logan Sharp.*

Jillian flashed a smile perfected in the course of cajoling her subjects into all sorts of poses and levels of cooperation over the years. More than that, enticing them to be open and candid with her. She had melted much tougher customers than this one. "I'm sure you'll find us nothing but cooperative. We want this assignment to really be something special." She shot a look at Mark that told him he'd better not make her eat her words.

"Right, Mark?"

"Wouldn't dream of anything else," Mark answered automatically.

"Would you care for a tour?"

"Do you have the time?" Jill asked eagerly.

"Sure." The major's hazel eyes held no hint of artificiality, and Jill decided she was a straight shooter—that she could be trusted and would be honest with them. The gods are on my side here, Jillian thought with bemusement.

"That sounds perfect, Major Sharp." Jill decided to use military rank. Since they were on a base, she would be addressing people by their ranks for the next two weeks. She might as well get used to it.

Mark tossed the backpacks they'd brought with them into the back of the Jeep and vaulted into the backseat. Jill climbed in beside the major, the tiny effort making her sweat more in the crushing heat. *Jesus. How do people here stand it?*

"I'm sorry, Major." Jillian couldn't help the whiney tone in her voice. "But this body armor makes it ridiculously hot. Do we really need to wear it?"

Logan smirked. "You should see it in July around here. It gets past sixty in the day. Even the nights are well above thirty."

Jill struggled with the mental calculation. Logan, a Canadian, was using Celsius, and Jill's metric skills were almost nonexistent. If sixty were hotter than this, she concluded, it must be extremely hot. In which case, she was very glad it was March and not July.

"Sorry," the major apologized. "That means about a hundred and forty in Farenheit."

It was marvelous how Logan Sharp seemed to read exactly what was going through her mind. Jillian indulged in the fantasy of getting answers before she even had to pose the questions. *Talk about a journalist's dream!*

"And to answer your question, yes. You need to wear that armor whenever you're wandering around out here."

"But *you're* not," Mark noted as the Jeep lurched ahead.

"You're right, I'm not, Mr. Kennedy." She gave Jill a sideways glance. There was surprisingly no air of superiority in her look or her voice. "When I signed my name on my induction papers almost four years ago, I consented to these risks. You did not."

Jillian gave a nod of agreement before checking on Mark, who sat hunched in the backseat. His defiance was gone—for now. He wasn't exactly an angel when it came to respecting authority, and Jill wanted to chuckle. At KAF, they were absolutely surrounded by authority figures, and their freedom would be tightly controlled. They were chattels of the military now, and they would play by their rules, whether they liked it or not. Major Sharp was probably being nicer about it than she needed to be.

There was gravel and sand everywhere on the flat, endless surface that was the base. There were mountains in the distance— big, brown, majestic ones and smaller ones, too, that seemed to sprout out of nowhere. But the immediate landscape was dotted with rows and rows of ugly buildings—domed tented ones, others that looked like giant sheds made of sheet metal, shipping containers, even a few concrete block ones.

Major Sharp pointed to one of the squat, cement buildings. "That's a bunker. There's some every few hundred yards. If you hear a warning siren, get into one of those as fast as you can."

"Does it happen often?" Jill swallowed. "The sirens?" What she really meant was *attacks*.

"Not really. A few times a week."

The answer was as casual as if Jillian had asked what time dinner was served, but Logan's indifference was hardly reassuring. A few times a week was a few times too many.

"Don't worry," Logan added with an enigmatic smile. "They're usually pretty tame."

Mark grunted in disbelief in the backseat, and Jill could tell he was no longer in a buoyant mood about being here. The Boy Scout adventure had worn off—at least for now.

"How long has this been your home, Major Sharp?" Jillian needed to change the subject.

"Ten months so far."

That was a long time to live in such ugly surroundings. The

absence of beauty surprised Jill. There were few trees, almost no greenery, no natural bodies of water. She knew from what she'd read that not all of Afghanistan was like this, but the base certainly was. Perhaps, she thought, studying Logan's profile, the people here were too busy to notice. They were here to work, after all, and the military didn't like distractions. "How much longer are you here?"

Logan smiled fully, and Jillian decided she was both pretty and handsome in an androgynous way—strong jawed and straight nosed, but with very much a feminine, sensuous mouth. She had a great face as a photo subject with those strong, symmetrical lines. Her hair was short and wavy, light brown. Her eyes were certainly to die for—alternately green and foggy gray, and Jillian was sure the young major had a full stable of admiring men...or women.

"Just a couple more months unless I decide to extend it," Logan answered. "Most of the Canadian troops are here for six-month rotations, but at the MMU, it can be anywhere from three months to eighteen months. My tour right now is for a year."

Jill turned away from the cloud of dust kicked up by a passing dump truck. There were loud, smelly, diesel-powered vehicles everywhere—tractors, front-end loaders, trucks of all types. She wondered how Logan truly felt about being here so long—the spartan surroundings, the noise and stink and dust, the threat of attacks, and, she knew from all she'd read, the too-frequent casualties, both military and civilian. Maybe, she thought, studying Logan's profile again, she would tell her about it some time. But then again, Logan looked a little on the hard-core military side, with her emotions firmly in check and her rules unbendable. Jillian would need to gain her trust if she expected her to reveal much of herself.

"That's our famous boardwalk." Logan pointed to a long, U-shaped covered boardwalk that ringed what looked like a hockey rink, complete with boards and lights.

Mark perked up immediately. "Is that a hockey rink?"

Logan laughed. "Yes. It's perfect that it's right in front of the

Canadian compound. It was all our doing, of course."

Mark beamed, barely able to contain himself. "Do you play, Major?"

"Every chance I can."

Mark gave Jillian a playful tap on the shoulder. "A woman after my own heart. I like it."

Logan stopped the Jeep but made no move to get out. "Later, you can check these places out on your own. But on the boardwalk you'll find a pizza joint, a couple of coffee shops, a general store, that kind of thing. There's even a sit-down restaurant."

"Do we eat at the restaurant or with you guys?" Mark asked.

"You can eat here if you want, but as our guests, you have full access to our dining hall. The DFAC is just ahead."

"DFAC?" Jillian asked, her stomach twisting at the prospect of eating institutional food for the next two weeks.

"Dining facility," Logan answered patiently. "The food's actually quite good."

Jillian smiled her response. *There she goes again, reading my mind.*

"Is it all you can eat?" Mark asked enthusiastically, his thoughts clearly on his stomach.

"Pretty much, yeah, but you'll have to fight your way through a line of some very hungry soldiers."

Mark grinned, his cocky self again. "I've played a lot of football and hockey. I can take care of myself."

Jillian rolled her eyes. She didn't doubt that within a day or two Mark would be hanging out with the soldiers, swapping sports stories, talking about what was going on back home, acting like one of them with all his swagger and easy humor. He was a guy's guy, in spite of his long and intense friendship with Jillian. They'd dated centuries ago, when they were teenagers, before drifting naturally into friendship. They were far better friends than lovers.

An explosion, somewhere distant, rang out, followed closely by the piercing wail of the warning siren.

"Ah, shit," Logan yelled. "Let's get to that bunker. Follow me."

She burst out of the Jeep, head down, and dashed off toward one of the squat, concrete structures a few dozen yards away. Mark easily kept up, but Jillian struggled a little. She was fit, but she was no athlete. Just then, a rocket whistled overhead, a short, thin stream of red light trailing behind it. It was all the incentive Jillian needed to move faster than she ever had in her life. She heard herself yelling "fuck" over and over, like a prayer or mantra. It was amusing, she thought a moment later as she sat breathless in the shelter, how she'd recognized instantly they were under attack by a rocket launcher, even though she'd never experienced anything like it before. It reminded her of the time she'd gotten caught in an earthquake in Central America. She had known immediately and with helpless clarity exactly what the noise and shaking meant. It was as though the body was keenly attuned to identifying immediate physical threats, even without prior experience.

"Hear that?" Logan asked.

Jillian heard the rhythmic thwacking of helicopter blades in the distance.

"That's the Apaches going out to have a look. They'll be back in a few minutes, and then we'll get the all-clear."

"Do you get used to them?" Jill asked, her heart rate finally returning to normal.

"The attacks? No. You don't ever want to get used to them," Logan answered coolly, and Jillian knew immediately what she meant. *Taking your safety for granted here could get you killed in one hell of a hurry.* But the major seemed so calm, as though she fully expected everything to turn out just fine. *Maybe that's the key to staying sane. Be ready, expect its inevitability, but trust you will be okay.*

Mark was sitting so close to Jillian their shoulders touched.

"This place reminds me of that old tree house in my neighbor's backyard. Where we first fooled around, remember, Jillsy?" He bumped her playfully.

Oh, God. Jillian felt her cheeks grow warm with embarrassment. He always did this sort of branding thing when he felt there was competition. He'd done it with Steph, too, when she and Steph had first got together. It was his way of intimating that they had a long and unbreakable bond—that he was important in her life. That they had *history*. Her more cynical side knew it was also his little way of trying to control her, protect her, even though he knew damned well she could take care of herself. That he would do this little act in front of Logan Sharp, whom they barely knew, bewildered her. She raised her eyes to Logan, who held her gaze with a curious, mildly amused look. *She is wondering just what the hell we are to each other*, Jillian realized, and it gave her a tiny and inexplicable flicker of excitement.

Jillian turned to Mark with a piercing glare. "It's also where I popped you in the nose when you tried to go too far. Remember that, *Markie*?"

"Yeah," Mark muttered, unconsciously rubbing his nose.

She noticed Logan's eyes drop to her ring finger in the quickest of glances, and Jillian suppressed the surprising sensation of wanting to explain. *Christ, she must think I'm married to Mark.* Not that it would be an unreasonable assumption under the circumstances, but she wanted Logan to know her companion was a woman, that the gold band on her finger didn't mean she was married to a man. Jillian was a private person, but explaining her situation to Logan mattered for a reason she couldn't name. The compulsion made no sense, so she resisted.

"Is the hospital ever attacked?" Jillian decided to change the topic.

"Occasionally. Not often."

"What do you do with the patients?"

"Are you interviewing me, Ms. Knight?" Logan asked mildly, the smallest hint of a smile at the corner of her lips.

"Not at all," Jillian answered smoothly. She wanted to avoid official interviews as much as possible, especially early on. She still needed to get her bearings, to get a feel for the people who would be her subjects. She knew instinctively that Logan would never be completely comfortable with her if she thought she was always on the record. "Just curious, that's all."

"It is mostly a photo essay you're doing, right?"

"I'll write a few hundred words to accompany the photos. Nothing major, but I will be interviewing you at some point. Will that be a problem?" Jill hoped Logan wouldn't start getting nervous and clam up on her. Cultivating cooperation would take precious time and effort away from her photography.

"No, but I expect you to tell me when we're on the record."

"Of course, Major Sharp."

"Thank you." Logan pointedly studied Mark. "What is your role here, Mr. Kennedy?"

There was the barest hint of a challenge in her tone, and Jillian cringed, hoping Mark didn't pick up on it. He was a little sensitive about Jillian's accomplishments. He was a news photographer, too, but far less successful than she was. He was good, but he was not at her level. And while they'd worked past much of this years ago, she knew his pride still stung sometimes over being her assistant.

"Well," Mark said, a touch contemptuously. "I'm her pack mule, gopher, secretary, good luck charm *and* bodyguard." He was purposely being a prick, marking his territory like a dog.

Crap. If these two were going to be like oil and water, she'd have to play mediator and be a buffer—again more precious time away from her work.

Logan stared at him for a long moment with her own brand of intimidation, then broke into a slow smile that would have melted the toughest foe. "I could sure use one of those. What are you doing when she doesn't need you?"

Jillian felt Mark relax beside her. *Thank you, Lord.*

"I'm always open to offers," he supplied quickly, and that pivotal moment of whether the three could work together or not had passed. *For now.*

The all-clear siren pierced the air.

"I'll let you two do some more exploring of the base later," the major said. "You're probably exhausted anyway."

That was an understatement. First they'd flown from Detroit to Heathrow and then to Dubai before catching a military transport to Kandahar. Jillian could use a long nap, but she was also anxious to get a feel for the base. The sooner she did that, the sooner she could get to work.

"I am pretty tired, Major, but I would love a quick tour of the hospital."

Logan slipped her beret back on. Jillian hadn't noticed her slip it off. Perhaps on the run to the shelter? "You're sure you're up to it?"

Jillian glanced briefly at Mark before agreeing to it.

"I'm game for it," he added. "Besides, I'm starving more than I am tired. When do we eat?"

Logan shook her head and smiled. "Let's check out the hospital, then I'll show you where you'll be lodged. *Then* we can have dinner."

The hospital didn't look very impressive. Made of plywood and steel with shipping containers for washrooms, it was nevertheless a source of pride to Logan. Despite such spartan conditions, the hospital's one hundred and twenty staff members were equipped to do everything from perform surgeries to conduct tests such as ultrasounds and X-rays. And they did all of those things very well. There were two operating rooms, a state-of-the-art CT scanner, an ICU ward, an outpatient area and even a tent for overflow patients. Conveniently located beside the runway to make for brisk transfers from the med-evac helicopters, the hospital was the best equipped in the entire province of Kandahar. Besides serving the thousands of NATO military troops in the province, it also provided care to Afghan army and police units and even some civilians.

"It's not exactly the Mayo Clinic," Logan said by way of an excuse. "But it does what it was designed to do."

Logan hadn't exactly been a crack trauma physician when she'd joined the army, but she could handle just about anything that came through the doors now—chest tubes, tracheotomies, severed arteries. It was her job to stabilize casualties before the surgeons got them or to make the kind of repairs that didn't require surgery. The critically injured, once stabilized, were usually flown to Landstuhl, Germany, ten hours away.

Logan's colleagues were excellent. They were dedicated, inventive, versatile. They could do some amazing work under extreme conditions, but better to let Jillian Knight and Mark Kennedy come to their own conclusions. She wouldn't "sell" herself or the hospital. It was what it was, and what conclusions this award-winning photojournalist came to were beyond Logan's control. If Jill was smart and observant and objective—and Logan suspected she was—she would quickly appreciate the hospital and its staff.

Jillian asked questions about lighting and where they could set up, and Logan went over the ground rules, discussing privacy issues and reminding them to stay out of the way as much as possible.

"It gets crowded in a hell of a hurry," Logan said. "And when the team is under stress, they can get a little…short. You won't be told things nicely when that happens."

Jillian nodded, and Logan tried to gauge the photographer's intentions. Would she try to take award-winning photos at any cost, or would she be patient and work with them? Would she blend in, know her place, stay in the background? Was she interested in them as people and not just as subjects? Would she take the trouble to really understand their work at the hospital? Logan could only hope so. She and the others would invest two weeks of their time in Jillian Knight and Mark Kennedy. And not just time. There would be an emotional investment as well. On display would be their fears, their disappointments, their victories, their strengths and their weaknesses.

God, why didn't I give Patterson a harder time over this?

Logan stared into Jillian's wide-set, brown eyes—so dark they were almost black—and searched for answers.

It was at that moment Meg Atwood rounded a corner carrying a tall stack of hospital gowns and nearly collided with them.

"Jesus, Atwood," Logan grumbled, straightening herself. She hadn't realized she'd put her arm out protectively in front of Jillian, but Jillian had definitely noticed, because she was frowning at Logan and moving away as though she'd just received an electrical shock.

Meg, meanwhile, was looking far too smug. It was obvious that she, too, had noticed Logan's instinctive, protective gesture, and Logan could see in Meg's eyes that she was itching to engage in a relentless round of teasing. *Oh, yeah. I'm not going to hear the end of this anytime soon.*

Logan's face grew warm. It was like she'd been caught at something, and she glowered at Meg even as she kept her voice neutral. "Captain Atwood, this is Jillian Knight and Mark Kennedy. Ms. Knight, Mr. Kennedy, Captain Atwood is one of our charge nurses. In fact..." She felt a mischievous smile spring to her lips. "If there's anything you ever need, and you can't find me, Captain Atwood would love to help."

Meg had Jillian strictly in her crosshairs as she homed in on her with her free hand and her interested eyes. "Of course I would be happy to help, Ms. Knight. Any time." Meg's glance swept appreciatively and unapologetically over the photographer, and Logan's patience dropped a dangerous notch. *Christ.* She did *not* want to spend the next two weeks keeping Meg from flirting with Jillian. In fact, the image of Meg trying to get close to Jillian, telling her little jokes, touching her arm conspiratorially as she whispered amusing little stories to her made Logan feel an inexplicable but undeniable anger. They were professionals, all of them, and there was important work to be done here. She did not want Meg cheapening herself, and by extension Logan, with her libidinous behavior. Not to mention that Meg had been effectively put on notice by the colonel. As much as she hated it, Patterson was right in forcing Logan to ensure Meg cleaned up her act.

Logan sighed loudly, wanting to kick Meg's ass but knowing now was not the time or place. She noticed Mark suspiciously eyeing Meg. He'd placed his arm possessively around Jillian's shoulders before stepping closer. What was with that possessiveness of his, anyway? Were he and Jillian an item? Married? She'd noticed the ring on Jillian Knight's left hand, though he didn't wear one. It didn't seem like they were a couple and yet…somehow it did.

Meg quickly shifted her charm to include both guests and was now inviting them to watch the hospital's ball hockey team play in a couple of nights. Logan took a slow, deep breath, relieved that Meg seemed to be getting a clue for once. Logan might not trust her with her girlfriend, if she had one, but she would certainly trust Meg with her life. As silly and over the top as she sometimes got, deep down Meg was one of the best soldiers and nurses Logan had ever worked with.

"Has Major Sharp shown you to your quarters yet?" Meg asked with a pointed look at Logan.

Bitch, Logan wanted to say, knowing full well what that look meant. The only available spot in the women's section of the hospital barracks was the second cot in Logan's cubicle. It had been vacant since her blood technician roommate shipped home a couple of weeks ago.

"I was just about to do that," Logan answered as innocently as she could, even as her eyes fired daggers at Meg. She knew Meg would have fun with this for a while, would tease her relentlessly about the gorgeous photographer bunking with her. And Jillian Knight *was* gorgeous, with that long, shiny black hair pulled neatly into a ponytail, wide-set dark eyes that were so big you could almost fall right into them, and a face that was heart-stoppingly exotic, yet openly friendly. Okay, so Meg had a point. Being in the company of a beautiful woman—something Logan hadn't allowed herself to think about in a long time—wasn't so bad. It could almost make you feel normal again…make you forget your surroundings. Logan hadn't thought that was possible here.

"You don't have us stuck in a tent next to the latrines, do you?" Jillian asked slyly.

Logan laughed at Jillian's unexpected humor. "Actually, I hadn't thought of that."

"Lucky for us," Mark said, biting off his words.

Moments later, Logan and Jillian were alone in Logan's tiny room with its two cots and two large chests for storage. The walls were plywood. A heavy wool blanket substituted as a door. It wasn't much, but it was at least a small sanctuary in a place where privacy was as rare as a cool breeze.

Jillian blankly surveyed her accommodations. She'd probably stayed in worse, Logan figured. Particularly since she'd been in Darfur. Her bags and cases of photography equipment were already neatly stacked in a corner, and Jillian gave her a weary smile of appreciation.

"You're welcome to join us in the dining hall in an hour or so."

Jillian shook her head. "I'm starving, but I'll probably just sleep for…oh, about the next three days." She sat down on her cot, her eyelids drooping.

"I'll leave you to get some rest, Ms. Knight."

"I'd really rather you didn't keep calling me Ms. Knight." Her voice was firm and in contrast to the tired eyes she raised to Logan.

"Sorry, I–" It was the military, and before that it was med school and sports. The habit of using last names and titles was long ingrained.

"Call me Jillian, or Jill." She laughed from somewhere deep in her throat. "Just not *Jillsy*. Please."

Logan sat down on her own cot, facing Jillian, and absently fingered the beret in her hands. "Childhood nickname?"

Jillian nodded. "Do you have one, Major Sharp?"

Oh, no, thought Logan. She wasn't going there. She'd had a few over the years. The worst had been Mouse, from her early years as a quiet, shy kid who took longer to hit her growth spurt than most, while her current one was Boomer, granted because of her booming slap shot in hockey. But nicknames were personal and certainly not up for discussion with strangers—especially visiting journalists. Her mood began to sour.

"Sorry," Jillian interjected. "I didn't mean to pry."

"You're not," Logan answered, a little too quickly. She would be polite and accommodating with Jillian Knight, because doing so would be in both their best interests, but she had no intention of being *friends* with her. She did not want to risk exposing too much of herself to someone who was intent on capturing her in photographs for strangers to pore over or breeze through at their leisure, or in dentists' offices and bookstores. It was best to keep a polite but friendly distance and to set the boundaries right away—to establish that they were on Logan's territory, that it was okay for Logan to ask personal questions, but not the other way around.

"You know," Jillian said, sitting back and leaning against the plywood wall. Her hands were limp in her lap. "I'm sorry you're stuck with Mark and me. I'm sure it's an assignment you'd rather not have, especially having me underfoot right in your own room."

The apology caught Logan off guard. Most of the journalists who'd visited the base were aggressive, entitled and even rude sometimes in their zeal to get the story or the photo. Sure, they'd suck up when they needed to, but apologize for simply being there? Never.

Jillian had her attention now, and Logan felt the urge to trot out the company line, but without the sharpness to it. "It's part of our job, having…" *people like you here…* "media people here and assisting them. It's in our best interests if you understand what we do here."

What she really wanted to say was that the media couldn't be trusted to wander around at will and that keeping them on a short leash was the military's way of trying to manipulate and control the information and the image that was presented for the world's consumption. She and Jillian were simply the characters in a play, each with their scripted role, each at the whim of greater forces. An experienced photojournalist like Jillian would understand the game.

Jillian smiled knowingly. "Don't worry. I have every intention of *not* giving you a hard time. I only have two weeks here. If I spend most of it with you pissed off at me, I'll never get what I need."

And what is it, exactly, that you need? Logan wanted to ask. And she *would* ask, but not today, though she knew Jillian must have a plan. Anyone could take photos of the medical teams at work. But award-winning photos? That must take something special. Something extra.

"Well," Logan said, feeling it was time to push Jillian a little, see what she was made of. "How far are you willing to go to get what you want?"

Jillian's mouth moved a little, and her eyes widened marginally. She studied Logan, undoubtedly trying to read if a double meaning lay beneath her words. She was trying even harder not to look shocked or insulted.

Shit. She thinks I just made a pass at her. Logan fumbled with the beret in her hands and nervously cleared her throat. "Ms. Knight—I mean, Jillian. What I meant was..."

"Something other than what it sounded like?" A mischievous glint ascended in the photographer's eyes.

"Exactly."

Jillian obviously saw the humor in it, thankfully. But still, giving this woman the inadvertent impression that Logan's cooperation or permission could be bought would be a huge mistake. Not to mention an irreparable chink in her own credibility. And to Logan—to most soldiers—honor and integrity meant everything. "I'm sorry," she said heavily, apologizing more to herself.

Jillian quirked a curious eyebrow, studied her again. "It's okay. I didn't really think you meant...you know." She absently twirled the gold band on her finger.

Logan couldn't help but wonder for just the tiniest instant what Jillian's reaction would have been had Logan truly meant that she was open to sexual favors. Would she have been outraged? Amused? Reported her immediately? Or would she have toyed with the idea, let Logan think there was a possibility...strung her along until she got what she wanted *without* having to sleep with her. Women were good at that sort of thing. It was called survival, and Jillian Knight looked like a survivor.

"I guess you realize by now it's not exactly the Shangri-La here." Logan went for blunt, wanting to test this woman's mettle.

27

"It's about the farthest thing from a vacation resort there is."

"I know." Jillian clamped her mouth shut.

"We're surrounded here by death and destruction. Senseless violence. There are people in this country who desperately want us here, and there are people who desperately want us out. At any cost. There are no rules of engagement in this war." Logan knew the lengths the insurgents would go to—the suicide attacks, the roadside bombs, the ambushes, the killing of helpless civilians. She hadn't so much seen them herself as seen the horrific results of them. "What we do and see here, Jillian, is not pretty."

Jillian's smile was razor thin, her eyes dark and impermeable, like black granite. "I realize that, Major Sharp. I'm not here to look at the pretty sights or to vacation. I'm here to work. And *my* work is to capture *your* work, in all its stark reality, no matter what that is. That is what I want. The truth."

Logan nodded once, feeling the tension in her body ease a little, but she wasn't quite finished with Jillian Knight yet. "How far are you willing to go? What risks are you prepared to take?"

Jillian's gaze remained fixed on her. "I'm not prepared to be totally reckless. I'm prepared to take as much risk as you think I should."

Logan studied her for a long moment before she finally answered, "Good."

"I want to do the best job I can, but I want to go home at the end of this." Jillian's expression softened considerably. Her eyes grew moist. There was a weakness there. "I have a daughter back home. She's almost two."

Logan seized this new information as evidence that Jillian wasn't going to do anything stupid to put herself or others in danger. She would be sensible. Responsible. She had a good reason to go home. "What's your daughter's name?" Logan smiled, trying to ease the tension. She wasn't truly trying to scare Jillian; she just wanted her to understand the risks and to understand that they were a team. If one person put herself in peril, they were all in peril.

"Maddie." Jillian's smile was dazzling and proud. "Madison,

really, but we've always called her Maddie."

"Your husband is with her?"

Jillian's smile faltered for an instant. There was a tiny bob in her throat. "My partner is, yes."

That's an interesting way to frame it, Logan thought, before quickly returning to formalities. "Tomorrow, Captain Atwood and I are taking a chopper out to do a polio clinic at a nearby village. Would you like to come?"

"Oh, yes," Jillian answered enthusiastically. "Thank you."

"Good." Logan stood and carefully positioned the beret on her head. "There's just one last thing, Jillian."

"Yes?" Jillian stood, too. She was a good three or four inches shorter than Logan. Trim and fit looking, too, Logan couldn't help but notice. Even if she did look out of place in those four-hundred-dollar fancy leather boots.

"Do you trust me?" If you don't, Logan thought, you won't have any success here.

Jillian didn't need long to think about it. She seemed to grasp the enormity of the question. "Yes, Major Sharp. I trust you with my life."

Logan was used to people putting their lives in her hands, but she never took that trust for granted—never thought to take the responsibility lightly. "Then help me. If I tell you to do something, you must do it without question."

Jillian smiled disarmingly. "I fully intend to."

CHAPTER TWO

Jillian studied the brand-new camel-colored combat boots on her feet, surprised by how good they looked and how solid and sturdy they felt. When she'd wakened this morning, after sleeping right through dinner, the boots were lined up beneath her bed, stiff and straight like little leather soldiers, the toes pointing out.

She thanked Logan, who only grunted in acknowledgment before casting a final, disdainful look at her Gucci boots that made Jillian want to laugh. How had Logan guessed her size so perfectly anyway? She pictured Logan holding up her boot in the dark to examine it, and she smothered a chuckle. Had Logan used a flashlight to do it? Had she snuck one of the boots out and taken it to the supply depot? Whichever way she'd done it, Jill was pleased Logan had gone to the trouble.

The heat so early in the morning came as a shock. That and the blinding, almost white sunlight. The dust was everywhere. So was the diesel exhaust and the roar of jet engines. It was a sparse, smelly and very noisy planet she'd landed on and one that she just couldn't seem to get used to, even though she'd only been here some twenty hours. It was as foreign to her as the refugee camps in Sudan had been, even though they resembled each other not in the least.

The chopper was loud, its rotors thwacking rhythmically as they lifted off. Both sliding side doors were open, for which Jillian was grateful. Her camera was at the ready, and she was buckled in so she wouldn't fall out while leaning for a shot. Logan sat in the seat beside her. Opposite them were two kneeling gunners, their automatic rifles pointed out, their goggled eyes constantly scanning the horizon for danger. Mark, Meg Atwood and a lab technician were in an accompanying Blackhawk.

Jillian wouldn't let herself think about the enemies below who might be hiding, waiting to take a potshot at them with a rocket launcher or even a rifle. She glanced at Logan, so stiff and composed, her face impassive, her hands perfectly still in her lap. She was so cool about it, but then, she probably did this sort of thing all the time. Jillian knew the medical staff often went out to VMOs—Village Medical Outreaches—to treat ordinary Afghans. It was important to the mission for villagers to get to know them, to see them helping and doing good. And today's clinic was the perfect opportunity for Jillian and her camera to observe Logan and her staff interacting outside the base.

The helicopter skimmed over the jagged mountain range, the same neutral brown as the flat ground of the airfield. They were going fast—so much faster than those twenty-dollar tour helicopters you could take over Niagara Falls or the Grand Canyon. It must be an imposing sight to anyone below, she imagined, seeing these black machines whizzing past, guns poking out, held by anonymous soldiers.

Kandahar City lay just behind the mountains, spread out flat and wide. The roads looked to be mostly made of dirt, and they were clogged with small cars, rickety trucks, donkeys pulling carts and people on foot and on bicycles. No one waved up at them. Few barely even looked in their direction.

"The village is just a few miles beyond the city," Logan said over the noise. "We've had a company of troops there since yesterday getting things ready for us."

Making it safe for their arrival was what Logan most certainly meant. The military's health-care providers were a precious commodity, and it would make sense that the army would do everything it could to make sure they were protected. As much as possible, anyway.

From the air, the village looked flat and the same shade of brown, the houses all one-story and made of bricks and mud. The chest-high mud walls were everywhere—around the houses and yards, along the dirt streets. Villagers waved up at them this time, turning wide, smiling faces skyward.

"They're happy to see us," Jillian noted, pleased.

"They usually are in the villages," Logan responded. "The kids really warm to the soldiers, though they're shy at first. The adults don't say much, but you can tell they're happy to be getting medical help."

"It must be very rewarding."

Logan's smile was one of deep satisfaction. "It is." She turned her face to the rapidly approaching ground, and Jillian had to lean closer to hear her. "Polio has been devastating in this country. You see people everywhere crippled from it." She turned back to Jillian, her expression one of professional detachment that was probably vital to keeping her emotions at bay. "The health care here is like stepping back to about the nineteen twenties in North America. They don't have enough trained medical personnel, and even if they did, they have such a poor supply of medicine and equipment. Sometimes, what we do here feels like we're only putting a Band-Aid on a sucking chest wound."

Jillian felt her heart sink a little as she watched the children huddle around the perimeter of the landing zone, shielding their eyes against the dust, clustered together in little groups. Their future was bleak, she thought starkly. But if the Band-Aid that Logan talked about worked for a day or a month or a year, then it had to be better than nothing.

Jillian started taking photos as the medical team and the soldiers began unloading the boxes of needles, vaccine and antiseptic. Mark joined her, handing her a second camera or a different lens when she looked up wordlessly. He took notes for her, too, freeing her up to concentrate on the photos.

Logan was right about the children. They were shy at first, huddling together or with the adult who'd brought them, glancing wide-eyed at the soldiers and medical staff, their smiles blooming slowly but surely. Meg Atwood didn't wait long for them to warm to her—she simply hugged as many of them as she could, talked cheerfully to them without waiting for an interpreter, and handed out smiles like they were candy. The littlest ones got a stuffed animal and a pat on the head or a final hug after their needle, while the others waited patiently in line.

Logan got down on her haunches and greeted each child in line, touching their hand or their shoulder gently, then their forehead, the back of their neck, asking, through an interpreter, if they'd been sick recently and if it hurt anywhere. She was methodical in her questions, careful in her touch, which, Jillian finally recognized, was more than just a warm salutation. She was covertly checking them for fevers, bumps, cuts, skin rashes, without them even knowing it. She smiled the entire time she spoke to them, letting them touch the floppy, camouflage fishing-style hat the Canadians wore in the field when they weren't wearing a helmet or finger the metal dog tags around her neck.

She's good with kids, Jillian thought as she clicked off more frames. Logan didn't smother them, didn't overwhelm them with her own personality the way Meg did. She was warm and affectionate without invading their space. She treated the kids with respect—listened to them even when they didn't speak, let them come to her. Maddie would instantly like her, it occurred to Jillian. Maddie was a little shy, just like these kids, yet she loved the affection and attention of adults. *Yeah, Maddie would definitely like Logan.*

How lucky her little girl was, Jillian thought. How lucky they all were. She gave Mark a sharp look, shook her head a little, felt a tear in the corner of her eye. He put his arm around her shoulder.

"It's tough, isn't it? Seeing all these kids," he murmured. His brief marriage had never produced any children, but he loved kids. Probably because he was like a big kid himself. He knew her well enough, too, to know she'd be thinking of Maddie. "How come there's no women here?"

"Logan says the women customarily aren't allowed at these. They only go out in public for specific reasons, and they're not supposed to mix with the men. There's too many men here," she said, gesturing at the soldiers.

"But how do they get help if they're sick?"

Jillian shrugged helplessly. "I suppose they have some sort of nurse or midwife visit them at their home, or maybe there's special clinics just for them. I don't know, Mark. But it's pretty lousy, isn't it? God, I'm so glad I'm not a woman in this country."

Mark glanced around at the few adult men there. They were toothless, most of them. Haggard, too, and looking far older than they probably were. Their life expectancy was no more than fifty. "Not much fun being a man here either, I expect."

An Afghan man began speaking frantically to Logan through an interpreter, waving his arms, his eyes frightened and desperate. Logan nodded calmly at him, asking pointed questions. Jillian inched closer, sensing something unusual. The man's voice and actions intensified, and Jillian felt a new sheen of sweat break out on her forehead. Something was terribly wrong. Just then she caught Logan's eye, for an instant. She caught just a glimpse, but she saw calm authority. And clear signs of a decision having been made.

Logan signaled to Meg and a young corporal in full gear, his automatic rifle snug and at the ready in his arms.

"This gentleman needs us to go to his house to attend to his wife. Captain Atwood, can you come with me? And Corporal, we'll need an escort."

"Can we walk there, Major?" the corporal asked.

"Yes. He says it's just around the corner."

"All right. We'll send a couple of troops ahead to make sure it's clear, and I'll stay with you and the captain."

Jillian stepped up to Logan. "Can we come?"

Logan's stare was so stony, Jillian felt sure she'd just made the most ridiculous request the major had ever heard in her life.

"I don't know how safe it is," she said after a moment, snapping off her words like twigs breaking beneath her boots. "It could be an ambush."

Jillian swallowed. If Logan and Meg were willing to take a chance, so was she. She'd never believed her line of work was without risk. And while she didn't plan on doing anything stupid, she knew that her best work often happened spontaneously, by taking a chance. By doing it just like this. "I'm okay with it if you are, Major."

Logan gave Mark and Jillian a final look of appraisal. After what seemed like several minutes, she gave them an abrupt nod. "Stick close to us, but when we're with the patient, step back and give us space."

Logan instructed the lab tech and another nurse they'd brought with them to continue the vaccinations, then picked up a hard plastic case that looked like a fisherman's tackle box.

"You," she said pointedly to Jillian. "Zip up your flak vest."

She wanted to protest, particularly since Logan wasn't wearing a helmet or a vest, but she didn't dare. Not after the stern order she'd just been issued. It was hot and the damned thing weighed about a dozen pounds, but she did as she was told, because she instinctively knew Logan would not accept defiance in any measure. She would not do anything to blow this chance now.

There was a window cut out in the mud house. No glass. The ceiling was low—Mark, at six feet tall, had to stoop a bit. Logan had to be about five-foot-nine, and there was only just enough clearance for her.

The Afghan man gestured to a room at the back. It was dark there and smelled like the sick. They waited for him to light a gas lamp, and while Jillian couldn't see past Logan and Meg, she could tell they had already started to work on the patient—Meg fastening a blood pressure cuff, Logan taking out her flashlight for a closer examination. The unseen woman moaned weakly, and Jillian caught a glimpse of her husband's eyes, darting about with worry. He must have been desperate for assistance to have allowed foreign men to see his wife's unveiled face and to have begged female caregivers—wearing pants!—for their help.

Jillian uncapped her camera, clicked on the flash and reeled off a few quick photos from different angles. Logan moved to fill a needle from a vial in the tackle box. Meg was taking the woman's temperature. Jillian could see that the side of the woman's face was swollen to the size of a softball. She wanted to ask what was wrong with her, but now was not the time.

Minutes later, Jillian followed Logan and Meg outside. She heard Meg warn Logan that the colonel was going to have their heads on a platter.

"What are you doing with her?" Jillian asked Meg, while Logan retreated with one of the soldier escorts.

"We're going to take her with us to the base hospital." Meg looked resigned to the decision, but a tiny frown revealed her displeasure.

"Is that common?" Jillian couldn't imagine them bringing every ill civilian back to the hospital. They'd never have the room or the staff.

"No, but with Logan…I mean, Major Sharp…" Meg's eyes drifted to her friend. There was pride, affection and a bit of puzzlement in her expression, which seemed to say that she loved her friend and yet sometimes wanted to throttle her, too. "Let's just say she's done this before."

What makes her do it? Jillian wanted to ask, but she knew there would be no succinct, easy answer to the question. She'd known Logan less than twenty-four hours, but she sensed that something as deep and instinctive as breathing compelled Logan to help others, even at risk or expense to herself. It was probably just the way she was wired, and the military's rules and threats wouldn't change that. Neither would a good scolding from a friend.

"What's wrong with the patient?" Jillian pressed.

"Severely abscessed tooth. She'll need it drained and then surgery. The infection's probably gone into the bone."

She had never thought of something as simple as a bad toothache being life-threatening. "Will she be okay?"

Meg nodded reassuringly, her tanned skin crinkling around her blue eyes. "We'll take good care of her."

"How will she get back here?"

Meg shrugged lightly and watched two soldiers carry a collapsible stretcher into the home. "Logan will probably pay for a cab to bring her back when it's time." She said it with the confidence of having seen Logan do it before.

Meg left to help and Mark sprang to Jillian's side. "Our Major Sharp is a real, genuine hero." He pronounced it *gen-u-wine*, and his tone was loaded with contempt. Jillian glared at him, waiting for him to show the tiniest shred of remorse for acting like a bastard. He wouldn't give her the satisfaction.

"Quit being an ass," she said curtly, not wanting to explore his immature reasons for disliking someone he had just barely met. She turned abruptly on her heel.

There was a childlike quality in the way Jillian scooped up her frothy iced cappuccino with the straw, using it as if it were a spoon. Logan's attention was riveted on Jillian sucking at the creamy drink, alternately using both ends of the straw, devouring it with sweet satisfaction.

"I take it you like the drink."

Jillian froze, looked up with an adorable frown of embarrassment. "Sorry," she said sheepishly. "Am I making a spectacle?"

Logan smiled, not wanting Jillian to stop on her account. There was something both sexy and innocent in the woman's actions. "Not at all. I'm glad you like it. They don't have Tim Hortons in Michigan?"

"I think I've driven past one or two, but I've never gone in. I live in Dunkin' Donuts country, I'm afraid."

They were sitting at a table on the boardwalk, sipping iced coffees that were more like milkshakes. She'd been surprised when Jillian had shown up without her sidekick, but neither had discussed his whereabouts. A notebook and pencil lay on the table between them, like a tiny barrier at first, but one Logan quickly forgot. It was...*different*...sitting quietly with a woman she hardly knew yet felt strangely comfortable with. She spent a lot of time with women—many of her colleagues at the hospital were women. But the rare times they sat around with nothing to do, work always loomed over them and ultimately seeped into every conversation. She knew it would this time, too, but Jillian's questions and observations would undoubtedly bring a new perspective to her work, allowing Logan to see it through the journalist's eyes.

"How do you feel about being here now?" Logan asked gently. It had only been a couple of full days on the base for Jillian, but it was a big adjustment for outsiders.

"I'm doing okay." Jillian sucked on her straw again, her eyes growing impossibly bigger with the effort. They really were like soft, shimmering, dark pools that were full of mystery and depth—the kind of eyes Logan had read about in fiction but was skeptical really existed. "I think what I notice the most, though, is the extreme lack of beauty here. No flowers, no trees, no grass, no sparkling water."

"The nighttime can be beautiful," Logan countered. "The stars. The constellations."

Jillian seemed to consider this for a few moments. A tiny crease formed between her eyes. "Would it be more...distracting here for you if the scenery was beautiful?"

"Probably." You're beautiful, Logan thought with the sudden intensity of a meteorite igniting as it falls to earth. *You could be a distraction.*

"No temptation to picnic by a river or sneak off for an afternoon at the beach," Jillian offered with a somber smile.

"That's true, but a little bit of beauty now and then might,

I don't know..." Logan was suddenly uncomfortable with the conversation—by her easy willingness to share such private thoughts. More than that, she was embarrassed by how easily her thoughts seemed to stray sideways in this woman's presence.

Yes, Jillian was a beautiful woman, and it felt like it'd been years since she had truly noticed and even delighted in a beautiful woman's company. But Jillian was here for only a short time, and they both had work to do, no matter what her friend Meg's imagination was cooking up. Meg could tease all she wanted; Logan wouldn't dream of trying to start something up with Jillian Knight. Even if Jillian showed the slightest bit of interest, which she hadn't, it just wasn't in Logan. She was no Meg. She was far too wedded to her codes of honor and rules and to deeply-ingrained gentlewomanly behavior. A war zone and the welcome presence of this intriguing stranger weren't going to change the habits of a lifetime.

Besides, Jillian was married...*or something*.

"What were you going to say?" Jillian asked quietly, her eyes kind but probing.

Logan shrugged a little and swallowed the lump in her throat. There was nothing to lose by answering the question. "I was going to say, a little bit of beauty now and then might be a welcome relief from all the ugliness, you know?"

"Yeah, I think I do know."

"I was a little shocked by it when I arrived for my first tour here."

"You mean this isn't the first time you've been here?"

Logan shook her head. "I did a six-month tour here just over two years ago." Her current tour was easier, because she knew what to expect this time around. She glanced around, suddenly grateful for the iced coffee that reminded her of home. She could have sat like this all afternoon, sipping coffees, just talking like friendly acquaintances. But Jillian was reaching suddenly for her notebook. Logan automatically stiffened a little, Jillian's gesture reminding her of the real reason they were sitting here.

"The Afghan woman you brought in yesterday. With the

abscessed tooth. How is she doing?"

"Nazirah? She's doing well. You can visit her, you know."

"I can?" Jillian brightened.

"Sure. You have carte blanche to go anywhere in the hospital. She might like a visitor who's not, you know, one of us for a change."

"What about others like her? Women who need help and can't get it?" There was indignation in Jill's tone.

"Jesus, it breaks your heart, doesn't it?" Logan blurted out, uncharacteristic emotion thick in her voice. She had never confessed so openly before about the frustration she felt regarding people she couldn't help or even the ones she could only temporarily help. She had to look away, her throat tightening and her eyes beginning to burn.

A fighter-bomber took off loudly, its jet engines roaring overhead and smothering any further attempts at conversation for a moment. It gave Logan time to compose herself, to remember that emotions only hampered her work. There would be time—much later—to worry about all the things she couldn't change. Besides, it would be appalling to go off on a stranger like that.

"We try to hold VMOs of some sort as often as we can," Logan said, much more controlled now. "Like the polio clinic yesterday, though most of them are more involved than that. We've had a couple specifically for women since I've been here, and I want to do another one soon."

"It's risky, isn't it?"

"Yes, but they can pay huge dividends. In addition to providing essential medical care, the clinics get the civilians on side with us. Hopefully they learn to trust us and to work with us."

Jillian leaned closer and set her pen down. "Is it worth it, being here, Major Sharp?"

Logan wondered for an instant if Jillian meant if it was worth it for her personally or worth it from a mission standpoint. She resorted to her scripted answer—the one for journalists, dignitaries and other outsiders. It was important to be positive about the mission, to be ambassadors, and mostly, Logan believed it. In her heart, she felt that they would never be able to do enough for this country and its people, but what they were doing was better than nothing. They were making at least a small difference, and that knowledge was what really kept her going.

"What about you?" Logan ventured. "Do you think we should be here?"

Jillian's face colored a little, and she wore her confusion and frustration plainly. Logan liked that about her—she didn't hide her feelings. "I don't know, Major Sharp. It just seems to me that it's all so futile sometimes. It pisses me off that we can't help these people more. And it pisses me off that there are some people in this country who seem to want everyone here to keep on suffering. I guess…I don't know." She deflated visibly, staring at her empty cup with disappointment. "I guess I thought that when we came into this country, we'd be able to set things right. That they'd see right away that there was a much better way to live, and that would be it. Our soldiers could go home." She raised her eyes to Logan. "It's not that simple, is it?"

Logan shook her head but wanted to smile. Jillian got it, all right. She got exactly how they all felt. "It's kind of like buying a fixer-upper house. You think it just needs a few coats of paint, maybe a new floor, that sort of thing. But you get in there, and you find it needs new wiring, new plumbing, a new roof, the foundation's cracking."

Jillian laughed, and Logan couldn't help but laugh, too. "Is that official military jargon?"

"Nope, not enough acronyms."

Jillian cast her eyes around, tracking two soldiers nearby who were speaking Dutch. "It's funny to be all the way over here and yet to have coffee with someone who grew up probably thirty miles from me. You're from Windsor, right?"

"Yes. I was there until the end of high school."

"Ever go to the Renaissance Center or Tiger Stadium?"

Logan smiled, nostalgia sending her back to a time she hadn't thought about in ages. "I used to go to Tiger Stadium all the time. God, it was a great place. The way people would stamp and clang against all that old iron. I can still hear it."

"Yeah, it was awesome. My dad used to take me there five or six times every summer. It smelled like decades of sweat and hotdogs and stale beer, didn't it? And fresh grass. Kind of a weird combination, but so unique."

God, what she would give to be sitting at a ball stadium again. Jillian's description was exactly as she remembered the place. "Yeah, it did, didn't it?"

"Maybe we were even there at the same games. It's funny how we move through the world, isn't it?"

Logan couldn't argue with that. As a high school student, the pull of medicine in her blood, she would never have guessed she would end up in Afghanistan. It wasn't even a country most people had heard of back then.

"Your work takes you all over the place. Is Michigan still your home?" Logan asked.

"Yes. I think it always will be. My parents still live just a few miles away from me. And for the record?" Jillian smiled wistfully. "The new Comerica Park is nice, but it's not Tiger Stadium."

Logan nodded. She had yet to visit the newer ballpark.

"Do you go back home often, Major Sharp?"

Home. She hadn't really had a home since those years in Windsor. After all her schooling, she worked in Toronto's Sunnybrook Hospital's emergency ward for a couple of years before a breakup and a lack of direction led her to sign on with the military. Dorms, apartments and bases had been where she'd lived for nearly four years now, but they were not *home.*

"My sister still lives in Windsor."

"What about your parents?"

"They moved out to British Columbia when they retired."

Jillian raised her eyebrows. "That's a long way from Windsor."

"They decided they wanted mountains instead of all that flat farmland."

"Where will you go, after the military? Or will you make a career of it?"

The bluntness of the questions threw her for a moment. She didn't have an answer, but she wasn't ready to share her uncertainty. The doubt she was feeling again was too vague to talk about. She was thirty-four years old. Young enough to take her medical career somewhere else. But where, she had no idea. She was pretty sure she was not meant to be a career military doctor. It was a great side street she'd veered onto, but not likely to be her ultimate path. It felt in her gut like there was so much more she wanted to do with her life. "It's hard to say, but no, I'm not a lifer."

"So you're on some kind of contract?"

"I am, and it runs out in a few months. I'm sure they'll try to extend it."

Jillian looked at her directly. "Are you going to?" She had put her notepad down, a clear sign they were off the record.

Logan began to fidget with her empty cup, finally crumpling it between her hands. This was all getting way too personal. She'd already revealed so much about herself…probably more than she had to anyone but Meg these last ten months. It was astounding how easy that was to do with Jillian. A small knot of panic gathered in Logan's stomach. Easy connection with a stranger was an unfamiliar experience for her. She looked up at Jill and felt her mouth harden. "I don't know." It was the truth, but the sharpness of her tone was also designed to indicate that the subject was now closed.

Logan stood to go. Jillian scrambled to gather up her things. She looked a little perplexed at the abruptness of it all.

"I hear Captain Atwood invited you and Mark to come watch the game tonight?" The question was as close as Logan could manage for an apology.

"Yes. I hear you're quite the hockey player, Major Sharp. Mind if I take some photos?"

"It's not for your photo spread, is it?" Logan didn't care to be a bug under a microscope, especially during her down time.

Jillian touched her forearm lightly. "No, it's not. I just thought you and your friends might like some photos. That okay?"

"Yeah." Logan smiled easily. "It is."

Jillian was amazed. How could these men and women run around a hard-packed rink energetically playing ball hockey in such oppressive heat? Evening had done little to cool the air. The players' shirts were stained with sweat, their hair was drenched, their smiles never left their faces.

"Don't you think this is even just a little bit insane?" she asked Mark as she squeezed in beside him on a wooden bench.

"Are you kidding?" He grinned. "I'd love to be out there right now."

"So why don't you go sign up with the media guys? I'm sure they have a team."

Mark gave her a look that said she was crazy.

"What?" The heat had sapped her patience hours ago. Not long after the iced cappuccino with Logan.

He patted the small paunch that threatened to bulge over the waist of his camouflage pants. With each passing day he'd begun to take on the look of belonging here, with his military-style pants and olive T-shirts. It was cute, in a little-boy, wannabe way. "It'd probably kill me. Don't you know we're just getting into heart attack territory at our age?"

Jillian frowned deeply. "I hardly think we're doomed at thirty-six."

"Yeah, well, you don't drink a case of beer every week and eat at Burger King like I do."

"You do have a point there." She patted his knee. "Best to leave this sort of thing to these fitness freaks."

Still smiling, she turned her head in time to see Logan striding out to the center of the rink, both hands gripping her stick. She'd been late, getting caught up at the hospital, Jillian supposed, and she looked much fresher and drier than her cohorts. Shielding her eyes from the unrelenting sun, Jillian watched Logan ready herself in the middle of the faceoff circle. It wasn't the heat clamping down on Jillian's chest now that squeezed the air from her lungs. It was the vision of Logan, looking like some kind of warrior goddess, all sinewy muscle beneath her tanned skin. Her frame looked strong, her muscles even stronger, and there was an unmistakable concentrated ferocity to her body's tautness, like she fully intended to massacre the opposition.

"I've got to shoot this," Jillian mumbled and scrambled away, raising her digital camera to her face.

She trained her telephoto lens on Logan, her motor drive knocking off action shots at the rate of a couple of dozen a minute. She couldn't seem to pull the camera's lens off the major, who was clearly the best player, man or woman, on the rink. She glided between and around bodies, legs pumping as she spun and glanced off a larger opponent, the ball like a yo-yo on her stick. She scored once, then again a couple of minutes later, never celebrating too much.

After several moments, Jillian disengaged from her viewfinder, wanting to watch this display of grace and athleticism without obstructions. She shook her head in awe at the burst of speed from Logan. Zero to sixty in about three strides. It was astonishing, her power disguised in almost elegant dexterity, like a cat. As an athlete, she was seductively beautiful and lethal at the same time. Her opponents got mesmerized watching her—like helpless prey. Jillian grew disappointed. She knew already that her shots weren't going to make the grade. No camera could truly capture the essence of Logan's athletic abilities.

A whistle stopped play for a moment, and Logan, dripping wet now in her shorts and tank top, her light brown hair dark with sweat, looked across at Jillian. She smiled unexpectedly, as though amused by Jillian's attention, but her eyes remained stone-like and unblinking with the intensity of the battle at hand.

Jillian took a few more photos, liking how Logan looked with that smile contradicting her fierceness. It struck Jillian just how similar Logan was at play and at work—profound joy coupled with such razor concentration. Cool competency softened by a quiet warmth and easiness. Confidence in her abilities, humility in her victories. Logan Sharp was the complete package at work and in sports.

"What's it like?" Jill asked Mark after claiming her seat again.

"What?"

"Being so fucking good." She knew she sounded annoyed, but she really wasn't. She was in awe.

"At sports?"

At everything, Jillian wanted to say, but she simply nodded.

Mark shrugged. "Truthfully? It feels fucking great!"

"Thought so."

Mark, a high school football and hockey star, had had his wings clipped a little in college, but he was still good. He had even played two seasons with a low-level professional hockey team, earning just enough to pay for a crappy apartment and a regular supply of beer and pizza. He probably would have kept at it longer, except his girlfriend at the time, who later became his wife for a few agonizing years, had convinced him to get a real job as a newspaper photographer.

"Don't tell me there's a closet athlete scratching to get out in that body of yours," he teased.

Jillian smiled at the absurdity of his comment. She'd never been an athlete, other than dabbling at dance and figure skating when she was young. Steph was no athlete either. In fact, her partner abhorred and mocked anything to do with sports. Yet Jillian had always found sports intriguing. It was why she'd spent so many hours in her youth watching Mark play hockey and football. It was as though she thought that by watching enough, she could decode the magic formula—unravel the mystery vicariously.

"I can't imagine," she said, watching Logan, "what it's like having your mind and your body in perfect sync like that."

"Sure you can. It's like when you take pictures, Jillsy."

She thought about that and realized Mark had made the perfect comparison. "You still have that ability to surprise me sometimes, Mark."

"What, you don't expect a nugget of wisdom from me every now and then?" He laughed self-deprecatingly.

"That's not what I meant, you big goof."

"I know, I know. That's what Steph's for, right? To give you all the smart talk in your life? I'm just the big idiot you haven't been able to ditch since high school." He said it lightly, but she knew he was looking for a good ego stroking.

"Oh, Mark. Shut up and watch the game, would ya?" She let him quietly sulk for a minute. "Look, you're the only big idiot I have, okay? Everyone needs at least *one* in their life. Jeez!"

"Ah, finally you appreciate me! It only took coming to a war zone to feel wanted."

Jill's eyes and her thoughts settled again on Logan, watching her as she ran along the boards carrying the ball, passing it off nicely as she reached the far blue line. She was aware as she did so that Mark was watching her watch Logan.

"She's good," he finally said on a long sigh.

"Why don't you like her, Mark?" The question was out before she'd committed to asking it, but she and Mark had been friends for so long, they usually reacted to each other without thinking first. Their relationship was one of cause and effect in its purest form.

"What makes you think I don't?" Mark answered sharply.

"Because you two are like lions penned up together, biding your time until you can get at each other's throats."

"Bullshit," he said, but there was no challenge in his words.

"I'm just trying to understand."

"Look, Jill, there's nothing to understand. I don't even know her, okay?"

"I know that. It's something baser than that, that's all."

"Well, if it is, then why are you asking me to explain it?"

Jillian shrugged. She was tired. Tired of fighting with Mark about the same things. Years ago it was over why he acted the way he did with Steph. Before that, it was anyone else she'd dated. Logan, however, was not in the same category as the others. They'd never dated and they were never going to. "You're right. It just seems like…I don't know, Mark. Like you get a hate-on for anyone who might vie for my attention or be the object of my affection."

He made a noise of derision. "Is that what Major Sharp is? Someone you have affection for?"

Jillian felt her face taking on a different kind of warmth. "Forget it," she said, not wanting to prolong the conversation. He was being juvenile, acting like a jealous ex-lover. Being overprotective as usual. Aside from their brief romantic fling as teenagers, Mark was like her big brother and best friend all rolled into one. He wasn't nearly the ass he made out to be, because certainly if he was, Jillian would have little use for him in her life. There were just times he couldn't help but act like that sixteen-year-old boy again.

"Hey." Meg trotted up to them. The game had ended without Jillian or Mark having noticed.

"Good game," Mark said, giving her a high-five. "You guys killed those poor dining hall bastards."

Meg glanced over her shoulder at Logan, who was trotting up behind her. "It's all Major Sharp's fault if they start feeding us pigs feet and cow tongues from now on."

"I don't think we need to worry," Logan said breezily as she joined them. "For some strange reason they're worried about getting a nasty needle prick if they ever need treatment from us." She gave Meg a nudge. "You wouldn't have had something to do with that, Atwood, would you?"

Meg gave her a what-me look and they all laughed.

"Listen," Mark said, lowering his voice. "I've got a bottle of Jack Daniels I managed to sneak through in my bag. You ladies interested?" He glanced sideways at Jillian, making sure she'd noticed he had included Logan, too. A peace offering, of sorts.

Meg's eyes immediately lit up. "Jesus, we haven't had a drink here since New Year's. They let us each have one beer to ring in the new year. Big of them, huh?"

"Is that a yes?" Mark grinned at them like he was Santa Claus bearing precious gifts.

"Oh, God, yes!" Meg swooned laughably, but Logan remained an enigma beside her. She was like the one kid in the group who, without having to say a word, was a visible reminder of how much trouble they could catch.

"Just let us do the world a favor and shower first," Meg continued. "Why don't you guys come to my room? My roommate's working nights."

Logan raised her eyebrows in a look of both amusement and disapproval. She hadn't committed either way, and Jillian irrationally hoped Logan would join them. What would the major be like, she wondered a little guiltily, with that armor of hers stripped away by alcohol? Would she be funny? Talkative? Would she be a sloppy, affectionate drunk? Or would she be grim and morose, retreating further into herself? Jillian considered the possibilities.

By the time Logan joined them, they were well on their way to happy intoxication. Meg and Mark looked like long lost best friends getting hammered together. Jillian, on the other hand, was much more contemplative, sitting alone on the opposite bed, quietly sipping and watching the other two.

"Hey, my friend," Meg said and ceremoniously poured Logan a shot into a small plastic cup. "Cheers!"

Logan took a sip of the burning liquid. She had liked the stuff once, but now it tasted much too strong. "Having a good time, I see."

Jillian patted the empty spot beside her. Logan sat down, noticing immediately the foggy look in Jillian's eyes and the lazy smile that was full of invitation. *Oh, boy.*

"Don't you wanna have a good time too, Major?" Jillian asked thickly, maybe even a little suggestively if Logan's imagination was accurate.

"Yeah, Sharp, you're badly in need of a good time," Meg added. "Drink up."

Logan had no intention of getting drunk. Tomorrow was Meg's day off, but not Logan's. "Some of us poor slugs have to work in the morning, Atwood."

"Work, shmirk," Meg countered. "Too much work makes us

49

as boring as…as this fucking dead fly in my drink! Jesus, where did that come from?"

"Don't worry, the alcohol will sanitize it," Logan supplied, trying not to laugh at her friend. Meg was by far the worst workaholic of them all, and seeing her like this was highly entertaining, though not surprising. When Meg did cut loose, she liked to have a good time. "So what have you three been talking about?"

Mark grinned at her. "We've been talking about your hockey skills, Major. You fucking rock!" He held up his drink in salute. He was being remarkably friendly, considering the dubious vibes he'd been giving her before. *Could just be the alcohol.*

"Thank you, Mark. Do you play?"

"Used to. In my day."

"Why don't you play with us this weekend? We're going to be short in our game against Bravo Company."

"Serious?" He looked like she'd just handed him the winning lottery ticket.

"Sure." She shrugged and caught the instant approval in Jillian's eyes. It was obviously important to Jillian that she and Mark get along. And though she didn't understand the reasons, there was really nothing to lose by being nice to him, after all.

Mark reached across and slapped her lightly on the shoulder. "Awesome, Major. Me and you. Goals!" He punched his fist in the air. "We'll be like Gretzky and Messier. Lindsay and Howe. Crosby and Malkin!"

The three laughed at him, Jillian most of all. She fell against Logan's shoulder in a quivering fit of laughter, and Logan snaked an arm around her for support.

Mark fixed Jillian with a scolding glare. "Quit laughing, Jillsy, or we'll make you stand in net!"

Jillian sobered a bit at his threat, stiffening slightly but still leaning against Logan. She seemed in no hurry to pull away, and that was just fine with Logan. The contact felt surprisingly good, Jillian so warm and soft against her.

"Oh, no. I'm going to be taking pictures of the dynamic duo

scoring all those goals." She laid her head against Logan's shoulder again, the move so endearing that Logan's pulse quickened in response. "Speaking of pictures, I think I need to take some tomorrow at the hospital. I'll be seeing two of everyone if I drink any more."

"I'll help you back to the room," Logan quickly offered. She didn't know how much longer she could endure Jillian leaning against her like this. It was making her feel so many things—nervous, thrilled, annoyed and yes…turned on. They were feelings she hadn't allowed herself to feel around a woman in a long time. She stood abruptly, because she needed to, and offered a hand to Jillian, who playfully batted it away.

"I'm fine. I don't need any help, Major Shhaarrp!" She giggled. "I like the way that shounds. Shhaarrp."

"C'mon," Logan said, thrusting her hand out again until Jillian took it.

"I told you, I'm fine." Jillian slowly pulled herself up. She took a step and stumbled.

"I've got you." Logan latched her arm around the shorter woman's waist. They slowly made their way down the hall to their room, Logan keeping her grip steady.

"Are you always so chivalrous, Major?" Jillian asked as Logan deposited her on her cot.

Logan smiled. "Only when there's a damsel in distress around."

Jillian, flat on her back, laughed heartily. "Well, you fit the role perfectly. But I'm not normally…in distress, you know."

"I know, Jillian. Let me help you get your boots off. Trust me, you don't want to fall asleep with those on. It'll just take me a sec." She spoke to her the same way she spoke to her patients—authoritative without being demeaning.

"Okay." Jillian sighed loudly, growing sleepy.

Logan deftly untied the heavy boots and gingerly slipped them off one at a time.

"Are you going to undress me, too?"

"I–" Logan raised her eyes to Jillian, and her heart began to pound in her throat. "Do you want me to?" She could see that Jillian had a great body, but she didn't want to see her naked or nearly naked. She'd been able to avoid that so far, even in the close quarters of their shared room. And tonight, she didn't want Jillian's body to be the last thing she saw before she went to sleep. She didn't want an aching reminder of how lonely she'd been these last few years—of how long it had been since she had let her eyes and her imagination feast on a gorgeous woman. *Please don't say yes.*

"Don't worry about it," Jillian murmured, her eyelids heavy.

Logan began to gently turn Jillian on her side, worried she might vomit in the night.

"I'm okay, doc," Jillian mumbled.

"Just making sure."

Logan quickly pulled off her own boots and pants and climbed into her bed wearing her typical boxers and T-shirt. They were a few feet apart, lying on their sides, facing each other, Logan's tiny reading lamp still on.

"Who's that?" Jillian pointed to the photo pinned to the wall behind Logan.

Logan rolled over and plucked the picture of two women from the wall. "It's my sister Lisa and her partner, Dorothy." She stared at the image of Lisa and Dorothy sharing an embrace at a family get-together a year ago Christmas. She kept in regular e-mail contact with them, but they'd not seen each other since Logan had shipped out almost a year ago. She missed them both terribly, alternately wishing they were here with her and glad as hell they were safe back home.

"Are you close to your sister?"

Logan pinned the photo back up and rolled over to face Jillian again. "Yeah, I am. We're twins, so I guess you could say we've been together since the beginning."

"Twins?"

"Fraternal."

"And her partner. How long have they been together?"

"Almost as long, it seems." Logan smiled. She loved Dorothy

52

like a sister, too. "They met in university fourteen or fifteen years ago. Dorothy was a grad student and Lisa was a freshman. They've been together since."

"Wow. That's cool." Jillian closed her eyes, and Logan thought she was asleep until she reached under her bed suddenly and pulled out a book. Inside the book was a snapshot, which she held out with trembling hands.

"I have one of those, too, you know."

"What, a sister?"

Jillian shook her head, and Logan reached for the photo, holding it under her light.

"Partner," Jillian said quietly.

Jillian didn't have a husband, Logan marveled, but rather a *wife*. The woman in the photo had one arm around Jillian's shoulder while Jillian held a toddler in her arms. The little girl looked just like Jillian. Dark wavy hair, big brown eyes, a playful smile and skin tone that looked perpetually tanned. The partner was tall and wiry, older than Jillian by a few years, her short blond hair going gray at the temples. They looked…Logan didn't know if she'd use the word happy. Content, anyway. They looked like a family, and Logan felt the familiar sharp tug of loneliness. Sometimes it felt like everyone was coupled but her, but thank God, moments like these were very rare. She really did cherish her alone time, and it was liberating to make decisions that only ever affected her.

When Logan went to hand the photo back, she discovered Jillian snoring softly, one fist curled under her chin, looking the way a small child might look. Logan carefully slipped the photo back inside the book. It was a hardcover, a lesbian novel by Emma Donoghue.

Well, well, Logan thought, clicking off her light and laying on her back. Why hadn't she picked up on the clues before that Jillian was gay? *Would it have changed anything? Probably not.* The rapport between them was easy, comfortable. And the undeniable need to protect Jillian would have been there, no matter what.

Now they were into personal territory, and things *would*

change between them. It would leave them both more open to each other, and that, Logan reasoned, was a mixed blessing. She was responsible for this woman for ten more days, and knowing her better would make their time together easier, but it might also make her care too much. And caring for someone too much was a danger here. A risky distraction. Maintaining her focus would be harder now, but not impossible.

She began to drift off with visions of Jillian, her baby, and this older woman sharing domestic bliss in a house that was probably three-bedroom, brick, and on a nice, leafy, Michigan suburban street with manicured lawns and houses with long front porches.

Good for you, Jillian Knight.

CHAPTER THREE

Jillian fumbled clumsily with her camera lens, her usual coordination stolen by the morning's hangover.

"How are you feeling today?" Logan had slipped quietly into the hospital's staff lounge. There was a playful gleam in her eyes as she watched Jillian curse at the lens.

Jillian was too annoyed with herself at the moment to feel guilty about her close encounter with Jack Daniels. "I don't know what possessed me last night. Jesus." Her fingers sought out the aching part of her forehead. "I haven't had anything hard to drink in three years—since before I got pregnant with Maddie. Guess it showed, huh?"

Logan's smile was one of pure enjoyment. "You weren't that much of a handful. Honest."

Jillian felt like crap and was in no mood to joke about it. "I'm sorry, Major Sharp. For you having to take care of me and all." Logan started to say something, but Jillian shushed her with a raised hand. "Please don't say you were just doing your job. I highly doubt your job includes looking after drunken photographers."

"Okay, you've got me there, but I'd really rather avoid the paperwork of having to explain some accident befalling you under my watch."

Logan didn't seem the least bit pissed at her. She was grinning, and Jillian decided now was a good time to find out just how poorly she'd behaved. "So…how much of a fool did I make of myself?" She swallowed. "Exactly?"

Logan, wearing cammo utility pants and a blue scrub shirt, crossed her arms over her chest. Her grin disappeared in a flash.

Oh, shit, Jillian thought. *What the hell did I do?* She'd begun to sweat a little just as Logan broke into another grin. She was obviously in a mood to torture her.

"You were fine. You were cute, actually."

Jillian's nerve endings prickled. "Cute?" she squeaked. She'd been accused of being cute all her life, and it had lost its charm a long time ago. She thought of herself as tough, capable, smart, independent, assertive. Fun, too, and her sensitive side was no secret. But *cute*? *Ugh!* Cute was for kids, not for thirty-six-year-old, award-winning photographers.

"Sorry." Logan shrugged, not looking sorry at all. "But you were."

"Hmm. Does that mean I was falling all over the place, or was I trying to hug everyone?"

"A little of both." Logan quirked her eyebrows playfully. "Okay, how about endearing? Is that better than cute?"

Jillian couldn't help but laugh. She liked that Logan could make her laugh, even when she was grumpy. "Not really, but do I have a choice?"

"Nope. Besides, I'd pick endearing and cute over stiff and reserved any day."

"What, you?"

Logan grew quiet and jammed her fists in her pockets. Her face closed up, like curtains sweeping across a stage, the joy quickly disappearing. She seemed so unapproachable at times, so fierce was her concentration and her formal demeanor. She followed rules, liked efficiency, had high expectations. She was probably a perfectionist, but Jillian knew that beneath Logan's exterior lurked a sensitive soul with an endless capacity for caring and giving. She'd seen Logan's selflessness and gentleness when she interacted with children or with her patients.

"Logan," she said, drawing closer. "You know, you–"

"Hey," Logan chimed, backing up a step, suddenly a little nervous. "You have a nice family, by the way. Your little girl looks just like you."

Jillian rubbed her forehead again. Fragments of the evening were coming back to her; it was like fitting a jigsaw puzzle together. She vaguely remembered something about a photograph now. She forced a gracious smile. "Thank you. I, um, didn't realize I came out to you."

Logan looked like she wanted to say something, but she didn't. Jillian took that as a sign of discomfort on Logan's part. "I didn't mean to be evasive about my home life. It's just...I wasn't sure how that sort of thing would be accepted on a military base."

"Actually, it's not the big deal you might imagine," Logan answered smoothly. "In the Canadian military, at least. They haven't been able to discriminate against us in any way since nineteen ninety-two. There's even a few gay couples on base who are married."

Jillian was still stuck on the first part. *Did she say* us?

A low-pitched alarm, like a buzzing alarm clock, rang out from the wall speakers, followed by the pounding of feet throughout the building.

"What's going on?" Jillian asked, her heartbeat quickening. "Are we being bombed or something?"

Logan rushed out the door, Jillian hot on her heels. Logan caught up to a woman in scrubs bustling toward the rear double doors.

"Mass casualties on the way," the woman said without turning around. "Roadside bomb. ETA's about eight minutes."

As the medical teams scrambled to get ready, so did Jillian, cursing Mark's absence. Just as she did so, he sauntered in, looking disheveled and unconcerned. She impatiently ordered him to set up her tripod and meter the light while she checked the remote camera which they'd earlier fixed in a top corner of one of the two trauma rooms. She could activate the camera by remote control, and it was perfect because it could take bird's-eye view photos while being totally unobtrusive. Moments later they sprinted after Logan's team and a second team, arriving just in time to greet two helicopters landing with their injured.

In clipped jargon, two medics explained what happened to the three casualties, yelling over the noise as they unloaded the stretchers. The soldiers' armored vehicle had hit a roadside explosive device, and as the soldiers tried to exit the vehicle, they were ambushed by waiting snipers. Jillian watched the first casualty, a big burly guy, hop off the stretcher and insist on walking into the hospital himself. He'd been shot through the neck, the bullet going clean through without hitting anything vital, according to the medic. The other two casualties looked lifeless, their camouflage uniforms soaked in blood—one from the waist down and the other a mirror image, his torso completely bloodied. The sight shocked Jillian, and she rocked back on her heels for an instant before taking refuge behind her camera lens. Things always seemed a little less real once she put her camera between herself and the subject. It was a welcome barrier at times like this—a window to what was happening before her but one that allowed her to be an observer or interpreter rather than a participant.

She followed the second medical team and the soldier covered in blood from the waist down, watching them cut away his clothing to reveal his mangled, bloodied groin. It was still gushing blood. The patient looked white and as still as a porcelain object.

"Pack that wound," the male doctor yelled to an assistant. "Pack it tighter than a freaking can of tuna until we get him into surgery!"

Someone else was trying to start an IV line, and Jillian snapped off shots—close-ups of one nurse checking the central line and another's hands thrusting gauze into the wound, close-ups of faces that were worried, determined, somber.

She signaled Mark after a few moments to follow her to the second treatment room, where she knew Logan was working on the other patient. Mark looked every bit as alarmed as she was at the blood and gore and bleakness of the situation, but they had jobs to do, just as the medical professionals did. There was no time to stop and process it now.

Chaos greeted them in the adjoining room, with Logan yelling for a surgeon, her hands on the chest of the young soldier whose uniform was blood-soaked and half cut off. She stood in a pool of blood. Jillian immediately began to shoot photos. This was exactly the sort of thing that struck her as so surreal—something as mundane as boots covered in someone else's blood.

Raising her eyes from her viewfinder for a moment, she studied the young soldier's face. His blue eyes were wide open and unblinking, his short hair slicked with sweat and blood. He looks like he hasn't a care in the world, Jill thought. *And he's so young. He's just a kid.* His skin was so white and bloodless; Jillian had never seen skin so white. *He's dying. He's dying right in front of me.* She began to root hard for Logan and her team to pull off some sort of miracle. She had never seen anyone die before. In Darfur, she'd seen things almost as horrible—emaciated children, people scarred by torture tactics, rape victims, some dead bodies. But not someone actually in the act of dying. Not someone who was alive and healthy only moments before. And this… She swallowed against the ache in her throat. This was someone who could have been her brother or neighbor or friend. This was someone randomly killed for just doing his job.

They were bagging the soldier through a tube in his throat. Again, Logan called for a surgeon, her tone impatient and imploring, but not panicked.

"We're losing him," she said, her voice barely audible. She glanced at the wall clock and seemed to make a decision, because she turned and reached for a scalpel from an outstretched hand. She ran it decisively between the soldier's ribs from his sternum and around to his back. His lungs bulged out of the incision, inflating and deflating in time to the hands that were squeezing air down his throat. Pints of clotted blood fell out of his chest in a gelatinous heap. Ignoring all that, Logan took a saw and began roughly cutting through his sternum, the sound of the procedure nearly sickening Jillian on the spot. Blood transfusions were being pumped in, but the blood was leaving him almost as quickly.

"Fuck," Logan cursed, more to herself. "His aorta is shredded."

A look passed between Logan and her team that Jillian knew couldn't be good. Their patient was slipping away. Their shoulders suddenly slumped a little, and their voices became rougher, more gravelly. They, too, had to recognize they were fighting a losing battle, but they weren't ready to concede.

The surgeon, a tiny woman who looked gruff and bitter, stalked in almost unnoticed. She quickly looked into the open chest and asked how long the patient had been down.

"Twenty minutes," came the reply.

"That's it, I'm calling it," she announced matter-of-factly, like a film director calling "cut."

The room went as still as the morning. It was eerily silent. After a quick shot of the grim tableau, Jillian respected the quiet and stopped taking pictures. She glanced one last time at the soldier, who, with his blue eyes and blond hair and youthfulness, managed to look incongruously cheerful even in death.

Later, in the hallway, Jillian saw Logan chatting with another soldier—a buddy of the victim, she concluded. She couldn't hear what they were saying, but she saw Logan put her arm around the man as he began crying—quietly at first, then more violently.

Turning back to Mark, Jillian cleared her throat roughly, her voice like sandpaper. She couldn't take another minute of this. "C'mon, let's get out of here."

Jillian let the tears fall as she scrolled through the photos on her laptop. Mark sat beside her, silently respecting her emotional display. It was hard looking at the photos, remembering what she'd seen a few hours ago. The doctors and nurses had all worked so hard to save that young man's life, and it had all been for nothing. They'd all gone through the emotional turmoil of trying to save a life that couldn't be saved, putting everything they had into it.

There was some comfort in the fact that the other soldier, the one with the severe leg injury, had survived and was going to recover. But Jillian didn't think she'd ever be able to forget the look on that young soldier's face in death or the haunted look of futility on the faces of Logan and the others. When it became apparent their work was done, that the fight was lost, they looked like they were barely holding back a torrent of emotions. But they had, and now Jillian's heart broke a little for all the things Logan and her colleagues couldn't express. Their stoicism was admirable, yet had to be so damned hard to maintain.

"I don't think I'll ever look at a young man the same way again," she said quietly, knowing their time here would change her and Mark.

Mark nodded, staring unblinking at the screen. After a long while, he said, "You know, when I was that age…" He shook his head sadly, his eyes moist with his own memories. "All I cared about was getting high or getting laid…scoring the next big goal. Jesus. To put yourself on the line like that for your country? I couldn't do it, Jill. I just couldn't."

She put her arm around him, thinking how differently men and women reacted to war and self-sacrifice. Mark, she knew, was examining his manhood, questioning his sense of selflessness and courage. She, on the other hand, was thinking of her daughter and the mothers and wives and husbands and how much there was to lose. She thought of the emotional costs, too, and her thoughts slid to Logan and the toll she paid here, day after day, week after week. How did she manage to cope with so much loss? And how would she come out of it?

She'd seen the flashing, haunted look in Logan's eyes after

the young soldier's death—the void where hope had sparked just moments before—followed by the supreme look of sadness and then the dulling of her emotions. Jillian felt her heart constrict again, as she remembered the overwhelming desire she'd had to take Logan in her arms and comfort her, to try to transfuse some light back into her. Hope, she knew, was something people had to discover and maintain themselves. But hope and joy for life were terrible things to lose, and she didn't want Logan to stop caring, to stop *living*.

Recognizing the deep need she felt to protect Logan gave Jillian a sudden, unexpected jolt. Logan was hurting, and Jillian's instinct was to go to her. "Mark, have you seen Major Sharp?"

"Nope. But I ran into Meg. She says the major's taking it pretty hard."

What did that mean, exactly? Did it mean Logan was curled up in a little ball somewhere, crying her heart out? Not likely. Was she in the gym pounding on the heavy bag? Was she in someone else's arms right now, getting comfort?

Her last thought rattled Jillian, uncomfortably so. Logan was gay. She'd as much as told her so this morning. Jillian now wondered, with more than a passing curiosity, if Logan had a girlfriend here or back home. *Who does she open her heart to, tell her sorrows to, find companionship with? Who does she think about when she turns out the light at night? Is there anyone she shares her innermost thoughts and feelings with? Or is she totally on her own?*

Jillian couldn't say if she honestly wanted to know the answers to her silent questions, because she felt a vague sense of loneliness herself. Maybe loneliness wasn't the right word, but aloneness was, for sure, even though she had the idyllic life back home with a reliable, loyal partner and the most wonderful child in the world. Her stable home life allowed her to go off exploring the world with her camera, and yet she felt as though a part of her had faded like an old photograph over the years. She shook her head to clear it. She didn't want to think about that lost, withering part of herself right now, because she really had no rational explanation for her feelings. It was like looking out on sunny skies even as the barometer on the wall warned of severe atmospheric changes.

"Jill," Mark said gently, interrupting her thoughts. "You need to back off."

"Huh?" She hadn't a clue what he was talking about. She only knew her stomach felt like it was bottoming out.

"Major Sharp. You need to step back. You're getting too close."

Jillian felt her breath leave her. He was right. She was getting close. But she'd done nothing wrong. She felt an undeniable connection with Logan Sharp, an emotional pull she could not ignore, but it was not wrong. Neither of them had overstepped any boundaries, and she resented the implication. Her voice tightened. "There's nothing to worry about, Mark."

He clearly wasn't buying it. Disbelief was in his eyes. "There's something going on between you two, Jill. And I think it's dangerous."

"There is *not* anything going on between us. Please. Do you not think I'm just a little more professional than that? Not to mention the fact that I take committed relationships very seriously?" Her indignation was about to explode. How dare he try to be her conscience, her morality cop. *Him* of all people!

"I didn't say you were fucking her," he whispered. "Jesus, Jill. All I meant was…" He sighed in frustration. "I don't know, okay? I can just feel this real bond between you two, and I don't want anyone to get hurt. I just don't want you getting too attached to anyone here."

And what would be wrong with that? she wanted to ask him. What was wrong with caring for someone? With sharing an emotional connection, even if it was only for a couple of weeks? What the hell was wrong with being human and having feelings?

"I swear, Mark, all you men think about is sex. That if I'm not *fucking* Major Sharp, as you put it, then I must want to. Or she must want to. Or we're going to commit some carnal sin here. Christ. What is so wrong with just wanting to be friends with someone? I mean, you and I are friends, and we don't have sex or do anything that's a threat to my relationship with Steph. So why are you so worried about Major Sharp?"

He shook his head, his jaw clenched. Her words had clearly stung him. "Look, just forget I said anything, okay?" He glanced at the pictures on the screen again, changing the subject by suggesting which ones she should edit out and which ones she should keep, but Jillian's mind kept wandering to the issue he had raised, to this supposed mutual attraction between her and Logan, to the obvious chemistry between them. Or at least obvious to him.

Jillian tried to corral her thoughts, because the sooner she got hold of them, the better. Mark was right in that there was something between her and Logan, but he could say or think what he wanted, because Jillian did have a firm grip on her morals, dammit. She'd never cheated on Steph in their seven years together and she never would. Their relationship didn't exactly make her want to scream from the rooftops anymore, but it was safe and it was solid. It was what relationships became when the sparks sputtered out and the chemistry dissolved.

"Are you going to the ramp ceremony at sunset?" he asked after a moment. She welcomed the new topic.

"I wouldn't miss it," she said firmly, though she was still quietly disturbed.

Logan had been to ramp ceremonies for fallen comrades too many times. Saying goodbye to them never got easier; in fact each time was worse. It was the layering of sadness upon sadness until it was almost too much to bear. This one hurt especially, because this was one she herself couldn't save. It wasn't often that someone was brought into the base hospital alive and left in a box, and she took it personally. Though she knew in her gut they'd done everything they could have done, it still felt like a failure. All deaths did, but this one most of all.

The Light Armored Vehicle carrying the casket pulled up to the assembled troops and civilians, its dust taking a long time to settle. At least six hundred people were on hand to give a final salute to the young soldier, to watch him depart for home soil for the last time. The LAV's ramp dropped with a loud, metallic thud, and the pallbearers—fellow soldiers in their cammos—hoisted the flag-draped casket on their brawny, weary shoulders and slowly began to move between the flanking lines of troops. Logan and the others were at least fourteen rows deep—Brits, Americans, Danes, Dutch, Estonians, Aussies, French, Romanians, Canadians. The casket was inched slowly toward the belly of the waiting Hercules C-130. A bagpiper walked slowly behind and played a wailing, haunting rendition of "Amazing Grace." It was both heartbreaking and breathtaking.

Logan felt the crushing weight of so many emotions—mostly despair and deep sadness—as she watched this final departure of a fallen comrade. Still, she felt buoyed by the enormous honor of serving in the company of such brave, selfless people. The brief ceremony was dignified, lovely even, but unspeakably sad. Already, people back home were grieving the loss of this young man. Again, Logan was nagged by doubts. Could she have done something more? Tried something different? Had they given up too soon? She hated second guessing, yet she always had to exhaust herself with it before she could find the peace to move on.

She turned her attention to the padre, who was uttering a brief prayer. Then the lieutenant-colonel, stiff as a flagpole, turned to face them. "Task Force Afghanistan, to your fallen comrade, salute!" They complied, some with tears streaming down their cheeks, and then they were commanded, "Carry on!" And they would, Logan knew, but with a small piece of them gone on that huge, dull gray military plane that soon would wing its way home. Each colleague's death left them just a little emptier, a little more exposed and sharper edged, like when a hunk of rock was chiseled away from a boulder.

The ceremony over, Logan milled around, talking quietly with her comrades. They hugged and comforted one another with simple words and gestures. None of them spoke angrily.

No one wanted to be responsible for being a negative influence. They all knew instinctively what it would take to carry on with their jobs, and it was support for one another and their mission, not fear or anger or regret.

Logan had been aware earlier of Jillian discreetly taking photos, but she had kept a respectful distance, letting the soldiers grieve together. *She is waiting to talk to me, to see if I'm okay,* Logan realized. The thought was both annoying and beautifully touching.

"Hi." Logan approached Jillian without hesitation. *If she wants to talk to me, fine. Here I am.*

"Hey, you." When Jillian looked up at her, Logan saw the depth of her worry and concern. They were so clearly etched on her face, deepening her fine lines just a little.

"Walk with me?"

The sun's last rays were nearly gone now, the sky darkening rapidly as they sauntered away from the crowd, their shoulders nearly, but not quite, touching.

"Are you okay?"

The question was inevitable, but Logan didn't know how to answer. She desperately wanted to say she was just fine, but Jillian would want an honest answer—she was not asking out of politeness. For reasons she couldn't quite decipher, Logan wanted to tell her the truth. But it was so hard. With her sister she was unfailingly open, but with no one else. Not with her former lovers, not with the rest of her family. Not with her friends. Even with her colleagues, it was rare to confess fears or weakness, raw emotion. It was natural for her to resist now.

"I…" Logan's throat was hopelessly dry, and words would only come if she forced them out. Even then, she wasn't sure. She was drowning in emotions right now, powerless against them. The churning inside her was like a swollen, raging river that had yet to decide in which direction it would thunder and carve its will. "It's hard," was all she dared.

"Oh, Lo– I mean, Major Sharp." Jill halted their progress with a gentle hand on Logan's shoulder.

"It's okay." Logan tried to smile but failed. "You can call me Logan. It feels like you should."

"Yes, it does." Jill's answering smile was reassuring.

They were quiet for a long time, walking again. The sky had grown inky black, and it was mercifully cooler now. The stars were clear and bright, like in northern Michigan or Canada, and yet they looked different somehow. The crescent moon was oriented sideways, its ends tilting upward instead of vertically like back home, and the stars and constellations were not in their usual positions. It was disorienting, and Logan still couldn't get used to it.

"You were right," Jillian said, tilting her face skyward. "It's beautiful here at night. Different but beautiful."

A star fell in the distance—a shooting ball of flame—and Logan felt Jillian stiffen at her side.

"Don't worry, it's not a rocket."

Jillian laughed nervously. She curled her arm around Logan's bicep and clutched it because they could barely see a step in front of them now. They walked again in silence for a while, heading slowly in the direction of their quarters. "Do you hate them, Logan?"

"Who?"

"The Taliban."

The question burned in Logan's throat. She had contemplated it so many times over the last ten months—before that even. Oh, she wanted to hate them, all right. But if she sank to their brand of evil and hatred, she would irreparably damage herself. She knew this just as surely as she knew anything real. "Hate's never changed the world for the better."

"No. It hasn't. But they're your enemy. They want to kill you, Logan."

"We're professionals. It's not necessary to hate the enemy."

"Ah, I see. More like a game of hockey. You're just playing the game for the sake of the game. You don't actually hate your opponent."

Logan felt a smile try to exert itself. Jillian, by her own

admission, was no athlete. And she was certainly no soldier, and yet she had a point, even if Logan wouldn't admit it to her. "Hate makes you lose your focus, distracts you, forces you to make mistakes. You'll lose the game if you let your emotions rule."

"And what about when your opponent hurts you or someone you care about? When they make it personal? When they *hate* you? What then? You said yourself there were no rules of engagement in this war."

Logan didn't want to continue this conversation. It was making her think about things she didn't want to think about right now. She had two more months to get through, two more months to keep her head in the game, to maintain her composure. "Jill, look. I have nothing more to say on the topic, okay? I'm just trying to do my job here the best way I can. And for me, that means not thinking about...*them*. Not letting them have that power over me."

Jillian clamped harder on Logan's arm to stop their progress again. "I saw the look in your eyes today. When you lost that soldier. You looked heartbroken, but then you bottled everything up again. You push those feelings down so deep, Logan. I'm afraid for you. I'm afraid there'll come a time when there won't be any space left to put those feelings."

Anger began to surge through Logan—in tiny waves at first, but then more powerfully. What did this woman know about war? About losing lives? About trying to do your job when everything around you is going to hell? What did she really know about *her* and what made her tick? It took all Logan's effort not to raise her voice. "What do you think I should do, Jillian? Break down in front of everyone? Throw up my hands and say I'm not doing this anymore? What?"

"Of course not. But is there anyone you can talk to?"

"Why do you care?" Logan's tone was abrupt and accusing, but she couldn't help herself. If Jillian wanted her to show emotion, fine, because that's exactly what she would get.

"Because." Jillian stepped closer, facing Logan. It was so dark, Logan could only see the outline of her face. "Because I don't want this place to steal the kindhearted, generous person you are. I don't want it to make you bitter and…I don't know. Different."

"You don't even know me."

"I know you enough to know you're a good person, Logan. The best kind there is."

Logan laughed bitterly. "Yeah, well, you know what, Jill? It's not your job to care about me, okay? It's not your job to worry about what any of this shit is doing to me." If it was one thing she didn't need right now, it was someone scrutinizing her every move and every look to see if she was okay. Someone peering into her very soul. She didn't want to feel like a specimen on a slide, didn't need someone worrying about her, checking up on her all the time like she was some emotional cripple.

Jillian, clearly stung, recoiled almost imperceptibly. Her voice grew strained. "Of course it's not my job, Logan. But I do…care, okay? I want to be your friend."

Logan felt the prickling of guilt for being such a heartless bitch. Was it so terrible that this woman had struck a bond with her and cared about her? She'd be gone in a little more than a week, after all. What did it really matter if her weaknesses were apparent to Jillian Knight? They would never see each other again. She was safe with Jillian, wasn't she?

"Jillian," she said roughly. Her need was so great right now, its enormity scared the hell out of her. She couldn't risk opening the floodgates because she had no idea if she could rein her emotions back in. Could you reverse the water after opening a dam? Recapture a breath once it escaped? Take spoken words back? *No.*

Suddenly, Jillian's featherlike fingers were on her cheek. The sensation that resulted was like an electrical current, one strong enough to nearly knock her on her ass. Her breath left her violently, and it hurt to suck it back in. *Jesus Christ.* What was happening to her? She felt dizzy from the touch and began to sway a little.

"It's okay." Jillian's voice was butterfly soft before it was carried off on the gentle, warm breeze.

"*No, it's not okay,*" Logan wanted to scream. *You have no idea!* The hand on her face, so tender, sparked an unexpected painful longing for all the things she didn't have—a home, safety at the end of the day, a woman's loving, caring touch. *God.* How she wanted to nuzzle her cheek against that hand, to fall into what she felt sure was a warm, waiting embrace...to let herself go, to let herself be consoled and nurtured in a way she had not allowed herself in so long. *Just this once.*

Instead, she forced herself to stand up straighter, to step away from Jillian's reach. *This is not the woman, Logan, and it's not the time.* It was foolish, maybe even dangerous, to grant Jillian the role of her emotional savior. With effort, Logan dragged her resolve back to the forefront, where it belonged.

"Look, Jillian, do us both a favor. Don't waste your time caring about me, okay?"

Jillian, rigid from the sting of the words, wasn't relenting. Her voice was thick with hurt. "I want to care, Logan. It's who I am, okay? I can't just shut that off. And neither can you."

The last part felt like a slap, but Logan refused to be baited. She wanted to lash out, to hurt the woman who had so easily seen right through her, who made her want to admit things and share things that were better left buried, like the soldier she'd just lost.

"Look, Jill. Just go back to your wife and child when you're done here and just forget about everything, okay? Go back to your nice life and leave me alone."

She turned sharply and strode away, leaving Jillian alone in the dark, knowing that Jillian was probably hurting as much as she was.

CHAPTER FOUR

Jillian flipped to another page in her *Michigan Today* magazine. She'd brought it with her more to remind her of home than as reading material, and it had occurred to her this morning that Nazirah might like the pictures in it.

And boy, did she ever. Especially the article on Mackinac Island...well, the pictures anyway. There was no interpreter available, so Jillian did her best to explain where Mackinac Island was, using a piece of paper, a pencil, and her rudimentary drawing skills. Her depiction of Lake Michigan looked like a drooping water balloon and Lake Huron resembled the jagged wing of a bird. Oh well. It wasn't like Nazirah would hold her to account.

Nazirah was touching the magazine like it was sacred, her eyes dancing with curiosity and awe. She stroked the glossy, bright pages reverently, almost afraid to turn them. Her wide-eyed joy and appreciation instantly lifted Jillian from the dark mood she'd awakened to. Logan was already gone from the room, removing any chance for them to talk about what had happened the night before, any chance for Logan to show remorse or guilt or discomfort for the way she'd treated Jillian. At least Jillian hoped Logan felt those things. And that Logan had lost as much sleep as she had. It would be divine justice.

Why, Jillian wondered again for the millionth time, does she think she needs to wall off her feelings from everyone? *Why does she need to be so goddamned stoic and stubborn all the time? What is she afraid of, that I'll mock her? Think less of her? Think she's weak? Or that I'll hurt her in some way?*

Jillian knew she could come on a bit strong sometimes. She liked to talk things out, even if it required lots of pushing and pulling. Introspection was fine to a point, but only if it ended in discussion. And sullenness or pouting? She had zero time for that. Some of the epic battles she and Steph had fought had resulted from the clashing of Steph's quiet, reflective ways and her own emotional openness. Steph liked to disappear into her study for hours at a time or sit at the table over a meal with her nose in a newspaper or book. If she was feeling angry or upset, Steph would vanish to lick her wounds. Jillian, on the other hand, would fume and storm about. They weren't exactly a good match that way. It drove Jillian nuts sometimes.

Nazirah's gesticulations drew Jillian's attention back to the pictures of horses and buggies in the Mackinac article. Nodding enthusiastically, she mimicked driving a car, and then, through hand signals, tried to explain that there were no cars on the island. It was some moments before she noticed Logan leaning against the plywood wall, watching them, a hesitant smile twitching at the corners of her mouth. Logan's eyes, though tired, looked much sharper and more alive than they had last night. It amazed Jillian how those eyes could be like the cold, November waters of Lake Michigan one minute, then lushly green the next, capable of skewering you one minute and cradling you the next, depending on her mood. That was the key to reading Logan, Jillian decided, studying her eyes.

"Did you want to see me?" Jillian finally asked.

"Not if I'm interrupting." Logan directed her attention to

Nazirah. "Salam. Chétori shoma, Nazirah?"

"Man khoobam, mamnoon."

Jillian smiled at Nazirah and motioned for her to keep the magazine. She followed Logan out of the room to an empty supply area. Walled off on three sides by plywood, its fourth side a curtain, it offered as much privacy as could be found anywhere on the base.

"How is she doing?" Jillian asked.

"Good, considering how bad the abscess was. We're getting the infection under control and in a day or two we'll do some surgery."

"Your Farsi is very impressive," Jillian said.

"Anyone can pick up a few words. But you…you're so good with her." Logan eyed her with obvious appreciation. Her voice was deep and soft and so far removed from the hollow, harsh tones of last night. "Maybe we should keep you here as part of our therapy program."

Jillian laughed politely, then grew silent at the emotion she glimpsed on Logan's face. It was there and gone so fast, like the falling star last night…almost too quickly for Jillian to catch it. Was it sadness? Longing? Regret? Jillian couldn't be sure, but whatever it was had burned intensely for an instant before disappearing. She gasped at the realization of how practiced Logan was at tamping down her emotions.

"Last night, I…I'm sorry, Jillian. I wasn't very nice to you and I just want to apologize."

Jillian crossed her arms over her chest, confounded. How could this intelligent, caring woman be so clueless? How could she not get it? No matter how much she wanted to choke some sense into Logan, she needed to gather the words she wanted to say, keep her temper in check. Castigating Logan would end their budding friendship in a hell of a hurry. "Logan." She took a deep breath and let it out slowly. "It's not about me. You don't need to apologize."

Bewilderment flared in Logan's eyes. "But my behavior…it was uncalled for."

"All right, fine. I accept your apology. But don't you see?" Jillian's temper threatened to surface again, and she had to push it back down. "It's about you, Logan. It's about you having a place to express your feelings. It's about you working through what happened yesterday with that soldier. I was trying to help you find that place because I was worried about you."

Jillian watched the handsome jaw predictably stiffen, the eyes darken. *There she goes, withdrawing again.* "I know," Jillian added softly. "You'll deal with it all later. After you get through this." She took a step closer and dropped her voice. "But what if later is too late? What if there's too much of it to deal with? What if it's too overwhelming?"

"It hasn't been yet," Logan said in a whisper.

Jillian didn't wait for another excuse or denial from Logan. She simply stepped up to her and put her arms around her. Not clutching, not desperate, just gentle and calming. It was what she had wanted to do and should have done last night. She waited for Logan to get past her surprise, to relax her body, to accept what she was giving. After a few beats, Logan's arms loosely returned the embrace and her body sagged a little into Jillian. A slight trembling began, and Jillian tightened her grip. The embrace became more of a hug—a hug that was sweet and warm and comforting.

"I can't, Jillian. I can't do this," Logan finally uttered, her voice cracking.

"Yes, you can. Sometimes this is all we can do for one another."

Logan shook her head and forcefully pulled away. "You don't understand." She waited until they were looking at one another. "My need is much greater than you can give, Jill."

It was said with almost clinical detachment. Jillian was stunned by how quickly and unequivocally Logan was willing to dismiss what she was offering. *How does she know that what I am willing to give her isn't enough? And even if it isn't enough, isn't a little bit of warmth and understanding better than nothing?*

"Logan," she started to say, but her words were met with Logan's retreating back.

It was a truce, of sorts. Logan tried her best to avoid Jillian over the next few days. When they crossed paths, she was polite but perfunctory. Keeping things businesslike between them was best, even though she knew it grated on Jillian. She'd catch the photographer looking at her sometimes like she didn't understand what was happening. Logan understood exactly what she was doing, however. She was closing up, retreating into a protective shell the way she'd done many times before with women who had tried to get too close. She had no choice. She was walking a minefield with Jillian, losing something of herself, and for her own protection, it had to stop.

Pushing the barbell up for another chest press, Logan's muscles strained, but her mind remained calm and razor sharp. Jillian might think she was helping, pushing her way into that deep, private place that Logan had only ever allowed two people into, but she wasn't at all. All Jillian was doing was making her feel vulnerable, exposed, weak. Her sister Lisa was allowed into that space and always would be, because Logan trusted her implicitly. Nicole had been once, but that had been a huge mistake. Logan was not about to repeat that lapse in judgment again. Family was different because they were with you forever. Friends and girlfriends, on the other hand, were transient. Logan was simply not a Meg Atwood, somebody who was everybody's confidante and buddy. Nor was she a Jillian Knight, so secure in her touchy-feely, confessional ways. No. She had to protect herself first. Rely on herself first because ultimately, she was all she had.

Logan replaced the bar on the rack. She lay on the bench, breathing hard, her chest burning. *God*. She hadn't thought of Nicole in months. Longer even. Nicole no longer elicited much bitterness in her, but she would never forget her betrayal, nor the years of hurt and doubt that betrayal had caused. That it still caused, she supposed. Thinking about Nicole now was like examining a scar. While the wound no longer hurt, its mark remained, a stark reminder of the pain.

They'd met in college, when Logan was halfway through med school and Nicole was starting her master's degree in English lit. They became lovers quickly and moved in together after just few months. She could talk to Nicole—really talk to her, be herself with her. They shared everything—their goals, their fears, their hopes and dreams. And then one day, three years into their relationship, Nicole announced that Logan's absences and long preoccupations with work and study had left her feeling isolated and lonely. So isolated and lonely, in fact, that she'd had no choice but to find solace in the arms of one of her fellow professors. It was bad enough that Nic had left Logan for someone else, but blaming *her* for it? Saying that it was her fault because she had had to spend long hours away from home in med school and residency, because she had not paid enough attention to Nic? The experience had taught Logan unforgettable lessons: that trust was transient, that the one you love most could be not only unreliable but untrue, that love more often than not was a veneer and not something that was solid to the core.

Nicole had been Logan's failure. It was her only failure in life thus far—and it had changed her, she knew. She hadn't the desire to make that emotional investment in anyone again. There was enough pain and disappointment in this world without slapping a sign on your forehead asking to be hurt again. And so she hadn't. She'd gotten quite good at putting distance between herself and any romantic prospects. She really didn't need anyone else, thank you very much. She had her sister as her long-distance confidante, she had people in her life with whom she could catch a movie or share a drink, and she had her left hand when she needed sexual release. She'd dated a handful of times since Nicole—just long enough to ask herself what the hell she was doing sitting across from someone she had to struggle to make conversation with.

Logan retrieved the heavy bar again, straining against the weight, feeling her anger burn with each rep. *Jillian.* Jillian was the first woman since Nicole who'd shown any interest in trying to strip away her aloofness and really get inside. And she didn't seem to want anything in return, unlike Nicole. It was mind-shattering. Intensely disturbing. Why did Jillian care about her? And why did she act as though dissecting and analyzing her heart was no big deal? As though talking about feelings was like talking about the weather? And how could she so selflessly offer herself as an emotional crutch? Did she not know that being needed by someone was a burden—a quagmire of responsibility that sucked both people in until they didn't recognize themselves anymore? Until their need for each other overshadowed and suffocated anything else?

Logan sat up, wiping the sweat from her forehead. Jillian was naïve, that was it. She must be one of those people who thought everything could be solved by watching Dr. Phil, or buying the latest self-help book, or confessing deep sins. She was simply foolish enough to think that love could overcome anything. *Please*. Logan had loved Nic once, and look where that had gotten her. And... *My God*. Did Jillian *really* think a hug could make everything better?

Logan fiercely held onto her silent admonishments, using them to justify the discomfort Jillian had seeded in her. Even if Jillian was right, and it was a big if, there was no way she could reveal her feelings or have a good heart-to-heart with an outsider. Jillian might be able to say all the right words and dole out another of those amazing hugs, but she would never understand the life of a military doctor. She could never know what it was like to be Logan—the need to be always in control, to be reliable, steady, dependable, decisive, courageous. To be able to produce all of those things on demand, without heed to the toll they took.

"Hey, Major! Pumping yourself up for the big game tonight?"

Mark swaggered into the gym, a towel slung over his shoulder, a water bottle in his hand. He was being decidedly friendly lately, even more so since she'd enlarged the distance between herself and Jillian.

When he sat on the bench across from her, it was with the casualness of having done it a hundred times before, as though they were best friends. "I gotta tell you, I'm so thrilled you asked me to play tonight. I heard those guys we're up against are huge, but I figure, if we've got speed, we–"

"Mark," she interrupted, not in the mood to talk hockey. The hot and cold way he'd been treating her was eating at her, she realized. She wanted to know what the chip on his shoulder was and why the hell he was carrying it. She addressed him as an officer would a subordinate—direct but emotionless. "You haven't liked me much since the first day we met. Care to tell me just exactly what I've done to offend you?"

Emotions rose and fell on his face—surprise and confusion at first, followed by denial. Then a cold, hard honesty sharpened his features. "You're right, I didn't." He sighed heavily, looking around before settling wary eyes on Logan again. "It nearly drives Jillian insane when I do that."

"Do what?"

"Act like an ass to someone she gets close to. It just usually takes me a lot longer than the first day."

"So you're jealous or something?" The shock of her words resonated in her own gut. *Yes. He wouldn't be wrong to be jealous, would he?* "You want all her attention for yourself? Is that it?"

Mark grinned. "I gotta hand it to you, Major. You don't pull any punches."

"I rather get the feeling you wouldn't have it any other way."

His grin dissolved. "You're right. This is good, me and you talking. And no, I don't want Jill all to myself. Been there, done that."

Logan had suspected as much. "Ancient history?"

"Yes. Very ancient."

"Then why does it bother you that Jillian and I…" What were they exactly? Fast friends? Friendly acquaintances? Buddies? It occurred to her that she really didn't know. She cleared her throat and decided to be as honest as she could. "I'm not exactly sure that I would call Jill and I friends, Mark. But I would like to know why her being around me or seeing her direct any attention my way seems to piss you off."

Mark looked away again. He seemed to be battling with himself about how to respond, his grip loosening and tightening on his towel. When he finally looked at her, it was with surprising openness. "You see, Jill and I go back a long way. She's like a sister to me. My best friend. I get very protective of her. And sometimes, I admit, I act like an idiot. But I can't seem to help it. She's very important to me, and I worry about her."

Logan nodded, having no problem with his answer so far. In fact, it was nice that Jillian had someone like Mark in her corner. "Where do I fit into all this?"

"Major Sharp, I–"

"Please. Call me Logan."

"I probably shouldn't be telling you this stuff, you know. I haven't even told Jill."

Logan felt her eyebrows arching skyward. "You don't have to–"

"Yes, I do, because I haven't been very fair to you." He leaned forward, elbows on his knees, and looked at her so earnestly that she could immediately see that this man, this sometimes rude, immature jock, had a sensitive side. He was a good guy underneath all that macho crap, and it shouldn't have surprised her. A woman like Jill would not place her trust and friendship in Mark if he wasn't one of the good ones.

"See," he continued. "Jill went and picked herself the wrong woman seven years ago."

"Pardon?" She was not prepared for this admission, because it had never occurred to her that Jillian might not be happy. *Why the hell is he telling me this?*

He nodded severely. "It breaks my heart that she's with someone who's just so…different from her, so not right for her. It's hard for me to explain, but if you walked into a room of a dozen people and were asked which of them were couples, you would never guess Jill and Steph were together."

All right, so Jillian hadn't been lucky enough or smart enough to choose Ms. Right. So what? "And what does this–"

"Wait, Logan. It's more complicated than that." He looked around nervously, is if expecting Jillian to walk through the door any minute and catch him in this act of betrayal. "God, Jill would never speak to me again if she heard me talk like this. All this time, I've never told her how I felt about her and Steph for that very reason." He shrugged. "Though I'm sure she's figured out I'm not Steph's biggest fan."

Logan smothered a laugh. "You're not exactly good at hiding your feelings."

Mark grinned back at her. "Ya think? Anyway, as close as we are, it's not my place to tell her she and Steph shouldn't be together."

"But aren't you her best friend? Aren't you supposed to tell your best friend when something isn't right for them?" She knew Lisa would certainly tell her if she thought she was unhappy or had made a mistake. More than tell her, she'd kick her ass.

"Yeah, right. Your best friend jumps all over you about your lover. Who do you think is gonna lose that fight?"

He had a point. "You're right. Probably not a good idea."

"Hell, when she told me I was nuts for marrying Linda…my ex…I was livid. I didn't talk to her for three months. Even though she ended up being right, of course."

"I'm sorry you don't feel Jill is happy, Mark."

"See, that's just it. She doesn't even really know she's not happy. She's just gotten into this place where she just, I don't know, accepts it. She accepts that they don't go out any more, don't really have any friends, don't go on vacations together. Going to bed at nine o'clock every night. She accepts second rate."

"Having a young child can take the pop out of a relationship, I'm sure."

He shook his head regretfully. "It's not that. Jill always used to be so much fun. So full of life. She's changed with Steph. And you…" He scrutinized her like she was the prize heifer in the ring. "You're the kind of woman she should be with, Logan. I can tell she feels *alive* when she's around you. She's different with you.

But she's not free. She's so far from available, it's not funny."

"What?" Logan wished she were anywhere but here, floored as she was by the absurdity of what he was saying. She grasped for the tiniest shred of understanding. "Jesus, Mark! Christ, we hardly know each other. How could you possibly think I'm the kind of person Jill should be with? That's absurd."

Hell, Jillian would never choose her anyway. Logan just wasn't the type to be nailed down, to live the suburban middle-class existence of working nine-to-five, two cars in the drive, a nice vacation once a year.

Mark's smile was devilish. "I'm not as stupid as I look, you know."

She didn't smile back. "This isn't about IQ levels."

"All right, it's not. But you are exactly what Jill would be attracted to, even if she doesn't admit it to herself."

"Look, this whole conversation is making me uncomfortable."

"Sorry. It's just that I know Jill better than she knows herself sometimes. And vice versa. I just don't want her, you know, doing something stupid right now. Realizing all of a sudden how wrong Steph is for her, compliments of you. I don't want you to be the cause of her turning her life upside down. She'd never forgive herself. Or you." He stood up and leveled a gaze at her that might have been menacing on anyone else. "Be very careful with her, Logan."

A small breeze could have knocked Logan to the floor. This had to rank as one of the most bizarre conversations she'd ever had with anyone. And she'd had a few, particularly during her psych rotation. "Look, Mark, I really think you're just–"

"No, wait." He held his hand up like a stop sign. "Please don't make me sound like I'm crazy or something. Christ, even though I know I must sound like I am. I just don't want her or Steph blaming their relationship failings on a third party. It's just such a bad way to end a relationship. Believe me, I know."

Logan stood, wanting to end this conversation as quickly as possible. "Look, Mark. I admire your intentions, I really do. I know you want the best for Jillian. But there is nothing going on between us, and I certainly don't want to cause her any problems." She wasn't just placating him. It was the truth. "There is nothing for you to worry about."

He shook his head. "That's where you're wrong, Logan. God, I know I haven't made myself very clear. But I do know this. The chemistry between you two is like an atom bomb. I just don't want it going off."

"I don't have any intention of making any bombs go off. Believe me."

Mark looked relieved but not completely convinced. "Good."

Jillian read through Steph's e-mail again, more hurt than angry. Last night, she had sent her lover a long, emotionally draining e-mail describing the young soldier's death and how valiantly the medical team had worked trying to save him. She described the ramp ceremony and how honored she felt to be a part of it all, how empty she felt afterward. And yet Steph barely mentioned any of it in her reply, other than to ask if the dead soldier was American or Canadian. Like that mattered, Jillian thought angrily. Steph wasn't even trying to understand what she was going through. Didn't care. Instead she went on about her classes and the crappy mid-term marks and how that was going to reflect on her as a professor. She talked a bit about Maddie, of course. She also made a list of all the bills she'd paid and things she'd had to tend to. Her little way, perhaps, of making Jillian feel guilty for being away.

Jillian angrily slammed her laptop shut. Did Steph really not care what was happening to her here? She'd been away on assignments before, but never this long, nor had she ever been in harm's way like this. Already she was feeling vested in this place, in what the soldiers and medical staff were doing day in and day out. Of course Steph wouldn't understand, but it'd be nice if she at least tried, Jillian thought. She could at least show her a bit of empathy, have a little conversation about it. Was that so hard?

Oh, hell. What was the use at getting angry at Steph? It wasn't like it would help anything. At least Steph was doing her part keeping the home fires burning. Really, wasn't that enough? Was she expecting too much of her? Shouldn't she just be happy to have the freedom to push her career into new territory like this? Shouldn't she be grateful to have a chance to show the world what the brave, hardworking doctors and nurses were doing over here?

Jillian *was* grateful and honored to bear witness to what was happening at KAF, and she wasn't going to feel guilty about it. If she couldn't get some understanding from home, there were plenty of people right here who knew exactly what she was feeling. She understood now why Logan kept her thoughts and feelings to herself so much. Perhaps she, too, had tried and failed to get support from those she loved.

Hockey was the furthest thing from Logan's mind as she dressed for the game. She kept replaying the conversation with Mark in her head, still disbelieving his words. If Jillian was unhappy in her marriage, even though she'd given no indication of it, it was Jillian's problem. It had absolutely nothing to do with Logan, no matter what sort of strange threat Mark thought she posed.

Jesus, what does he think Jillian and I are doing in that little room every night? Does he think we're getting it on? Or at least that we're secretly wishing we were getting it on?

It was disappointing he didn't give her more credit than that. That he didn't give *them* more credit than that. Jillian had never so much as hinted that she was anything but monogamous, and Logan wouldn't dream of seducing someone in Jillian's situation and playing the role of home wrecker. She had far more respect for herself and Jillian than to engage in such destructive, juvenile games.

She jogged out to the rink and greeted her closest teammates with a high-five, distracted and grouchy and uncharacteristically just wanting to get the game over. She gave Mark a cursory nod

83

and lined up at center to take the face-off.

Logan ran hard, determined to let the action cleanse her mind and ease her mood. She quickly scored a breakaway goal, then set up Mark for a two-on-one that just missed scoring. After a few minutes, she jogged to the bench for a substitute, her mind remarkably liberated. When she played sports, especially ones as fast as hockey, there was little time to think about anything but the task at hand. That was a damn relief today. Her lungs and legs burned, the pain and her breathlessness keeping her focused on the game, even while on the bench. After a minute or two, she let her gaze wander lazily over the few dozen spectators standing or sitting behind the boards. She was thinking of nothing much at all when she spotted a familiar figure sitting quietly among them—and everything thundered to a halt. Her racing heart. The breaths she'd just moments ago been struggling for. And most of all, the serenity she'd been enjoying.

She blinked hard, making sure the dark beauty in the stands was indeed Jillian, then calmly reminded herself to breathe again. She tried to remind herself not to stare, too, but she couldn't help it. Jillian had cut her hair. It was short, just below collar length, and thick and wavy and almost black. The new shape made her face, with its impossibly big eyes and soft mouth, look more youthful. More carefree. She looked almost boyish, in fact. Except…Logan's gaze dropped a notch to the turquoise-ribbed tank top clinging to her perfect curves. Jillian was unquestionably all woman.

Logan got through the rest of the game without getting injured or making a fool of herself, but she was not exactly stellar, missing three one-timers and blowing several passes. Her mind was fixed irrevocably on Jillian, and neither the game nor shaking hands afterward with the opposing players could dislodge it. How had this woman sneaked inside her so easily? How could Jillian get to her like this? Kill that razor-like concentration she prided herself on and turn her into a walking, sappy greeting card? *Jesus.* It was like being back in college or high school, all butterflies and getting giddy and stupid over a girl. A girl who hadn't even shown *that* kind of interest in her and, worst of all, wasn't even available. *Could I have a crush on anyone more inappropriate?*

A crush. The word felt so childish, but her feelings certainly had all the hallmarks—the nervous tension when she saw Jillian, the little thrill she felt when Jillian looked at her or spoke to her, the pull to be in close proximity to her.

It was also so much more than a crush. Jillian made her think about things that were better left alone. Made her both love and despise the deep conversations Jillian and nobody else could involve her in. Made her wish—*pray*—that Jillian would just hop on the next flight home.

Logan, determined to make a quick exit, was on the sidelines hastily gathering her things in a duffel bag when she felt the inevitable tap on her shoulder.

"Good game, Logan. You and Mark looked like you've been playing together for years."

Logan spun around, immediately pinned by Jillian's eyes. Panic surged in her, the kind of panic that made her want to flee, the kind that turned her instantly into a coward. "I, ah, didn't realize you were here." *Liar.* "Um, your hair," she said as if she'd just noticed. "It looks great."

Jillian gave her a quizzical smile. "Really? I haven't had short hair like this since I was a kid. It feels strange, but it's just so incredibly hot here, I couldn't stand it anymore."

Logan still wanted to run but not as fast or as quickly as she did a moment ago. "You look like that singer, Norah Jones."

Jillian tilted her head contemplatively. "Well, that's quite a compliment, especially since I'm a fan of Norah's music. How about you?"

Reluctantly, Logan let herself relax. Yes, they could do this. They could chat like friendly acquaintances after all. There was nothing wrong with this, nothing to suggest they were doing anything unscrupulous or dangerous. "Who wouldn't be a Norah Jones fan? Anyway, it really does look great. You're lucky to have such nice hair." She was trying so hard to sound friendly but not too friendly, polite but not aggrandizing. Except...*God.*

She wanted to reach out and stroke the silky strands, feel the curling thickness between her fingers. Her hand trembled at the temptation.

Jillian was thankfully oblivious to the little battle Logan was waging inside. Her smile broadened with the accepting of a compliment. "It's my Cuban heritage. My mother's side," she clarified at Logan's raised eyebrow.

"Ah. That's why you looked tanned before you even got here. I certainly never would have guessed by your name."

"My middle name is Amparo, so I'm at least glad there's something of my heritage on my birth certificate. It's my daughter's middle name, too."

Logan was getting sucked in. She knew she shouldn't continue such a personal conversation, shouldn't breach the decision she'd made to keep her emotional distance from Jillian. It was like knowing you shouldn't go out on that snowy icy night to play hockey, but dammit, it was hockey and she wanted to play so badly. "What does Amparo mean in English?"

"It means protection or shelter."

Logan nodded. It made sense. Jillian was lovely. Breathtakingly beautiful. *And* hot. Was there nothing that wasn't extraordinary about this woman? Why had she not noticed before how just being in her presence melted her heart like ice in a warm drink? Jillian made her feel so many things—awkward, protective, comforted, energized. The feelings were confusing, even disturbing, and yet when she was around Jillian, everything in her world suddenly seemed to click into place. It was like a spinning wheel coming to rest.

Logan's knees trembled and not from physical exertion. Her chest hurt, too, as realization slammed into her. This was no girlish crush or small infatuation. Mark was right. There was something deep and dangerous and intense between them, a chemistry that could explode in their faces if they weren't careful. And even if Jillian wasn't aware of it, Logan was, and that was enough. She would have to be careful for both of them.

"Do you–"

"Sorry, I've got to run," Logan blurted in a rush of air. She walked away without looking back, wondering only later what Jillian had been on the verge of asking her.

An hour later, showered and re-energized, Logan headed for the hospital and the lure of familiar territory. She needed to escape from Jillian. It was vital right now to keep physical and emotional distance between them, because she was no longer sure she could rein in her growing attraction to Jillian. Maybe Meg could distract her with a few laughs, if she could find her.

She was directed to the supply room by a nurse, who said she'd last seen Meg heading there. Logan jiggled the handle, which was either stuck or locked. *Goddammit.* She pulled her plastic ID card from her pocket, knowing from experience it would work just as well as a key. She slid it along the inside of the doorjamb, and the simple lock slipped free. She pushed the door open and halted abruptly.

The back of a naked woman greeted her. She was sitting on a metal cart, her hair dark and short. Her head was tilted back a little as she moaned her ecstasy. Meg, the source of the woman's pleasure, was kneeling in front of her.

Oh, Christ! Meg, fully clothed, was spiritedly performing oral sex on a woman who—*Jesus!*—looked remarkably like Jillian from behind. *Oh, God, please don't let it be her! Meg, I'll fucking kill you if it is!*

"Christ, Meg, what do you think you're doing?" Logan demanded, her heart in her throat.

The woman squeaked her alarm as Meg extracted herself and grinned up at Logan.

"Please, have you no manners, Logan?"

Logan's heart pounded, feeding her panic. She stepped around the cart. She had to see the woman's face, had to be sure it wasn't Jillian. She blinked hard against what she might see. "Thank God," she uttered on a loud sigh. It wasn't Jillian. She stalked to the rumpled uniform on a chair in the corner, glancing at the name sewn on the front. "Private Evans, do you not have anything better to do right now, like perhaps fighting a war?"

The young woman glanced down sheepishly, trying hard to cover herself with her hands. She was squeezing her legs together in a vain effort to hide her private parts. "Yes, ma'am."

"And you, Captain Atwood, I'll see you outside."

Logan didn't have to wait long in the hallway for Meg.

"Christ, Meg, what is with you? Anyone could have walked in on you fraternizing like that. You could have been immediately busted down to lieutenant."

Meg looked completely unconcerned, as though she were almost happy about it. "The door was locked, you know."

"Yeah, well, an eight-year-old could have gotten in there like I did."

"Sorry, I didn't know we had children roaming the halls."

Logan's temper flashed hot. "For fuck sakes, Meg, this isn't fucking high school."

"No shit, Einstein. It's a war zone where we could all be scorched meat tomorrow. And if I'm going to be dead tomorrow, then I'm going to have a little fun first."

Logan expelled a long, exasperated breath. She was angry at herself because she was supposed to be keeping an eye on Meg, ensuring she toed the line. The colonel would have both their heads if he found out about Meg's latest indiscretion.

Logan looked squarely at her friend and softened a little. She didn't want to pull rank and play the heavy. She needed to talk to Meg as a friend now. "Ah, Meg. I know you're just having a little fun." And she was. Meg never meant anyone any harm, but she was a little too cavalier about the consequences. "You know as well as I do that the brass around here would freak out if they knew what you'd just been doing in there." Logan held up her hand to forestall a protest from Meg. "And it's not the gay thing. You know that. Hell, they've had enough years to get used to us all by now."

Meg rolled her eyes. "Look, we were both consenting adults in that room, Logan. Though I'll admit I could have picked a more private place. Not that there is such a thing around here," she added sarcastically.

"We knew when we joined up that privacy was a thing of the past. And Meg. A private? What the hell is with that?"

"I know, but I don't technically have any authority over her. She's not in our unit. She's in communications."

It was Logan's turn to roll her eyes. "Meg, why are you always courting trouble for yourself? You've only got a couple more months here, same as me. A quickie in a supply closet is not worth harming your career over, okay?"

Meg shook her head. She was trying her best to remain staunch in her defiance, but she looked close to tears. "The army takes something out of you, Logan, something that you might never get back again. It's called your spirit, your personality. And dammit, they're not going to steal mine. I'm not going to become some cookie-cutter soldier or nurse."

Logan didn't entirely agree, but then maybe she was better at molding her own personality to what the army needed. Meg obviously wasn't. "Can I ask you something Meg?"

"Sure."

"What made you join up?"

Meg laughed. "Besides the fact that they paid my nursing tuition and that I get to be surrounded by women 24/7?"

Logan granted her a smile. "Yes, besides that."

"And besides the fact that I get to see wonderful parts of the world like this?"

Logan laughed. "Yes, besides all the glamorous travel."

"Well." Meg grew animated. "I like the challenge. I mean, it's life-and-death every day, and not just for our patients, but for us. I love taking risks. I love the thrill of it. And I love helping people who really, really need it, you know?"

"Yeah." Logan did know. Treating ear infections and addiction withdrawal in a typical hospital emergency room got stale rather quickly. "So that's my point, then. Don't blow it all by taking that need for thrills and risks in your personal time, too."

Meg crossed her arms over her chest and looked down. "I know, Logan. You're right." She raised her eyes to Logan, the defiance gone. In its place was a quiet look of determination. "I have given the army everything for the last seven years now, and they will probably get another eighteen out of me. I do the best job I can do, day in and day out."

"I know that, Meg. You're an awesome nurse."

"C'mon," Meg said, leading the way down the hall. "Let's go outside for a little walk."

The hot air hit them like a wall, and Logan felt her breath leave her for a moment. She waved to a couple of soldiers she knew, slowing her stride for the shorter Meg.

"The thing is, Logan, I want to keep a tiny part of *me* that the army can't have. I can't survive in this environment if I don't. And that part of me needs to be a little wild sometimes. Not crazy, but just a little bit wild. It's who I am."

"I know, I know," Logan conceded. She couldn't totally relate because she wasn't like Meg. She was conservative and cautious by nature. A follower of rules and mostly an introvert. She also didn't think she was a lifer the way Meg was. "I'm just asking you to be smart about it. Don't take silly chances and don't rub their faces in it."

"What? Don't rub their faces in our sexuality? Logan Sharp, you disappoint me."

"I'm not embarrassed by the fact that I'm attracted to women, Meg. I'm just saying it's a conservative, male-dominated institution. They can still make it uncomfortable for us if they want. And they will."

"Well, I for one can handle a little discomfort."

Well, I can't. Not as easily as you anyway, Logan wanted to say, but didn't. She knew the world—and the army—could use a whole host of Meg Atwoods, people with the guts and indomitable personalities to challenge the status quo and force change and acceptance. But people like Meg were better off picking their battles. "Just be careful," she said ominously. "They're watching you."

"Ah-ha. Is that what Colonel Patterson took you aside for? To tell you to make sure I didn't jump Jillian Knight's bones or something?"

"Something like that."

"Bastard," Meg muttered.

"Well, it's not like it would be new territory for you." She knew her tone was laced with contempt, because the thought of Meg trying to seduce Jillian made her ridiculously jealous.

"Oh, for God's sakes, do we have to go over *that* again?" Three months earlier Meg had been caught flagrante delicto with a visiting journalist. It might not have been a problem, except another visiting journalist who'd caught them, jealous she wasn't getting the same favored treatment, spilled the beans.

"You don't think Patterson's likely to forget that sort of embarrassment for the hospital, do you?"

"I suppose not, but you know I promised you after that I would keep it in the family, so to speak."

Meg and her constantly adjusted rules were laughable. "Okay, look. Here's the deal. If you want to keep tempting fate, fine. Just don't tempt mine, too, okay?"

"Logan, you should never have consented to being my keeper."

"No? Who else? Would you rather it be someone who'd turn you in at the drop of a hat, without the slightest remorse? Someone you didn't like or couldn't trust?"

"All right, all right. You have a point. I'll behave on one condition."

Oh, no. Logan stopped because Meg had. She looked with trepidation into her friend's face, where she found an expression that was predictably filled with mischief. "What?"

"Stop being such a shit to Jillian."

Logan's heart skipped a beat. "What are you talking about?"

Meg glared at her. "You've been trying to avoid her lately, and when you can't, you're being a rude bitch."

"I am not," an indignant Logan replied. *Well, at least the rude bitch part isn't true.*

"What is it about her that scares you so, Logan?"

Logan shook her head. As close as she and Meg were, this

was not something she could share with her. "Okay, look, you caught me. I'm afraid I'll start adopting her Michigan accent."

Meg laughed, but only for an instant. "You are so full of shit, Logan Sharp. And I say that with all due respect."

"Yeah, right."

"Anyway, you can keep your little secrets. But I know that at night in that little cot of yours, with hers just inches away, the obedient and very professional Logan Sharp is thinking some very unbecoming thoughts."

"Shut up." Logan punched her friend lightly on the arm. "Not every dyke here is as horny as you."

Meg shrugged. "Too bad."

CHAPTER FIVE

Jillian fixed her eyes on the image of her daughter on her laptop's screen. Maddie was smiling that gap-toothed, adorable smile, her coal dark eyes glinting with mischief. She would turn two in a couple of weeks, and Jillian was thrilled she had been able to arrange to be home for the event. Steph had put Maddie on the webcam once since Jillian had come to Afghanistan, and Jillian had cried throughout the entire conversation.

She missed Maddie so much, missed the feel and smell of her in her arms, the constant chatter and endless curiosity, the hugs and kisses at the end of a day, Maddie falling asleep in her arms. The emptiness today was almost too much to bear. She wanted to cry again. Afghanistan was the most distant and most dangerous place she'd visited since she got pregnant with Maddie, and while it was a great opportunity for her career, she now calculated the cost in a way she'd never done before.

Being a mother had been so new and strange to her at first. It was like making her way through a foreign land without aid of a map or an interpreter. She'd read all the baby manuals, talked to other women who'd had kids. She had known to expect sleepless nights, bone-weary exhaustion, obsessive worry over a cough or sniffle. What she hadn't been prepared for was how she had changed inside and so quickly. It wasn't just Maddie's well-being she worried about now, but her own. Motherhood had made Jill aware of her own mortality. She tried harder to eat right, to sleep well, to exercise, to not take foolish chances with her body. All because she wanted to be there for Maddie for as long as she physically could.

Maddie made Jill hesitate, made her question the worth of assignments like this one, made her weigh the benefits and the detractions in new ways. Yet, she could not quite shake the hunger she still had professionally. She still relished the big assignments, visiting exotic places, meeting interesting people, trying to capture it all with her digital camera. Her job, she had come to feel, was much more than providing a window to history; it was living it. Her emotional involvement in assignments like this one made her feel not only like a witness to history, but also like someone *invested* in it.

In truth, Jillian knew, she had begun approaching her work differently long before she became a mother. When she'd started out, she'd tried to be objective and emotionally disconnected from her subjects. It was the way she thought she was supposed to be.

And then one day, her mask not only slipped, but it fell off for good. She had been doing a photo feature on homeless people, all the while telling herself that these people were drunks or psychos or that they had somehow chosen to be homeless. They were people in unfortunate circumstances, but not people she could identify with, because they weren't *like* her. Then she met a woman her age with a young daughter. Orphaned as a teenager, she bounced around from relative to relative. Raped and impregnated by a cousin, she dropped out of school and ran away. She didn't want her daughter taken from her, and so she kept on the move, prostituting herself periodically, stealing food and petty things. It was sad and sadder yet to look into the eyes of her young daughter and see no hope there.

After encountering the pair, Jillian cried herself to sleep every night for a week. Then she set out to find the woman and the little girl with the ghostly eyes again. She was determined to get them connected to a social agency that could help them. Oh yes, she was going to save them. Be the Good Samaritan. But she couldn't find them again. Their hollow expressions still haunted her sometimes.

After that, Jillian was never good at distancing herself from her subjects. She let herself feel their pain, their joy. She listened and watched, absorbed everything she could from them. Her photos became stronger as her involvement grew. She began to win awards, get noticed in her profession. It took a lot out of her—too much maybe. Her family was her salvation. Maddie brought so many things to her life every day—joy most of all, worry sometimes—but always, *always* Maddie made her feel needed, made her feel a part of something much bigger than herself or her career or her relationship with Steph. It was that love that acted as a counterbalance to her career. If you weren't careful, work, especially the kind you became deeply emotionally involved with, could suck the life right out of you. She could see that happening to Logan, because Logan didn't appear to have a life outside the military.

Jillian clicked to an image of her lover. Steph looked studious and serious in the photo. She had her reading glasses on because Jillian's camera had surprised her. Jillian looked closer. Truth be told, Steph looked irritated, the tiny, familiar wrinkle between her eyes revealing how she felt. Steph didn't like interruptions when she was working. She liked to compartmentalize her life, and even though she'd made the transition to parenthood better than Jillian had expected, Steph disdained anything she hadn't accounted for or planned on. Her obsession with organization made her a very dependable parent and partner, but it didn't exactly make her fun and outgoing. In fact, Jillian couldn't remember the last time they'd gone out on the spur of the moment and done something fun—and not just because they were parents. Even before Maddie, they hadn't done much of anything that could be called spontaneous. Jill had turned down many impromptu offers of barbecues, boat rides with friends, ball games, because she knew Steph wouldn't want to go.

Jillian clicked to another picture, this one of the three of them playing in the park. Hell, what did she have to complain about really? Though obsessively and admirably devoted to her own job as an economics professor, Steph had always supported Jillian's career and her time away working, making sure when she was gone that every bill was paid on time and that birthday cards and Christmas cards got sent out. She took the cars in for regular service and did the laundry, too.

She had also supported Jillian when she wanted to have a baby despite the disruption it would bring to their lives, and she had done more than her share with Maddie after she was born. Though their relationship was not legally sanctioned, they were committed through Maddie.

Steph was steady and solid as a rock, for which Jillian was grateful. Though she realized gratitude wasn't the same as heart-pounding love, that Steph wasn't exactly a meteor setting her heart or body on fire, there was much to be said for the predictability of her life. Though mundane, her life at home was her shelter, her sanctuary, after difficult assignments like this one—assignments she knew she would be doing less frequently now.

Mark strolled into the media tent, whistling an old Aerosmith tune. He looked especially jaunty.

"Oh, good, Jills, I was hoping you were here."

"You look pretty energetic for a guy who had to run his ass off playing hockey last night. Aren't you sore, you old stallion?"

"Ah, there's good sore and there's bad sore. And hockey is definitely the good kind of sore."

"You sure looked like you were having a good time."

"Oh, yeah, it was awesome!" Mark couldn't stop grinning. "I knew playing with Logan would be so much fun. I think she's actually a better setup person than a pure scorer, though you'd never know it most of the time. She has to do so much of the work herself. She needs a good playing partner, that's what it is."

Yes, she probably does, Jillian thought, her mind drifting from hockey. She didn't much feel like bantering about last night's game or talking about Logan. She was still hurt and confused by the cold shoulder Logan was giving her.

Mark was talking excitedly and in minute detail about the plays he and Logan had made together. Jillian nodded as if she were interested but let her mind wander. Why was Logan working so hard lately to avoid her? Why was she so skittish around her when they could not avoid one another, like in their tiny room? She shouldn't care. She and Mark would be gone in a few days, after all. But Logan fascinated her. Pulled at her heartstrings. She needed to know what Logan was so afraid of. She had a pretty good idea, though. Jillian clearly posed a threat to the control that was so essential to Logan. Jillian felt both sorry and glad about that. A little vulnerability, a loosening of that control, was exactly what Logan needed, or the pain she surely must be suffering inside might do irreparable damage. Jillian was no psychologist, but she'd seen plenty of damaged people in her life. *She's running from the very thing she needs. And what she needs is to let her emotions out once in a while, to lean on someone else from time to time.*

"I hear there's a convoy heading out tomorrow. We should hook onto it, Jill."

Jillian forced her attention back to Mark. "Sorry, what?"

"I stayed up half the night looking at all our images so far. You've done a great job here on the base. The ones when that young soldier died…incredible. The ramp ceremony. And those shots out at that polio clinic are fantastic, too. But we're missing the whole medic side of things. You know, out in the field. There's a couple of medics heading to a forward operating base tomorrow to relieve a couple of others there. I think we need to go with them."

Jillian knew exactly what Mark was talking about. It *was* the missing element—photos of medics putting themselves in harm's way in order to provide injured soldiers with immediate life-and-death assistance. She closed her laptop with a whoosh, her heart pounding with uncharacteristic dread. "You're right, Mark. I've been putting it off, I guess."

He pulled his chair closer and looked at her sympathetically. "You can stay here and I can go, you know."

Jillian smiled at her long-time friend. He'd always been willing to fall on swords for her. It just never felt so real before. "No, Mark. It's my project. I need to go."

"It could be really dangerous, Jill." He'd never looked more serious, and Jill felt a prickling of fear.

"I know, Mark." She couldn't dither if they were going to do this. *Dammit.* She should stay on the base where it was safer. Stay for Maddie's sake. But when she'd accepted this assignment, it was with every intention of doing the best job she could. She couldn't come all this way, meet all these incredible, selfless people, only to come out of it with something half-assed. "This project won't be complete without those shots. I won't feel like I've done my best—or done right by the men and women who have to be out there."

She hated it when her sense of duty and professional pride won out over common sense and self-preservation. Playing it safe wasn't what made her a great photographer, though…never had, never would. And she would never get this chance again.

"Dammit."

"I'll be with you every step, Jill."

She smiled haltingly, consoled that Mark would be by her side, just as he had for much of her life. "I know. And I'm very grateful to have you as my friend, Mark."

"You're not going to e-mail Steph, are you?"

"Hell, no. She'll tell me I'm nuts." *And she'd be right.*

"I guess we have to get Major Sharp's permission, though."

"Yup."

Mark looked uneasy. "I'll talk to her."

Mark and Logan seemed to be getting along much better now, but they were far from best buddies. Jillian knew she had better odds of getting Logan to agree. "I'll go talk to her while you go arrange things with the commander of the convoy."

"All right. By the way, it takes most of a day to get to this FOB and another day to get back. We'll just be able to squeeze it in before we have to leave."

Jillian nodded solemnly. It was only two days. *Two days. Convoys come in and out of here all the time.*

When they walked out of the media tent, they were blasted by a swirling sandstorm. It nearly knocked Jillian on her ass.

"Jesus Christ!" She turned to go back inside, but Mark grabbed her arm in a death grip and pulled her toward the hospital.

"It's just a sandstorm! It won't kill you!"

No, but it could maim you, she thought. The hard sand stung her skin relentlessly. It was like being sandblasted. Instinctively she pulled the collar of her shirt up to cover her nose and mouth. She could hardly see more than three feet in front of her. It was like a snowstorm, only brown, gritty and painful.

"You son-of-a-bitch, Mark," she mumbled from behind her shirt.

Logan gently tilted Jillian's head back and squeezed a couple of cleansing drops into each eye. Jillian blinked rapidly and gave a quiet moan of relief.

"Oh, that feels so much better, Logan. Thank you. I feel like I have sand in every single pore and orifice in my body."

Logan laughed; she could totally relate. "A shower will do wonders, but even then, I don't think you ever feel like you're not covered in it here." The ubiquitous sand barely registered any more, she was so used to it. It was like the constant soil under her nails when she was a teenager and worked in the tomato fields. It simply became a part of you.

"God, my camera equipment has been taking a beating from all this dust, too. I have to spend a good hour a day taking it all apart and cleaning it."

Logan smiled. The dust played havoc with their medical equipment sometimes, too. "It's amazing how good you get around here at cleaning grit out of things."

Jillian was looking at her quizzically. "Will you miss this

place?" The question was sudden and formidable, like a large stone splashing into a pristine pond.

Logan handed Jillian a tissue for her eyes, buying some time. She would not miss the place, that's for sure, but she would miss abstract things, like the camaraderie of the hockey games, the fast friendships, doing a good job under adverse conditions. "I'll miss the people," she said simply, feeling her emotions bubbling dangerously just below the surface.

Jillian gazed at her with bold affection. "I'll miss you, Logan."

Logan's stomach fell to her boots. She blinked once, twice, felt her mouth tighten. Her chest took on a heaviness that her shallow breaths could not alleviate. She would miss Jillian, too. More than she probably should, and certainly more than she could reasonably justify. This woman had come closer than anyone had in a long time to unlocking the secrets of her soul, to listening without judgment or agendas, to caring about her for who she actually was and perhaps could be.

Someone once said you don't miss what you don't have, but that isn't true, thought Logan. She would miss the deep friendship she nearly had with Jillian...could have had, if they had more time together. But she could not say these things to her. There was no point. Their time together was almost over. Investing any more of herself in Jillian now would be tantamount to stepping over a cliff.

Jillian cleared her throat impatiently. "I came here to see you for a reason, Logan."

"Okay," Logan replied. She saw a shadow pass over Jillian's face. She leaned against the treatment room's wood counter, arms across her chest. *Please, no more soul-baring confessions. I couldn't take another one.*

"Mark and I want to join B company tomorrow on a convoy to FOB Hawksbridge. They're taking supplies and relieving a couple of medics." Jillian spoke with surprising detachment, as though she'd done a dozen convoys before and they were just routine business. Which, of course, they never were. "It'd be a day there, then back the next. It's essential to our assignment here. I'd like your permission to go."

Logan said nothing for a few moments. She couldn't, because her voice had completely deserted her. Jillian outside the wire, without *her* to ensure Jillian's safety... It was unthinkable. Irresponsible. Convoys were incredibly risky. They were susceptible to land mines, ambushes, suicide strikes. She would not be the one to write Jillian a ticket into such dangerous territory.

"No," she declared.

"What do you mean, no? Why not?" Jillian looked hotly indignant, her eyes flashing. "Mark's squaring it away with Bravo's commander."

"I'm responsible for you here. You know that. And I won't give you permission."

"You have no reason to deny me. I take full responsibility for Mark and myself."

"Nope. Sorry."

Jillian hopped off the treatment table, affront stiffening her body, coloring her face, making her look adorably angry. "Why? Why won't you let me go?"

"It's not safe. In fact, it's unbelievably dangerous. You have a child waiting for you back home." *And a partner, but I don't want to think about that.* "I won't let you do it. It's not worth it, Jillian."

Hands on her hips, Jillian fumed. "The people in that convoy have children waiting for them, too, Logan. They have a job to do, just like I do. *I* should be the one to decide what it requires, whether it's worth the risk."

Logan knew she was being a prick by using the authority card and taking the decision out of Jillian's hands. But she had a bad feeling in the pit of her stomach. It was telling her, the way her athlete's knees told her a rainstorm was coming, that Jillian shouldn't go on this convoy.

A cool shudder raced through her. She'd felt something similar three months earlier, when a young medic—Guy Forrester—was assigned to a week-long mission heading to Kabul. He'd been nervous about it and had talked to Logan about his forebodings. It had felt all wrong to him and all wrong to Logan, too. But they were powerless in the face of his orders. So he had gone. He never returned.

"I'm sorry, Jillian." Logan swallowed hard against Jillian's visible disappointment and anger, but she was doing the right thing, dammit.

Logan watched the armored vehicles maneuver into position. The loud, smelly, dust-spewing monstrosities looked imposing and impenetrable, but she knew they were not. Right now, that knowledge scared the crap out of her. For Jillian was in one of those Bison ambulances, which were unmarked in order to deny the enemy a target. With their mottled brown paint, eight big tires and mounted machine gun, they were indistinguishable from the rest of the vehicles in the convoy.

Jillian should not be in there. Though Logan had denied Jillian's request, it meant nothing, as it turned out. Jillian had gone over her head to the colonel, who'd summarily decided that if traveling with the convoy was what Jillian needed for her photo essay, then that's what she would do. Logan had argued with him until moments ago to reverse his decision, but he refused. To press further would have been futile, so she had stormed out, hoping to catch Jillian and change her mind. What she would have said if she had caught her, she wasn't sure. A feeling of helplessness had sucked much of the fight from her, but she might not have been above begging.

What she might or might not have done didn't matter now, because it was too late. Anger and worry rooted her in place. She did not want to say goodbye like this—standing rigid, hands behind her back, staring helplessly at the big machines slowly wheeling into position, while Jillian sat somewhere inside likely not even knowing Logan was out here watching. She felt like a tiny pebble in a sandstorm, exposed and completely powerless against much greater forces. She wanted to run to the nearest Bison, pound on its trapdoor and haul Jillian out if she was in there. But Logan Sharp wouldn't dare think of interfering with a military operation. She would go to the wall for a patient, but she would not break protocol and run like a fool to Jillian's Bison.

An arm slipped around her waist.

"She'll be okay," Meg said quietly.

"I know." Logan's voice held not an ounce of conviction.

CHAPTER SIX

The medic and gunner riding in the bowels of the Bison with Jillian and Mark were good guys—not at all like the sadistic soldier who had been her seatmate flying into the base nearly two weeks earlier. Their friendly chatter helped pass the time as they bumped along the endless gravel road. It was almost as though they were on a country road back home, on their way to the local fruit and vegetable stand.

Jillian was sweating heavily beneath her vest and helmet, even though the vehicle was supposedly air-conditioned. Hot air continually descended like a heavy, invisible cloud from the gunner's rooftop turret, which was constantly open. The gunner, a pleasant young man from the Canadian prairies, sprang up and down from the opening like a Jack-in-the-Box on steroids.

She didn't want the soldiers to feel like they had to entertain her and Mark, but she suspected they couldn't stop talking because they welcomed the fresh company. They talked incessantly about their families back home. One had a wife and two kids, the other was single but had a steady girlfriend and a golden retriever. They talked about the other things they missed, like their sports teams, their pets, their cars, a friend's in-ground pool, a favorite neighborhood bar, backyard barbecues, the hockey playoffs around the corner. Everyday things you didn't miss until they were gone.

The radio crackled to life with a warning. There were reports that the women and children had suddenly deserted the next village—a sure sign, the medic said in an almost complacent tone, that the Taliban were in the area and digging in to fight.

"What does that mean?" Jillian asked, her senses prickling to heightened awareness. "Are they going to ambush us?"

The gunner, Sergeant Jack Wolfe, looked decidedly unhappy, but not particularly worried. "It might mean nothing. Or it might–"

His words were cut off by a hail of bullets erupting from somewhere in front of them. The radio sprang to life with curses and hurried exclamations. The convoy—a dozen or so vehicles—was under attack from the north side of the road where a wadi, or dried-out ditch, ran parallel. Wolfe leaped into his turret, rotating his machine gun in jerking motions and loudly popping off rounds, his whole body shaking from the reverberation. Empty shells from the gun rained down like hail, some landing right at Jillian's feet.

Jesus! Could this really be happening? She stole a look at Mark, who'd gone a little pale. He gave her a quick smile that didn't reach his eyes. "Don't worry," he whispered. "This thing's armored."

The medic, Corporal Towers, was looking through a periscope that poked through the vehicle's roof. "Sons of bitches are just trying to harass us. Doesn't look like they got any heavy artillery for us today."

His words failed to reassure Jillian. The bullets still bounced off their Bison, giving off a *tink tink* sound as they hit. She scrunched in tighter to the rear corner, trying to make herself smaller, and then, just like that, it was over. The gunfire faded like a distant echo, and she let out a long-held breath at the merciful silence.

"First time under fire?" The young corporal grinned at them both, relief clearly etched on his face.

Mark nodded. "Guess it shows, huh?"

"Nah. You did good. Hopefully that's it for this ride. We should be at FOB Hawksbridge in a couple more hours."

Jillian hoped he was right. *Please don't let this be the warm-up act.*

The soldiers at the Forward Operating Base were thrilled to see the convoy. They high-fived the new arrivals and gave them a loud cheer, greeting them loudly and enthusiastically like they were a sports team bringing home the big trophy. Jillian knew it was mostly because they were happy to get more food and clothing, ammunition and medical supplies. The happiest were the half-dozen men who, for one reason or another, were being relieved. She would say goodbye to Corporal Towers, who was replacing another medic who'd been stationed at the small, mountainside base for three weeks.

Jillian and Mark ate with the soldiers, played cards, took pictures of them. The soldiers couldn't get enough news and stories from home and even from KAF. There was no Internet access at Hawksbridge. No television or radio either. The temporary base was effectively cut off from the outside world. It was like camping, with tents and a wooden hut, latrines that were just fancy holes dug into the ground. The night was beautiful, the moon and stars providing the only light, and Mark and Jillian, exhausted from the day's events, rolled out their sleeping bags inside the Bison. She felt almost safe in its thick, steel confines. Sleep quickly claimed her, and dreams carried her home for a time that was too brief.

After a breakfast of powdered eggs and beef jerky, they began to prepare for the trip back to Kandahar.

"Damn, I don't think we're going to get any shots of the medics doing their thing in the field," Mark said with disappointment. "We'd have to stay here for a few days and go out on some exercises with them. Maybe then."

Jillian shook her head grimly. "Can't. You know we have to head home in something like thirty hours." *Is it really that soon?* She knew Mark would have loved for her to say yes, but they couldn't miss their flight home. Their travel plans were pretty much carved in stone, since the military didn't like diverting from their precious plans and protocol. She gave him a playful wink. "Maybe someone will accidentally cut their finger or something."

Mark shook his head, but he was smiling. "Yeah. That's about the only action we'll probably see."

Spectacular photos of medics racing to bloodied, injured soldiers would be the crowning piece to her assignment in Afghanistan. It was morbidly selfish to want them, though, since they'd come at the cost of someone else's pain or maybe his life. Jillian also didn't know how much more blood and gore she could stand, how much more death and fear and loss she could cope with. Coming under fire in the convoy had convinced her that her job wasn't worth dying over. She wanted to get home to Maddie. She was ready to leave Afghanistan behind—the country and the violence anyhow.

They pulled out as the sun climbed higher, their Bison taking up the rear again. It was only when they were transporting the injured that they raced ahead of the pack, explained the new medic, Corporal Simon. As he talked on, Jillian's thoughts turned to a photographer she'd met in the early part of her career. He was an old dog, a veteran of El Salvador's civil war in the early 1980s. He'd spent months there, alternately embedded with both sides, until one day, the small company of soldiers he was traveling with was ambushed. He'd flung himself on the ground when the shooting started, as he'd been instructed to, and when it finally stopped, he was the only one to get up. Even now, Jillian recalled the haunted, far-away look in his eyes when he'd told her the story. His brush with death instantly ended his days as a war photographer. He went back to work stateside for a newspaper, shooting pictures of country fairs and fender benders. It just wasn't worth his life, he'd told her simply. Now she understood what he meant.

She also understood now why Logan hadn't wanted her and Mark to make this trip. Logan had only been trying to protect her. Still, Jillian didn't like others making decisions for her, even if they were well intentioned. It was one of her great faults and had caused her grief with people she cared about many, many times. Her sense of duty, her commitment to reaching for the highest standards in her work, had overruled her common sense. *Please, Logan, don't be right this time.*

Their armored vehicle began to slow and finally ground to a halt. Jillian and Mark shared a look of concern as their two companions wordlessly slipped out through the steel trapdoor in the roof.

"I don't like this, Mark," Jillian whispered urgently.

"Relax. I don't hear any shooting or anything." He grinned. "Maybe they're lost, and they're just looking at a map."

"Very funny. How can you get lost on the one road leading back to Kandahar?"

"All right, so maybe they ran out of gas or something."

Jillian's pulse quickened, and a sick feeling edged into her stomach. Stopping meant something was wrong. Mark could joke all he wanted, but she was scared.

Minutes went by. The only sounds were muffled voices and the *clank clank* of steel being hammered. Mark could no longer stand the suspense. Ignoring Jillian's protestations, he poked his head out into the afternoon sun.

"The truck ahead of us seems to have broken down," he announced to Jillian. "I'll go find out what's happening."

"Oh, no you don't. I'm not staying in this thing by myself."

He had scrambled out already and was crouched on the roof, peering in, his face silhouetted against the sun. "Well, c'mon then!"

She stared for only a moment at his outstretched hand, then grasped it and pulled herself up. *What the hell.* The whole convoy was here, after all. It was a broken-down vehicle that had thrown them off their stride, not an ambush.

After more hammering and a short strategy session, Corporal Simon told them that most of the convoy would move on, while their Bison and another would sandwich the disabled vehicle in a slow escort back to Kandahar. They'd managed to jam the truck into second gear, but the transmission was otherwise shot, he told them. Their Bison would lead the trio back.

Jillian considered hitching a ride with one of the faster-moving vehicles, but then dismissed the idea. She didn't want anyone thinking that the "girl" on this mission was a baby, a wimp who needed to be coddled. Women journalists constantly had to prove themselves in war theaters, and she wasn't about to set her colleagues back another decade or two by hightailing it back to KAF.

Their mini-convoy began to meander back, the return trip to the base lengthened now by at least a couple more hours. It would be dark by the time they arrived, and for once, she looked forward to her little cot and the cramped room she shared with Logan. She smiled a little. Logan would give her lots of attitude when she returned, but she would be able to counter by telling her that her worry and overprotectiveness had all been for nothing.

She leaned her head back and closed her eyes, feeling the heft of the camera in her hand. She always had it at the ready, like a soldier's loaded gun. If anything should happen, she did not want to be searching for it. Not that she *wanted* anything to happen. Tomorrow she would be winging her way back home. Back to her daughter. Back to Steph, who by now was probably far behind on her work and anxious for Jillian to take over the parenting and household duties. Steph's students' final exams were only a month away, which meant a mountain of prep work for Steph. Jillian smiled. *Yup*. Steph would be going crazy about now, hating that she was falling behind schedule, probably cursing this Afghanistan assignment, though she—

She felt it before she heard it—a wave of energy convulsing through her, sucking as it went until her insides felt like they were being pulled out of her. And then the sound of the explosion came, so loud that it stunned her. The ringing in her ears temporarily deafened and disoriented her. For a flicker of a moment or maybe longer, Jillian's mind went completely blank. And then, as if slowly coming out of sleep, she tried desperately to grasp the meaning of all this. *God, what's happening, what's happening?* The question tumbled through her mind, even as she felt the heavy armored vehicle tip and slide on its side, metal screeching like a wild animal. She was in the air, then bouncing off something hard, and still she struggled to make sense of everything as her body absorbed more cuts and bruises.

Someone was screaming—a man's voice, so she knew it wasn't her.

Oh, God, I will not die like this. I will not die like this. Not here. I will not die here, in this place, so far from my daughter. This godawful place.

She would fight this force that was trying to claim her. She would fight for all she was worth, because she was worth more than dying like this.

She pulled herself to a sitting position, disoriented because everything was sideways. But the movement and the noise had mercifully stopped. It was eerily quiet, as though time had frozen. Then Mark moaned and cursed, gingerly pulling himself up.

"Oh, Mark, thank God!"

"Are you okay?" A tiny stream of blood trickled down his cheek.

"I, I think so."

Corporal Simon appeared to be in one piece as well. He reached for the rifle that had been knocked from his hand. The knee in his pants was torn and bloody, his chin scraped raw. "We've got to get out of here. There's ammo and oxygen in this thing and it'll start cooking off. Let's move. Now!"

Her camera still somehow clutched tightly in her hand, Jillian scrambled to her knees and followed the two men out of the roof hatch. Since the Bison was on its side, it was only a short hop to the ground. The dust and smoke and diesel fumes instantly choked her. A cloud surrounded the three twisted, broken armored vehicles, which now looked like crunched Tonka toys. She nearly tripped over her gunner, who, she only realized then, must have been blown clear of the turret. He was writhing on the ground, clutching his shoulder, his neck a bloody mess from shrapnel.

The medic bent down to him, took a rag from a cargo pocket and pressed it to his buddy's neck. "Hold on, Wolfie. We'll get a chopper here and evac you out, okay? You're going to be fine. Kennedy," he shouted at Mark. "Find a radio that works before these goddamned things blow up on us."

There were more bodies strewn around the vehicles. A soldier's arms dangled loosely from the driver's door of a second Bison, as if he had tried to crawl out and given up. On pure instinct, Jillian ran to him, slinging her camera behind her back, and tried to pull the heavy door open. At first it wouldn't budge. She pulled as hard as she could, grunting from the effort. Finally it creaked open, the soldier tumbling into her arms as the door finally gave way. She grabbed him by the scruff of his vest and slowly dragged him away from the vehicle, his boots scuffing a jagged trail in the dust behind him. Mark sprinted to her side.

"Jesus Christ, Jill! Next time you want to be a hero, don't do it all on your own, okay?"

Just as Corporal Simon had predicted, the ammunition soon started exploding from the heat. The bullets detonating inside sounded like popcorn being popped. Fire licked at the underbelly of first one of the Bisons, then another. There was a loud explosion, and it wasn't long before all of the wreckage was in flames. Black smoke rose in an ominous column, like a cloud of vultures circling roadkill.

Simon and another soldier were on their knees tending to the two or three survivors, and Jillian finally thought of her camera. She brought it to her eyes, not even sure if it still worked, and began taking photos. She looked through the viewfinder without really seeing, taking the pictures by rote. She had no idea how they would turn out and she didn't care, because right now, taking pictures was the only thing that felt normal about all of this. She needed to feel like she had a job to do, too.

"Christ," Mark said next to her. "I hope the Taliban doesn't see that goddamned smoke and start gunning for us."

She pulled her camera away and looked at him. She wanted to strangle him. Did he have to be such a goddamned pessimist?

Logan was about to change out of her scrubs when Meg stuck her head around the door of the staff lounge. Meg looked more than just alarmed. She was uncharacteristically somber, and immediately Logan felt her heart skip a beat.

"Thought you'd want to know, Logan. The convoy Mark and Jillian are on…"

Logan felt the blood drain from her face. *Oh, fuck.* "What happened?"

"They hit an IED about twenty minutes ago."

Logan's eyes slammed shut against the news she'd been dreading and yet half expecting since yesterday. Her worst fear had come true. She pounded her fist into her palm to stop whatever it was inside her that wanted to explode right now. "Goddammit! I fucking knew it."

Meg went to her and rubbed her arm. Logan barely registered her friend's concern. For the moment, she'd stopped feeling, stopped thinking.

"It happened only a couple of hours away," Meg said without being prompted. "Choppers are on the way to evac casualties."

Logan forced herself to look at Meg. She needed to see the truth in her face. "Casualties? Dead, injured, what?"

"Both," Meg answered flatly.

Logan felt herself swaying. She needed to think, but it was so damned hard. Impossible, actually. Meg reached for a chair, but Logan waved her off. She had to get it together, had to be ready to help the injured, whoever they were and whatever their condition.

"We don't know which vehicles were hit, Logan. The odds are that she's fine."

Logan took a deep, steadying breath, knowing full well that

Meg's attempt to reassure her was like spitting in the wind. There was no tonic for the realities of war. No looking on the bright side. It was what it was, and it was horrifyingly random in dealing the cards of death and destruction. A dozen different scenarios competed in her mind. Jillian might be just fine. Or she might be dead. Or she might have suffered any number of injuries, ranging from superficial to life threatening.

"C'mon," Logan said with contrived calmness and authority. If ever she needed to get by on experience and the mechanics that had gotten her this far in her career, it was now. "Let's get ready for them."

Six casualties in all—three DOAs, three seriously injured. Fortunately Jillian and Mark fell into neither of those two categories. Logan could not believe her good luck. Well, it wasn't exactly her luck, but Jillian's and Mark's, she supposed. Except for her it was every bit as good as winning a lottery. She'd nearly fainted from joy when she was told they were okay. There was no doubt in her mind that she would have blamed herself had Jillian been seriously hurt. Probably would have tortured herself with guilt, even though it wasn't anyone but the Taliban's fault for planting the mines that the convoy had run over.

Logan worked methodically on the injured soldiers, doing it by rote because her mind was not entirely there. She wanted to go to Jillian, because the quick glimpse of her in the hall and the brief reassurance from Meg that she was okay hadn't been enough. She'd tersely ordered Meg to closely check Jillian over again, X-rays and all, and while she trusted Meg absolutely, her mind would not rest until she could see with her own eyes that Jillian was okay.

It was another three hours before Logan finished up. She impatiently checked her watch again. It was late, well past midnight. Her mind kept returning to Jillian's pale face and the blankness of her stare. Something about her look had pierced Logan like an arrow. She'd looked so small, so vulnerable, so haunted, that Logan's heart ached for her. She'd wanted to take Jillian in her arms and smooth away the shock of the horrible things she'd seen. To hell with it being inappropriate or unbecoming or dishonorable or against the goddamned rules. If she could give Jill comfort, she would, no matter what the optics or the cost.

"Meg." Logan caught up to her friend in the locker room. "Is she really okay?"

Meg looked exhausted, but her smile was energized. "Yes, Logan. She'll be fine, I promise. Some cuts, bumps and bruises. A little traumatized, as you can imagine. Mark has a sprained wrist. They both got off very lucky."

Logan's heart still thumped with worry. Jillian was not used to war, had never seen such violence before, had undoubtedly never been a part of it like this. She didn't have layers upon layers of war experience thickening her heart and dulling her feelings the way Logan did. The fact that Jillian had managed to cheat death might mean there would be survivor's guilt on top of everything else. How could she possibly be all right in the face of all that? "Where is she?"

"She's gone to bed."

"You let her just go off on her own?" Logan's tone was accusatory, her adrenaline infusing her emotions. "Why isn't Mark with her?"

Meg leaned against a locker, calmly absorbing Logan's anger. "Mark was getting treated himself, then he was running around trying to take some photos. There was no one on staff available to stay with her. You know it was all hands on deck. She's a smart lady, Logan, and a tough one. She'll be okay."

Logan ground her teeth, a habit when she was stressed. She supposed Meg was right. Jill would be okay. Eventually. But not now, not when it was still so horrifyingly fresh. She would be remembering for days, maybe weeks, every sound, every ghastly detail of what she'd seen. The smells would stay with her the longest, Logan knew from experience. Jillian would be fragile and possibly in shock.

Goddammit, why didn't you listen to me, Jillian? Why did you insist on going?

"It's not your fault, Logan." Meg said, reading her mind. "She wanted to go on that convoy, and she made sure she did."

Logan drew a deep, ragged breath. She could go on blaming herself, the colonel, Jillian and Mark. But what good would it do now? Blame would not help Jillian, nor would it give Logan the strength she would need to help Jillian. It would be wasted energy.

"Meg..." Her voice deserted her suddenly. Meg stepped forward and put her arms around her.

"I know, Logan. I know how much she means to you."

"You do?"

Meg pulled out of the embrace and smiled up at her. Gone was her habitual smart-ass attitude. "Yeah, I do. Now hurry up and shower so you can go to her."

Logan gave her friend a grateful smile before sprinting for the shower. She was relieved she hadn't had to explain her feelings for Jillian. That would have been difficult since she didn't entirely understand them herself. On the surface, their bond made little sense. Other than having grown up just a few miles from each other, they were worlds apart in so many other ways. She was unsettled and directionless professionally and personally, and Jillian was the polar opposite, settled in both her work and her home life. Jillian's future couldn't be any more apparent to Logan.

She's married and has a kid, for god's sake. This can't be happening. I can't feel what I feel for this woman. There is no future in feeling so attached to her.

But it was too late; she did care for Jillian. And deeply. All she wanted was to hurry to their shared quarters, where she would offer Jillian the kind of love and protection Jillian had earlier offered her.

Her mini flashlight found Jillian in the pitch-black room. She lay in a fetal position on her bed, facing the wall, either asleep or feigning sleep. Logan hesitated for only a few seconds before lightly sitting on Jillian's bed and laying a gentle hand on her shoulder. Her heart lurched at the trembling that her touch ignited.

"Oh, Jillian," she whispered, trying to keep her voice steady as she bent closer. She rubbed Jillian's shoulder, clothed in the thin cotton of a T-shirt, waiting for a signal. Perhaps this wasn't what Jillian wanted or needed. Maybe *she* was not what Jillian wanted right now. Maybe Jillian really just wanted to be left alone, though surely if things were the other way around, she would not leave Logan alone.

Logan had been briefed on what had happened—how Jillian had helped save a soldier's life by dragging him from a vehicle before it went up in flames. That Jillian, a non-soldier, would do that for a stranger, gave her a whole new level of respect for the photographer—and newfound fear for her well-being. She could have died trying to save that soldier's life, and it wasn't even her job.

Oh, screw it, Logan thought. *She* needed to hold Jillian right now, whether it was the right thing to do or not. As gently as she could, she lay down next to her. Their bodies softly touched, and her hand remained on Jillian's shoulder. Heart pounding furiously, she waited for Jillian to acknowledge her—to signal what she needed. She would give Jillian anything right now. Whatever she required.

It was only a moment or two before Jillian rolled over and buried her face in Logan's chest, her body heaving with silent sobs. Logan tightened her hold, pressing herself against Jillian, trying to cover as much of her as she could, trying to physically shield her from her pain.

"Oh, Jillian, you're here now. You're safe now," Logan comforted softly. "It's over. It's over. I promise you, it's over now."

Jillian continued to sob against her chest, saying nothing in reply. Logan stroked her head, her neck, her back, and let her cry, never loosening her hold on Jillian, even when Jillian tried to pull back a fraction. Their bodies molded together perfectly, as if they'd done this a hundred times before, and Logan twitched in shock at the sudden surge of arousal between her legs.

Oh, Jesus, she thought in panic. *Not now, Logan, not now. And not her. She is someone else's wife, you idiot! And I am supposed to be comforting her right now, not getting turned on. How could I even be thinking of sex at a time like this? Christ!*

Jillian moved against her neck as though reading the change in her. Logan could feel Jillian's mouth against her skin and Jillian's tears on her skin, too. *Oh shit.* It had been such a long time since she'd held a woman in her arms like this, and knowing the inappropriateness of her arousal did nothing to extinguish it. Frankly, her body was pissing her off right now. Reasoning with herself was accomplishing nothing. She was growing wet. She needed to pull away, to put distance between them. Except she couldn't physically wrench herself away. Where was her iron will and her inflexible codes of conduct now? *Dammit!*

Jillian mumbled something against her neck.

"I'm sorry. What?"

Jillian's mouth slid up to her cheek. Next to her ear, she whispered, "I'm so sorry, Logan."

Logan swallowed the aching lump in her throat and stroked the back of Jillian's head. "Oh, Christ, Jill. Don't be sorry." *Don't be sorry for going on that stupid convoy*, she wanted to add, *and don't be sorry for being in my arms.*

Jillian shifted to look into Logan's eyes. They could barely see one another in the dark. "I should have listened to you. I should—"

"Stop." Logan drew her finger to Jillian's impossibly soft lips. "You're here now. And you're safe. I won't let anything happen to you, okay? Do you believe that?"

After a moment, Jillian nodded.

Oh, God, I want to kiss her. It was more than just a thought, more than a passing fantasy. There was a certain destiny to it in Logan's mind.

Before she could think about all the reasons why they shouldn't kiss, their lips found one another of their own accord. It was a soft, tender kiss. The kind of communion of their souls that only intimate contact like this could bring. It was the most peaceful Logan could ever remember feeling. Then she froze. This simply could not be happening between them.

Logan abruptly ended the kiss. Hell, it was just the stress of the situation and an antidote to the stress, she told herself. Jillian needed the physical contact to feel safe, to feel alive, and she…she needed it to convince herself that Jillian was indeed safe and alive. Her body cried out for what Jillian could not give her and for what Logan would never allow. *I wouldn't, would I? God, why do I always have to be the noble one?*

"Jill," she whispered.

Jillian leaned forward, reestablishing a firm connection. Oh, God, Logan thought, just before her rational mind completely abandoned her. *I am going to go to hell for this.* Passion welled within her…consuming her like a fire being fed oxygen. It was licking its way up her legs and straight into her soul.

If this were a dream, she should wake up now. But…this was real. Jillian in her arms. Jillian's mouth on hers just a moment ago. Their bodies molded together again. Logan's thigh just inches away from insinuating itself between Jillian's legs. It was really happening. As Logan opened her mouth, to say "yes," Jillian moaned—a soft, desperate, lost moan.

The forlorn sound crystallized…everything. In that instant Logan realized she was prepared to do anything for Jillian. Anything, that is, except make love to her tonight. *That* she could not do, not with a married woman and not with a woman in such obvious distress.

Logan put a little more distance between them. "You need to sleep, Jill. I am going to keep my arms around you and hold you, okay? And in the morning," she ground her teeth, "in the morning, sweetheart, you get to head home. Home to peace and quiet and greenness and some people who are going to be very, very happy to see you…"

Jillian nodded against her, her body sagging into Logan's. Logan clutched the smaller woman tightly to her and felt Jillian begin to drift off. There would be little sleep for Logan tonight.

She wanted to remember every minute of how this felt before it was gone forever.

It was daybreak when Jillian slipped out of Logan's arms. She perched wearily on the edge of Logan's nearby cot, studying the form sleeping in her bed. She shook her head, trying to clear it. She had packed the night before. It wouldn't be long before she and Mark would board the plane for home.

Home.

Jillian had a hard time fathoming the word at the moment, even though she tried with all her effort to focus on it. The word sounded good. It sounded safe. It sounded sensible. It sounded like something she should welcome and look forward to. And she would...if she didn't feel so numb and more than a little lost. Home was nothing more than an abstract concept to her at the moment, a foreign word she couldn't translate.

God, I should want to get the hell out of here as fast as I can. I almost died, for Christ's sake! I came close to never seeing my daughter again, close to being another innocent casualty of war. A few paragraphs in a newspaper. A few photographs to remember me by. Another fool journalist caught in the crosshairs.

She had cheated death, and in less than twenty-four hours she would see her daughter. The joy that thought gave her was accompanied by an unexpected stab of pain. She would never see Logan Sharp again. She gazed intently at the doctor, memorizing the planes of her handsome face, her strong and capable body. She had never felt so physically and emotionally connected to another human being as she had last night when Logan had held her and comforted her, giving her exactly the nurturing she needed to feel safe and alive. Logan's selfless gift, her...love...had taken her breath away. Still did.

Jillian knew she needed to leave, but she wanted to remember Logan this way...her arms protectively draped over the space where Jillian had been lying just moments before, her body curled slightly as if to shield her from harm. She watched a moment longer, aching inside. She wanted to crawl back into

Logan's arms and take shelter there. Maybe even find solace in her lips again.

Memories of their kiss came rushing back to her. *Oh, shit.* Not just any kiss, but the most wonderful kiss she'd ever had. It had gone no further. *Thank goodness.* Jillian brought her fingers to her lips, the softness reminding her of the same softness she'd felt on Logan's mouth. It'd been wrong to kiss her. Or had it? *I am essentially married to Steph. I am not supposed to go around kissing other women. I kissed Logan and it must be wrong.*

Jillian hadn't kissed any woman but Steph in more than seven years. She had never before even considered it, and yet she couldn't have stopped the kiss with Logan even if she'd tried. She'd needed it like she needed to breathe.

Jillian stood, lifted her two suitcases, looked over her shoulder one last time and slipped quietly out of the room. The blanket hanging in the doorway fluttered back into place, sparkles of dust drifting lazily through the early morning rays.

CHAPTER SEVEN

<u>PART TWO</u>
Detroit-Windsor, fifteen months later

It was warm for early June—a sure sign of a hot and humid summer ahead in the most southern part of Canada.

Logan flicked the sweat from her forehead as she glanced again at the three-towered, dark glass and steel Renaissance Center across the river. It was Detroit's signature building, and while not the highest structure in the city, it was still the most beautiful. Logan never got tired of looking across the river at the cityscape. It was a little private joke among Windsor's citizens that Detroit's skyline had been built to offer the best views from the Canadian side. *Thank you, Detroit*, Logan thought with a smile.

"It never gets boring, does it?" Logan's twin sister, Lisa, matched her stride as they jogged their way along the paved riverfront trail. "Did you miss this?"

Logan slowed to a halt to catch her breath. With college, medical school, residency and then the service, it had been fifteen years since she'd lived in Windsor, and it was about as different from a military base as you could get. "Yeah, I did." She rested her elbows on the waist-high iron fence, her gaze on the gray-blue water. Pleasure boats zipped around their watery playground, keeping their distance from the occasional freighter. "I don't think I realized it until now."

It wasn't the architecture of the American skyline that impressed her so much, but rather the peaceful co-existence of these two countries that had fought only once, almost two hundred years ago, and with much of the conflict taking place right here. *War*. Such an abstract concept until you lived it. It was ugly and evil. It treated lives as expendable and made chaos the norm. It was hell on earth.

All she'd really known about war when she'd signed with the military was what was in the history books. She'd signed on to help. Her profession and her intentions made her different from the career soldiers, she'd thought. Because she was all about saving lives, not taking them. But it was semantics, really, because most of those soldiers didn't want to take lives either, she'd learned. In a world of hate and violence and greed, they didn't have many alternatives, though. She'd learned early on that there was no way to make sense of things in Afghanistan—and no way to make things right. Not in one tour of duty or even the two that she'd put in. She'd never felt as useless and powerless in her entire life as she had during her tours in Kandahar.

"Deep in thought, are you?" Lisa touched her arm lightly.

Since Logan had moved back to Windsor nine months earlier, Lisa and her partner Dorothy had been particularly attentive. Mother hens, more like. They doted on her constantly, less because they thought she was fragile and more because they were thrilled to have her around. But Logan knew they also worried about her and how she was adjusting to civilian life. She caught Lisa looking at her sometimes with her lips pursed and that worried wrinkle between her eyes. Sometimes Lisa was more direct, like now, probing her thoughts.

"Just wondering why our two countries only went to war once."

Lisa gave her a bewildered laugh. "What on earth would make you think about the War of 1812 and all those boring seventh-grade history lessons?"

"I like history, remember?"

Science and medicine were the sisters' shared obsessions, but Lisa hated history, while Logan loved to lose herself in good books about different eras. It made her feel somehow connected to her ancestors and to others who'd once walked these same grounds.

"Yes, I know you do. People always thought you were smarter than me because you could always produce those obscure dates and events and stuff."

Logan laughed. "It didn't exactly make me the life of the party back in high school and college, if you remember."

"True. It always seemed to fall on me to fix you up with dates."

Logan punched her on the arm a little harder than she intended. Lisa was nearly the same size, but softer and less muscular. She was not half the athlete Logan was.

"Ow!"

"Sorry. I forget how fragile you are."

That got the intended response, with Lisa screwing her face up into a scowl reminiscent of their teen years when Logan would handily win all their play fights. "Logan Sharp, have you still not learned how to treat the ladies? Punching them in the arm is a big no-no, okay? Have you not learned anything in all these years?"

Logan didn't intend for her sigh to be audible. "Guess not or I wouldn't still be single."

Lisa's expression softened into sympathy. "You're still single because you close yourself up tighter than a drum. I know you don't like to let people in, but it's kind of important to open yourself to your partner, Logan. Sharing is everything in a relationship. That's my tip of the day."

Logan started walking, and Lisa fell in beside her. "Been there, done that, got the T-shirt."

"Seriously, Logan. Don't you ever want a real girlfriend again? Especially now that you're out of the military?"

"What, instead of Betsy, my blowup doll?"

Lisa punched her on the arm this time, but Logan barely felt it.

"You're such a girlie-girl, Lisa."

"Shut up. How is Betsy these days?"

"Not bad, though she's not so great at giving head. It seems she's missing a vital organ for that."

Lisa began laughing so hard that she doubled over, and soon her mirth became contagious. Logan laughed, too, from deep in her belly, and tears quickly streamed down her face. She loved that she could say things to her sister she wouldn't dream of saying to anyone else. By the time they straightened up and resumed walking, others on the trail were giving them furtive looks, as though one or both of them might be slightly crazy.

"Damn, Logan, it's good to see you laugh."

Logan smiled. It'd been a long time since she'd laughed that long and hard. Too long.

"So," Lisa persisted. "About women. Seriously. Dorothy has a colleague who might be fun for you to get to know. She's smart, funny, good—"

"Sorry to rain on your parade, Lisa. But honestly, I am not looking, okay?"

"You never are."

"Maybe that's the way I want it."

They were silent for a while, neither anxious to start running again. Both had worked at the hospital the previous night, and Logan was still feeling the effects of a busy shift in the ER. She'd slept for only four hours this morning, so it was like having a hangover, but without the good memories.

"I think," Lisa finally said, "you only want it that way because it's easier for you not to put yourself out there. To not have to trust anyone, or leave your heart vulnerable since Nic was such a horrible bitch to you. It's all crap, though, just so you know you're not fooling anyone. Including yourself."

Logan was starting to get annoyed. Once a year they had this talk—Lisa riding her ass for not dating and Logan reminding her that she liked it this way. "Do we really have to go through all this again, where I remind you I'm perfectly happy on my own, and you tell me I need to get laid or fall in love or whatever it is you want me to do with another woman?"

Lisa's sigh was one of amusement rather than annoyance. "All right, all right. I just want you to be happy, Logan. And I just thought, now that you don't have the military as an excuse to remain single…"

"I am happy, Lisa. Reasonably, at least." She would never have admitted that last part to anyone other than her sister.

"I know. It's the reasonable part that pisses me off. I just happen to think that you are the second most wonderful woman in the world—next to Dorothy, of course—and so I want to see you more than reasonably happy. I want you to be ridiculously happy!"

That elicited a smile from Logan. She just couldn't see herself being ridiculously happy. And she was mostly okay with that. Hell, at least she would never be hurt or disappointed in someone again. "They have pills for that, doc."

Lisa shook her head, but she was smiling. "Stop being a shit. Hey, have you ever heard from that photographer woman you met in Afghanistan? Jillian Knight?"

Lisa had made a big deal out of the *National Geographic* piece. She'd saved a copy for Logan, of course, and had given copies to everyone they knew. She still trotted the article out whenever possible, proudly showing off the pictures of Logan. But this was the first time she'd brought Jillian up since Logan had moved here, and hearing Jillian's name now nearly made her stumble.

"No, I haven't." She'd hoped Jillian would contact her, but she hadn't. Not even when the article came out.

It was Mark who had e-mailed her to let her know it had been published, and it was Mark who'd informed her that Jillian's KAF photos had won national recognition—a National Press Photographers Association award and two awards at the National

Magazine Awards.

"Doesn't she just live outside of Detroit?"

"Yes, I believe so." Logan was being deliberately vague. Back at KAF, she'd made the mistake of e-mailing Lisa about Jillian. Not the details, of course, but enough for Lisa to get the idea that Jillian was a special woman and that they had become friends. *Friends.* A useful, all-purpose word, but it fell far short of how Logan had come to feel about Jillian.

"So why haven't you gotten in touch with her?"

Logan shrugged. "She's probably crazy busy with her life. She might even be off traveling on assignment somewhere."

"Well, you could find out, you know."

"She probably wouldn't even remember me." Okay, that wasn't true, but it was worth a try as a stalling tactic.

Lisa guffawed loudly. "As if she would forget about the subject of her award-winning photo shoot! Jesus, Logan, you need a little more ego. You should have become a surgeon."

"Well, I'd be a rich prick at least."

Lisa swatted her on the arm good-naturedly. "Rich pricks seem to get all the women, that's for sure." They liked to joke about surgeons and their higher pecking order in the world of medicine. Lisa was a pediatrician and absolutely loved her work. Neither would change anything about their chosen specialty. "I thought you and Jillian had become friends over there?"

"I guess so." Logan could not bring herself to talk about how Jillian had reached in and touched a part of her soul she'd thought was long dead. It would shock Lisa how quickly and deeply Logan had let Jillian in. But no matter how good it had been between them, no matter how much Jillian had made Logan *feel*, it just wasn't meant to be.

"Call her, okay? You don't have many friends around here. It might be good for you."

"Oh, so that's it! You and Dorothy are trying to dump me on someone else, eh? Sick of me already?"

Lisa laughed and shook her head. "God, I missed you, Logan. It's so great to have you back in my life like this."

126

They stopped to face one another, and Logan enveloped her sister in a tight hug. It had been a long time since they'd lived in the same city. Too long. And the older Logan got, the more she realized she needed family and roots. She was just not cut out for a long and transient life in the military. A home base had its appeal, and if she ever got bored, there were things she could do and places she could go for short durations that didn't require rejoining the military.

"So, tell me," Lisa said after a moment. "Is Jillian Knight single?"

Logan rolled her eyes. "Oh, stop, for God's sake!"

"Just checking!"

Logan didn't want to think about Jillian and her perfect life with her suburban house, professor "wife" and young daughter. Since their kiss, Logan had wondered many times if Jillian had just gone back to her life and quickly banished all thoughts of Logan and what they'd shared. She didn't really blame her if she had, but it still hurt.

"Sweetie," Lisa said. "You look sad. What's wrong?"

"Nothing." Raw emotion burned in her throat. For an instant she wanted to cry, and the thought appalled her.

Jillian felt a bag slip from her grasp and caught it just in time, the new wineglasses perilously close to smashing to bits on the pavement. If not for Maddie at her side, she would have blurted out her favorite expletive, "shit." It was tame by most standards, but nevertheless, it was not something she wanted a three-year-old to adopt. Kids had a knack for choosing exactly the wrong moment to say something completely inappropriate, and Maddie had a spectacular memory for a word she only heard once, especially if it was a bad word.

"Mommy, I want to try it now! Can I please?"

Maddie was pushing the new scooter Jillian had just bought her. She'd wanted one for months, and the red one in the store they'd just left was more than a three-year-old could resist. Jillian had relented, probably too quickly. It was so hard to say no to her lately. Of course there was guilt behind it. Jillian didn't need the expensive family therapist they'd hired to tell her that, but right now she just wanted to see her daughter happy.

"No, honey, you have to wait until you have a helmet on and we're at home, okay?"

Jillian let go of Maddie's hand to place the bags in the trunk, her mind already thinking ahead to what she would cook for dinner and the items she would need to get at the grocery store.

"Look, Mommy!"

Behind her back, Maddie had hopped on the scooter and taken off, pushing it as fast as her little leg could propel her. She was heading straight for a parked car, oblivious to it because her head was turned to smile back at her mother.

"Maddie!"

Jillian was off and running, her heart in her throat. All she could do was watch as Maddie collided with the car, smacking her forehead on the fender before crumpling into a heap. She began wailing immediately, which both reassured and scared the living crap out of Jillian.

"Oh, honey!" Jillian gently swept her daughter into her arms. It was a few seconds before Maddie calmed enough to let her examine her. There was a bloody scrape on her forehead, and a nice bump was forming. *Shit*! It was probably nothing, but head injuries were not to be taken lightly. She would take no chances. "Honey, how do you feel? Are you okay?"

There were still tears in Maddie's eyes and on her cheeks, but the sobbing had quieted. "It hurts, Mommy."

"I know, honey. I want to take you to a doctor to make it all better, okay? Would you do that for Mommy?"

Maddie shrugged doubtfully as Jillian wiped the last of the tears from her cheeks and gently wiped the blood from her forehead. "You can have your favorite ice cream after we're done. How about that?"

Reluctantly she nodded, and Jillian scooped her up and into the car before she could change her mind. They had driven across the border to Windsor for a little shopping. She was only marginally familiar with the city, but Jillian knew the downtown hospital was somewhere on Ouellette Avenue, the city's main street.

The ER was quiet, and the intake clerk assured Jillian it wouldn't be long. Maddie, seemingly no worse for the wear, quickly busied herself with the toy box in the waiting room. There would be some scolding later over defying her mother's orders with the scooter, but not now.

"The doctor will see you now."

Jillian collected Maddie and followed the slender woman in scrubs down a sterile, cream-colored hall and past brightly painted arrows and signs. They were left alone in the treatment room, where Jillian tried to keep Maddie occupied with a word game, pointing things out and asking Maddie if she knew what they were.

Jillian had her back to the open door when the approaching and then halting swoosh of soft-soled shoes indicated that the doctor had arrived. She turned to make her greeting, a polite smile firmly fixed upon her face. It was ripped away in a nanosecond.

"Logan!" *My god!* Jillian's lungs protested painfully at her sharp intake of breath. It felt as though every nerve ending was on fire, so acute was her physical reaction at the shock of seeing Logan Sharp standing before her again. She could not breathe for a moment. Could not even blink. Her mind went blank.

Logan, her expression equally frozen, stood perfectly still, her clipboard tightly clutched by knuckles suddenly white. It seemed at least a minute before she spoke, and Jillian watched the emotions flicker across her face—surprise, confusion, delight, concern. She reined them in quickly, offering a smile that was somewhere between polite and warm.

"Jillian Knight," she said smoothly. "Wow, this is a surprise." She held out her hand without any special enthusiasm, and Jillian shook it with disappointment. A hug would have been so much more appropriate. "How are you, Jillian?"

"I'm doing okay, Logan. How about you?" Jillian began to smile like a fool...How could she not? A woman she'd come to deeply care for and whose company she'd enjoyed so much under such adverse circumstances was standing before her—stiff and a little too aloof—but the connection was still there. "When did you come back to Windsor?"

"I'm well, Jillian. I moved back here last fall."

A tickle of pleasure fluttered in Jillian's stomach at the knowledge of Logan living so close. *God!* It was good to see her again. She'd wondered so many times over the past fifteen months how she was doing, whether she'd finished her tour safely, whether she'd stayed in the military or gone into private practice somewhere. She should have written...but life and all the drama with Steph over the past year had left her little energy to think about anything or anyone else.

It was undeniably more than that, too, of course. The last moments she had spent on the base with Logan had been so intense, the sensations that had ripped through her so shocking, she'd not dared revisit any of it. Admitting the yearning in her that Logan had released could bring nothing but trouble, so Jillian had left her need and her unwelcome desires behind in Afghanistan. Where they belonged.

"So," Logan continued, her eyes moving to the tiny hands clutching Jillian's thighs from behind. "What brings you here?"

Jillian swallowed, hoping like hell her face had not divulged her thoughts. "My daughter, Maddie." She stepped aside, gently prodding Maddie forward. The little girl stood awkwardly, in full shyness mode, as Jillian recounted what happened.

Logan knelt down, looking Maddie in the eye but not touching her. Her voice was low and gentle, patient, too, like she had all the time in the world. "That wasn't very nice of that new scooter, was it?" She waited for Maddie to agree. "Now, if I lift you up on that table there, will you let me have a look at your bump, Maddie?"

Maddie complied, and Logan lifted her up like her thirty pounds was nothing.

"How fast was she going when she hit the car?" Logan asked Jillian. "Say, on a scale of one to ten, with ten being extremely fast, as though a teenager were on a scooter."

Jillian thought for a moment, remembering the helpless panic at seeing Maddie about to crash. "About three, maybe four because it was a bit downhill."

Logan was checking Maddie's legs and arms, bending them gently, asking her if anything hurt. She felt her neck, manipulated her head, all the while talking quietly to Maddie and letting her finger her stethoscope. Her gentleness and rapport with children did not surprise Jillian, but it pleased her even more than watching Logan treat children in Afghanistan had, because this time it was *her* child. It comforted Jillian, because she knew if anything was wrong, Logan would find it and take care of it.

Logan asked more questions of Jillian. Had Maddie cried right away after it happened? Had she been acting any differently in the hour since the accident...sleepy, sick to her stomach, overly energetic? Her answers seemed to satisfy Logan, who smiled once, then began checking Maddie's eyes with a penlight.

"She's okay, right?"

"Yes," Logan replied, and Jillian saw the truth in her eyes.

Logan plucked a small teddy bear from a cupboard and handed it to Maddie, who accepted it all wide-eyed and shy. Logan stuck a Band-Aid on its head.

"Now, your bear has a little boo-boo on its head just like you, Maddie. So your teddy bear needs to be careful for a few days and not do anything to hurt it again, okay? Can you remember that?"

Maddie nodded, clutching the bear to her, and Jillian's heart surged a little. She was grateful Maddie was not seriously hurt and overjoyed that it was Logan making her daughter feel safe and special and cared for.

"I'm going to get you an ice pack to apply to that bump," Logan said to Jillian. "And I want you two to stick around for at least another hour to make sure nothing changes. I don't want you stuck in traffic twenty minutes from now and have her suddenly get sick to her stomach or something, okay?"

Logan disappeared before Jillian could say anything more,

then returned with a small ice pack. "How about if I take you two up to pediatrics and you can stay there for awhile? They have a nice playroom I know Maddie will enjoy."

"Sure, thank you." Jillian really wanted to ask if Logan could sit with them, but she knew that would be impossible. She had so many more questions for Logan, most of which revolved on how she was doing. Was she happy back in civilian life? Had she come to some sort of peace with her time in Afghanistan and everything she had been a part of there? Had she found someone to share her life with yet? Jillian's face had begun to warm at her next secret question. Had Logan given much thought to *her* over the last fifteen months, or had she pushed the thoughts aside as Jillian had, afraid they were too unsettling?

Logan gave nothing away in her voice or manners, treating Jillian more like a distant acquaintance than the close friend she had become to her on the base. It was as though nothing special had happened between them—not the deep talks, the sharing of their feelings, their tears, the hugs, the heart-melting and bone-rattling kiss. The sadness of it all struck Jillian with surprising force. She swallowed the painful lump in her throat, grieving the loss of something that had been very special, at least to her.

Logan ushered them up a floor and showed them where to wait, instructing Jillian to apply the ice pack as best she could. She promised to come back and check on them in an hour. Her eyes were remote, her body language formal, as if she and Jillian barely knew one another. Once, back at KAF, there had been pain in Logan's eyes, pain that she had allowed Jillian to see. Trust, too. She had given no small part of herself to Jillian, and now it was gone as if it had never been given.

Well, Jillian thought morosely. *It's not like I have anyone to blame but myself. I left her without saying goodbye and I never contacted her again.*

Jillian read Maddie a story while keeping the ice pack on her daughter's head, trying not to think of Logan. Trying not to remember how safe and loved and alive she had felt in her arms that night. She'd called on those feelings many times in the months of discord with and finally separation from Steph but had refused to link them directly back to Logan, had refused to name Logan as the person who had unleashed such wonderfully reassuring but damnably inappropriate feelings in her.

"Excuse me, are you Jillian Knight?"

A woman in a white lab coat approached, her expression friendly but curious. She looked vaguely familiar. Jillian stood and squinted at her name tag. Dr. Lisa Sharp, Pediatrics.

"Hi," Jillian muttered, noticing the resemblance now. They shook hands, Lisa clasping both hands over Jillian's. It was a much warmer greeting than the one with Logan earlier. "You're Logan's sister." Jillian couldn't help but smile at the woman, who seemed so genuinely pleased to meet her.

"Yes, or rather, Logan is *my* sister." She laughed. "I'm the one with seniority around here." She turned her attention to Maddie and squatted down in front of her. "And what's your name, big girl?"

Maddie shrugged and tried to melt into the sofa.

"That's my daughter, Maddie."

"And how old are you, Maddie?"

Again her daughter shrugged, and Jillian reached down and patted her head affectionately. "Maddie just turned three this spring."

"I see you have a boo-boo," Lisa muttered sympathetically. "Did you fall down and hurt your head?"

Maddie nodded, and Jillian filled in the details. "Your sister is looking after us."

"Logan knows you're here?" Lisa beamed. "I'll bet she was so pleased to see you!"

Pleased wasn't exactly the word Jillian would have chosen to describe Logan's reaction. Surprised, unsettled, confused and finally resigned, perhaps. "It was quite a surprise to run into one another," Jillian offered quietly, disappointed all over again that Logan had not seemed happier to see her. Was Logan upset with her for leaving the base without saying goodbye? Disappointed she had never reconnected with her? Or did she remind her of too many painful things she'd rather not think about?

Dammit, Logan, can't we talk about it? Can't we talk about what we went through? How intensely we cared about each other? How much we willingly gave of ourselves and how protective we felt of one another? Hell, maybe we can even talk about that kiss and how it scorched me like my insides were lava, making me forget everything about my entire existence except for that moment. Yes, we will talk about that some day, Logan Sharp. Count on it.

"Well," Lisa said, standing up. She was about an inch shorter than Logan and built more finely, but their eyes were the same blend of gray, green and blue, and their quick smiles were identical. "I'm glad you ran into each other." She nodded toward Maddie. "It's just too bad it was under these circumstances." She turned quizzical eyes on Jillian, as though waiting for an explanation of why she had never contacted Logan again.

"Yes, it is." An unwelcome tear rose in Jillian's eye. Something hard and painful shifted inside her. "You know, Lisa…" She stammered, pushed down the panic attempting to exert itself. How could she explain the hell she'd been through over the past fifteen months? The months of alternate suppression and eruption of so many raw emotions, the growing and finally irreparable chasm between her and Steph, and her almost desperate worry about her own mortality and that of her loved ones. For days after her return from Afghanistan, she did not let Maddie out of her sight. And ultimately, she'd taken a hard look at her career aspirations, concluding that she would never do another assignment again that put her in such grave danger. She mostly did work for the Detroit newspaper and local magazines now, sticking close to home. She didn't know when she would be ready mentally and emotionally to venture further afield, and being the primary parent of Maddie now made her want to stay close.

"It's okay," Lisa said soothingly, taking a step closer. "I can't truly begin to understand all the things that went on over there. Logan's told me a few things. Not enough." Concern raced across her face. "She told me a little bit about what happened to you."

Jillian nodded, glanced quickly at her daughter, then back at

Lisa. She knew Lisa wouldn't press the issue, and she did not.

"You know," Lisa added warmly. "I have a wonderful idea, and I hope you'll at least consider it."

Logan hesitated outside the door. She took a deep breath, then another. She was over the shock now of seeing Jillian. Her racing heart had settled quickly enough once she'd started examining Jillian's daughter, the duties of her job taking all her attention. She'd tried hard not to look into Jillian's eyes too often, did not touch her again after the handshake, and had hoped like hell the little walls she put up would protect her. They hadn't. Now she wished she'd asked Lisa to examine Maddie one last time, so she would not have to see Jillian again and again feel the rush of so many emotions pulling at her like the invisible undertow of a lake current.

She pushed the door open, surprised to find her sister and Jillian conversing like old friends. They stopped abruptly, as though caught in some sort of conspiracy. Logan was not used to being the outsider where Lisa was concerned, and she frowned deeply. "How is Maddie doing?"

Lisa answered, eyeing her sister in an enigmatic but critical way, as though Logan had done something wrong and Lisa would take her to task for it later. "She's doing well, Logan. No signs of sluggishness or nausea. Mom says she's behaving normally."

Logan looked at Jillian for confirmation.

"She's no worse for the wear." Jillian looked worse for the wear, however. She looked weary and resigned to the distance Logan was bent on keeping between them.

Logan stepped up to Maddie, asked her a few questions, and examined her quickly. "Will you be sure to get her to an emergency room right away if anything changes?" she said to Jillian.

"Of course I will, Logan."

Logan smiled, but it was out of politeness, not pleasure. She found no joy in seeing Jillian, only reminders of some of the most fearful moments she'd ever had in her life, when she thought

Jillian had been killed or hurt badly. Seeing Jillian also reminded her how easy it had been to open herself up to this woman, how she had given something of herself that she would never get back again. "I know you will."

Lisa cleared her throat, looking from one to another. Something was most definitely up with her sister.

"I've gotta run," Lisa said quickly. "It was nice meeting you, Jillian." She reached for Jillian and gave her a hug, the spontaneity and warmth of it startling Logan and making her rock back on her heels for an instant. *Why is it so easy for Lisa to give Jillian a hug? And for Jillian to return it?*

Lisa disappeared while Jillian busied herself getting Maddie ready. She would be gone in minutes, and the thought made Logan shift uncomfortably. She wanted Jillian to disappear from her life as quickly as she'd come back into it, and yet the prospect of this woman walking out of her life again left an undeniably sick feeling in the pit of her stomach. It was bad enough to have lost the connection with Jillian all those months ago. Her breath caught in her throat. If she were not careful, she might even do the unthinkable and cry. *God, anything but that!*

"Well," Jillian said through a thin smile. Her eyes looked moist, as though tears were close at hand for her, too. "We're on our way. Thank you for looking after Maddie."

Logan dropped her eyes, unable to look into those dark pools anymore without needing far more from Jillian than Jillian could ever give her.

Jillian had taken Maddie's hand, and Logan smiled at the obvious bond between mother and daughter and at how much they looked alike. She stared at the intertwined hands, sensing something was different. She crooked her head, trying not to be obvious. Christ, why hadn't she noticed before now? Jillian's ring was gone. There was not even an indentation to indicate that it had been there until recently.

Logan's breath caught in her throat. She knew that her eyes were wide with surprise, confusion, excitement. That her face was burning and probably alive with all the emotions fighting for supremacy in her. When she looked up again, Jillian had turned her head and was reaching for her purse. Before Logan could think of something to say to make her stop, she was gone.

CHAPTER EIGHT

It was rare nowadays for both Steph and Jillian to tuck Maddie into bed. Jillian watched from the doorway as Steph pulled their daughter's sleeping figure from the car seat and carried her up to bed. She let a wave of sadness descend upon her. She knew Maddie still longed to wake up with both her parents in the house, crawl into their bed in the mornings, and have them take turns reading to her at night. Maddie still cried some days over not having her family living under the same roof, and it broke Jillian's heart every time. Maddie had had a hard time getting used to going back and forth between the two, and so they'd agreed for her sake that she would spend most of her time with Jillian, who retained primary custody. They hadn't fought about it, thankfully, but for Maddie the result was the same—a broken home. It made Jillian sad for Maddie's sake, but not regretful. As much as Jillian wanted to mollify her, she could not go back to a relationship in which the two people involved no longer had much to say to one another.

Steph blamed her for the breakup. There was no mystery in that. According to Steph, it was the trip to Afghanistan that had been their undoing. She accused Jillian of having left part of herself there. She'd not returned the same person, she said.

Jillian had to agree: She wasn't the same person. She hadn't wanted to go back to closing herself off, to being Steph's wife and Maddie's mother, to fulfilling her roles to perfection with no time to just be herself. No time to just breathe. To sleep in late or leave the dirty dishes in the sink. To forget to pick up the dry cleaning or let an unpaid bill lapse. To spend a whole evening reading if she chose. She'd had the urge to do all of those things when she'd returned from Afghanistan, and it had given Steph palpitations.

It was depression, Steph impatiently told her over and over again. She needed help. And while it was true that for a few weeks she had been numb from the trauma she'd witnessed in Kandahar, the malaise of a marriage dying on the vine had deepened and prolonged that numbness, had made something deep within Jillian want to cry out and escape from its smothered confines. She had finally realized that she would never reclaim herself and her happiness under the choking weight of her relationship with Steph.

"How about a glass of wine together?" Steph asked hopefully downstairs. She leaned casually against the kitchen counter as though she still lived there.

"Why? Something on your mind?" If it was something to do with Maddie, they didn't need to discuss it over a glass of wine.

Steph looked uncertain for a moment. "No, um, not really. I just thought it would be nice, that's all."

Okay, Jillian thought cynically. *What is it that she wants? Does she want to change the schedule with Maddie? Borrow something? Announce some kind of news?* It was hard sometimes for Steph to be blunt and just say what she meant. "All right," Jillian conceded, feeling tired suddenly. Steph did that to her. Made her feel as if she might collapse from exhaustion. A kind of heaviness seemed to descend upon her soul when she was around Steph. It had been that way since Kandahar. Before that, too, probably, except she hadn't noticed.

A half a glass of wine later, Steph finally got around to her agenda, moving closer to Jillian on the couch. "So," she said softly, her arm creeping over the back of the couch. "I just really wanted to tell you how much I miss you."

Oh, God, Jillian thought. They'd been living separately for seven months now. Weren't they past this crap? The guilt trips and the neediness? Steph playing the lonely card?

"Look," Jillian said matter-of-factly. "You know I don't want to have conversations like that, Steph."

"I know. I was just telling you what I feel, that's all."

There was more to it than that, and Jillian just looked at her former lover, feeling a little sorry for her but not too much. Getting out from under Steph the last few months had been like awakening from a deep slumber, a slow emerging from the unhappiness she had mistaken as boredom or fate.

"Steph, is there something you want?"

"Yeah," she answered quietly. And then her mouth was on Jillian's, softly at first, but quickly harder and more insistent. Desperate almost, and it was unpleasant.

"Steph," Jillian mumbled against her mouth. "Stop this."

She didn't stop, and her hand cupped Jillian's breast.

"Goddammit!" Jillian leapt up, anger flashing hotly through her veins. "What the fuck do you think you're doing?"

Steph jerked back as if she'd been slapped. "Jesus, take it easy, Jill. I just thought—"

"What? That I needed some and you're just the woman to give it to me?"

"Okay, you don't have to act like you wouldn't come to me if I was the last woman on earth, for God's sake. You didn't seem to mind having sex with me before."

"Yeah," Jillian answered bitterly. "The six times a year we had it."

"Oh, no." Steph hopped up off the couch, her face reddening. "Don't put that all on me. You hardly wanted me to touch you after Maddie was born."

Maybe it's because I was no longer in love with you, Jillian wanted to scream out. "It's time for you to leave, Steph."

"What, are you afraid of the truth?" Steph demanded angrily.

"I'm not afraid of the truth. I just think it's too damn late for the truth, Steph."

"Fine. Whatever." Steph was at the door in a few quick strides. "Don't expect me to ever offer again."

"Don't worry," Jillian said to the slammed door. "I won't."

Logan couldn't remember the last time she had felt so free, so relaxed, so unencumbered.

She let the warm breeze ruffle her hair as she sped along EC Row Expressway, the T-bar roof of her 1978 Corvette safely tucked in the back hatch area. She loved it like this, flying down the highway, the sunshine-and-warm-air feeling of almost being in a convertible, the tunes cranked to near deafening levels. Buying the classic silver beauty two months ago had made her feel like a kid again. It was the first indulgent thing she'd done for herself in years. She loved how low she sat to the ground, how the car seemed to nearly lift off the ground on a straightaway, how people looked at her like she was a jerk. Yes, a jerk. Corvette drivers had the reputation of being hairy, mid-life, gold-chain-wearing guys full of testosterone and fuck-you manners, but she didn't care. She almost felt like one of them every time she sat in the leather driver's seat and started the throaty engine.

She smiled as Bachman-Turner Overdrive's "You Ain't Seen Nothin' Yet" poured from the six speakers. She had just been a baby then, but the old rock tunes of the 1970s always made her feel good. Same with old Motown tunes. She'd gotten away from listening to music the last four years. Everything in the Army was so regimented, there wasn't much time or privacy in which to listen to music. Well, no more. Logan listened to music now as often as she could—in the car, on her iPod while jogging or at the gym, when she had time to cook. She would love to go out to a club, but she was reluctant to go on her own and she hadn't made many new friends yet. Maybe she could get Lisa and Dorothy to go with her some night. That would be a blast. She'd heard there was a new lesbian and gay dance club in the city. It was time to put some serious pressure on her twin sister and her lover to paint the town red with her. She'd get on them about it at dinner tonight.

Logan loved the fact that Lisa and Dorothy lived only a few blocks from the old family home. An old town with old colonial or Victorian homes, Walkerville had been gradually swallowed up by Windsor and now looked like a small enclave of the city. She slowed as she passed her old high school, a majestic stone structure built around the turn of the last century. God, had it really been twenty years since she'd roamed the hallways, the star of the basketball and soccer teams? Top of the class in academics, too, along with Lisa. The sisters were envied, sometimes even targets for the jealous, small-minded kids who'd never gotten to know them. Especially Logan, the more introverted one. She was mocked sometimes or avoided, but her genuine humility and honesty always won people over eventually. Once they realized she really didn't think she was better than everyone else, wasn't trying to prove anything to anyone but herself, they took her on and became her friend.

Boston was playing on the car stereo now, and Logan closed her eyes for just an instant. She wouldn't want to go back to high school, not really. It was such a cathartic time—realizing she liked girls, trying to figure out who she really was and how to get comfortable in her own skin, deciding on a career path, really learning how to deal with all those adult emotions for the first time. It was bliss and it was hell, and yet she wouldn't trade any of it. So many doors had opened for her then…doors to her own self. It had been the real beginning of the person Logan Sharp would one day become.

Logan turned onto Lisa's street. She envied her sister and her idyllic life—living in her wonderful old house with the love of her life. It was how she imagined herself living one day, though she was not yet convinced that was anything more than a fantasy. She was not Lisa. She was not "marriage" material. She was not the kind to settle in anywhere for a long time, to really open herself up and trust someone again. To lose herself with someone. She'd convinced herself that it just wasn't her.

Going off alone for long bike rides, or walks, or rides in her Vette—that was the Logan Sharp she knew and was comfortable with. So as much as she liked to entertain the idea of a life like her sister's, in those quiet, weak moments before sleep or when waking, it was about as likely to happen to her as a meteorite falling from the sky and landing on her precious car.

Logan didn't recognize the new Chevy Malibu with Michigan plates in Lisa's driveway. Lisa hadn't mentioned anything about another dinner guest, but Lisa and Dorothy were popular, and so was their swimming pool. It wasn't exactly unheard of for a friend to drop over for a late afternoon swim. Logan had come over a couple of months ago for what she thought was going to be a quiet dinner for the three of them, only to find it was a dinner for seven.

Dorothy, her warm brown eyes twinkling with pleasure, greeted Logan enthusiastically with a kiss on both cheeks. Then she tossed her a withering look that Logan knew she didn't mean.

"Oh, Logan. It's been twenty-six days since you were here last, you know. I almost thought you'd moved away again."

Logan rolled her eyes playfully. Dorothy, six years older, was like a mother hen to her, and Logan secretly enjoyed the attention.

"Have you been eating?" Dorothy swept discerning eyes over her.

"Yes, Mother, I've been eating."

"Well, you're taking home leftovers tonight."

Dorothy was a good cook, and since she was the queen of casseroles, Logan was confident there would be plenty of good leftovers for the freezer. "You don't need to tell me twice!"

Lisa strolled into the foyer, wrapped in a large towel, the straps of her bathing suit peeking through. "Hey, sis." She wrapped wet arms around Logan for a quick hug. Her eyes glinted with mischief.

"What?" Logan asked, eyeing Lisa dubiously.

"What do you mean, what?"

"Don't give me that. What are you up to?"

"Nothing," Lisa answered slyly, a smile in her voice.

Logan looked to Dorothy for help, but she simply shrugged and sauntered back to the kitchen.

"Care for a swim, Logan? It is rather hot out today. Or did your Vette cool you down?"

Logan shook her head, resigned to submitting to her sister's rather obvious machinations to get her into the pool. Perhaps Lisa was in the mood for a good ass-kicking water noodle fight. If that were the case, Logan would gladly oblige. Stronger and a little bigger than Lisa, Logan had always been able to physically dominate her twin in their little games of one-upmanship.

"Sure, just let me get my stuff on. Hey, who does the mystery car belong to?"

Lisa shrugged, feigning indifference. "Just a friend who dropped by."

"Uh-huh." Logan's Spidey sense was tingling, but she let it go. She reached for the gym bag she'd set down by the door, then trotted off to a guest bedroom to change. She was not the bikini-wearing type and never had been. While she appreciated a bikini or a sexy one-piece on a hot woman, Logan personally preferred the comfort and functionality of swim trunks and a sports bra.

Dorothy pressed a beer into her hands and gave her a complicit smile as Logan headed out the sliding glass doors to the pool. What was going on with those two, anywa—

Logan halted suddenly. Everything stopped except her eyes, which swam with the image of Jillian and her daughter sitting on the steps of the pool, playing with a rubber duck, making water spew from its beak as if by magic. With desperation, her eyes sought out Lisa, who sat on the edge of the pool, her feet dangling in the water, looking sheepish but not exactly remorseful. She gave Logan a smile of helplessness, as if to say, "I'm only doing this for your own good."

Logan scowled back at her. Damn her anyway for thinking she knew what was best. Lisa had always been like that, dragging her out to parties, trying to set her up on dates, running interference for her with their parents. She had always mothered her, come to think of it. Had always looked at Logan as emotionally fragile. Maybe it was all part of their bond. Where one was strong, the other was weak. Lisa looked after her emotionally, while Logan protected her physically. Only right now, she'd like to go over there and dunk her in the pool for a good minute or so. *That would teach her! Okay, it wouldn't, but it'd sure as hell be fun.*

After what seemed like minutes, Jillian finally noticed her. She didn't look at all surprised. Far from it. In fact, she looked as though she'd fully anticipated Logan's arrival.

Goddammit, I'm going to kill you, Lisa! But the thought was only a flash, because when she looked back at Jillian, she felt only joy—the kind of joy that lifted her soul, infused her heart, and made her feel lighter than air.

"Hello, Logan." Jillian's smile was genuine but tentative, as though she was worried about Logan's reaction.

It took Logan a moment to find her voice. "Hi." *Yes, that was brilliant. Way to go, Logan. Way to show her what just looking at her does to you.*

Maddie was being shy, clutching onto her mother, and Jillian mumbled something encouraging to her.

Logan crouched down in front of them, thankful for the diversion of Maddie, because she really didn't want to take a good look at Jillian in that white bikini. It should be illegal on a body like hers. She'd noticed enough of it to know that much.

"Hi, Maddie. Are you feeling better after your little accident?"

She nodded once, looked at her mother to answer for her. It had been a week, and Jillian explained that Maddie was back to her old self, the mishap long forgotten. Only a scratch and a faint bruise were evident.

Dorothy emerged with a tray and called to Maddie. A snack of animal crackers and a juice box chased away her shyness and had her little legs running to the patio as fast as they would take her.

"Hey, Maddie, no running near the pool," Jillian called out, then turned back to Logan. "She has a pretty big appetite for a little kid." Jillian smiled. "She takes after her biological father that way."

Logan sat down on the edge of the pool and dipped her legs into the water, careful to avoid accidentally touching Jillian. She had never managed to dislodge the memory of Jillian's last day at KAF. She'd been so scared at first that Jillian had been hurt—or worse. More scared than she'd ever been in her life. And then she'd wanted nothing more than to hold her, to soothe her, to erase all the terrible things that had happened to her. Holding Jillian in her arms, kissing her, comforting her, had felt like the most natural, wonderful gift to her soul and body. She'd felt more alive, more full of purpose holding Jillian than she had felt in years. Jillian's body against hers had dissolved all the protective layers she'd cocooned herself in. It should have been frightening or threatening, but it had felt surprisingly good. So good, in fact, that she had inappropriately wanted so much more. It was just as well that Jillian had slipped away from her at daybreak and out of her life for what she'd thought was for good. She would not have been able to forgive herself if anything more had happened between them that night.

Logan fought to regain her concentration, because things were stirring in her. Things she'd learned so well how to shut down and ignore. Jillian had said something about Maddie's father, and it was the perfect opportunity for Logan to ask the question she'd always wanted to. "Is Mark her biological father?"

Jillian just looked at her for a moment, gauging whether to answer perhaps, and then any shred of discomfort quickly passed. "Yes. How did you know? Was it the appetite comment?"

Logan smiled. It was almost like old times again. "Yeah. That and I just thought, who else would you go to but your best friend?"

"You know me better than I thought, Logan." Jillian said it so quietly, but the words were full of meaning, and something sparked in Logan, like a flame catching.

They slipped into the water at the same time, standing in the shallow end, trying not to look at one another, but it was useless. Logan was mesmerized.

Jillian was gorgeous, with her short, dark, tousled hair and those dark eyes so full of intelligence and compassion. Logan had found Jillian entrancing long before she'd ever spoken to her, and now she didn't want to stop looking at her. Her eyes dropped with a seeming mind of their own, and when she took all of Jillian in, she felt her breath stall in her chest. Her heart began to hammer in earnest. She knew her eyes had widened with the pleasant shock of the stunning vision before her and that her lips had parted in anticipation.

Yes, she probably looked like a teenager on hormone overdrive. And yes, she felt like the faintest breeze could knock her over right now, but she was beyond caring. She could no more control her reaction to Jillian in that revealing bikini than she could control the weather. Jillian was simply stunning. She was the sexiest woman Logan had ever seen, bar none. Her breasts were absolutely perfect. Round, full. Not too big or too small. Nipples like rosebuds beneath the thin fabric. Her waist was trim, her skin taut and tanned, her legs beneath the water muscular. A tiny bulge in her bikini bottoms made Logan's mouth water.

God. She hadn't felt this insanely attracted to a woman's body in ages. The primal urge in her was both disconcerting and delicious. It was all she could do not to reach out and touch.

Jillian dove headlong into the water and began slicing her way to the deep end. Logan couldn't be sure how much of her reaction had resonated with Jillian. *Shit.* She needed to behave, call on her former soldierliness or her medical persona. Show a little professional detachment and respect. *Yeah, right. Like you showed her that last night in KAF when you clung to one another so desperately in that tiny bed?*

Logan's eyes drifted to her sister. Lisa was grinning like the know-it-all she was, and Logan hauled off and splashed her with as much water as she could. Lisa squealed, but it did nothing to wipe the smirk off her face.

"So," Logan said quietly, sidling up to Lisa. "Are you going to tell me what this is all about?"

Lisa didn't try to deny it. They were beyond feigning innocence with one another. "I wanted to get to know her better."

"And?"

"And..." Lisa watched Jillian pull herself out of the water, wrap a towel around herself, then go to her daughter. Her gaze settled back on Logan, a steely don't-argue-with-me look. "Logan, I know how long it's been since you've been with a woman."

Logan's jaw stiffened. "Christ, Lisa. If I just wanted to get laid, don't you think—"

"Of course it's not just about sex. That's not what I meant, Logan."

Logan blew out an exasperated breath. She didn't want to think about sex with Jillian. It was too hard to contemplate something as impossible as that.

"I meant," Lisa continued in a whisper, "that you got really close to Jillian back in Afghanistan. I think something really profound happened there between you two."

Logan's eyebrows shot into her forehead. She'd never told Lisa how close she and Jillian had grown in that brief time together at KAF. Had never mentioned how Jill had reached inside her, had touched her the way no one else ever had. She'd intimated a few things perhaps but had never even come close to giving Lisa an idea of how much she'd come to care for Jillian.

Logan swallowed hard. "That was well over a year ago, Lisa. We haven't seen each other or even been in touch since then. It was just a brief moment that something...I don't know. It just doesn't matter anymore, okay? It's over. Whatever it was." She had resigned herself to that a long time ago. And she'd been more than okay with it until Lisa started meddling.

"Logan, I think that woman makes you happy. Happier than

you've ever been. She's good for you, so admit it."

"She's married," Logan hissed. "Christ, Lisa. What the hell do you think you're playing at?"

"I'm not playing at anything, and don't be too sure she's not single."

"Just because she doesn't wear a ring anymore?"

"I wouldn't know about that. But Maddie blurted something out to Dorothy about her other mom's house and that she stays with her other mom sometimes."

Logan shook her head fiercely, the burning of tears just below the surface. She didn't care whether Jillian was single or not. Didn't *want* to care, at least, what her living arrangements were or if she was with anyone. Logan was doing just fine on her own, thank you very much. No drama, no angst, no worrying about someone else's feelings or marital status or any of that bullshit.

She started to get out of the pool, but Lisa rested a hand on her forearm. "You're not going to leave, are you?"

Logan stopped herself from saying something bitchy. She wanted to leave, but she wouldn't do that to Lisa and Dorothy. Or to Jillian, who surely must be as confused and uncomfortable with all of this as she was. "Promise me this is it, Lisa. No more doing crap behind my back where Jillian is concerned, okay? I need you to leave this alone."

Lisa nodded severely. "All right."

Jillian was well aware that Logan couldn't take her eyes off her in the pool. It *had* been kind of cruel to wear the crisp white, skimpy bikini. She had wanted Logan to notice her, and boy, had she! Logan's eyes had covered her like an artist stroking paint on a canvas, filling in every indentation, every stroke smooth and thorough and textured. She looked away quickly, feigning disinterest, whenever Jillian tried to catch her at it, but Jillian felt Logan's warm gaze on her like the sunshine on her skin. It hadn't been her imagination, the way Logan had touched her, had kissed her with such feeling, back at the base in Kandahar. And it was all still there, every last wisp of their bond, visible there in Logan's

149

eyes. It was almost as though no time had passed.

Crap, Jillian thought. *What the hell am I going to do now?* Logan was not someone to be toyed with, and neither was she, for that matter. They were just not the kind of women who indulged in mindless, meaningless sex, and so a tryst was out of the question. Logan was too honorable for that sort of thing, anyway, and Jillian was straight out of a long-term relationship and still dealing with all its mind-numbing baggage. There was Maddie to consider, too. Jillian had no intention of introducing women into her child's life who might not be around for breakfast or dinner the next night.

Logan's fingertips brushed her arm as she handed Jillian a towel, and with that electrifying touch, it was painfully, annoyingly clear that they could never just be friends. The time for that had come and gone.

"Thank you," Jillian mumbled, a tickle in her stomach at the soft smile from Logan.

"Any time."

She had to look away, because those hazel eyes were moist and penetratingly full of something Jillian didn't want to decipher right now. She had accepted Lisa's invitation for a swim and dinner because she thought maybe it was time to renew her friendship with Logan. It was clear that idea had been a mistake. There could be no innocent friendship, because lust and desire and something so much deeper were firmly rooted in both of them. Exploring a relationship with Logan, while deeply appealing, was just not possible right now. Jillian decided she and Maddie would eat dinner and leave as soon as was politely possible.

Jillian tried to avoid looking at Logan. She focused mostly on Lisa and Dorothy, who were extremely curious about her work and all the places she'd been. The two doted over Maddie, who ate the quintessential kids' favorite, mac and cheese, while the rest of them dined on Dorothy's pasta and chicken alfredo casserole. Logan didn't exactly seem sullen, but she did seem preoccupied.

"So," Dorothy said pointedly to Jillian after a long pause over lemon cake. "Have you started dating yet?"

Jillian nearly choked on her mouthful of cake. From the corner of her eye she saw Logan do a double take while Lisa gave her lover a smack on the knee.

"W-well," Dorothy stammered, her face turning pink. "I'm sorry, it just slipped out. You don't have to answer that."

Jillian wasn't perturbed. Dorothy was a social worker, and so asking personal questions was no surprise. That the question had been asked in Logan's presence made Jillian wince internally for a reason she didn't want to think about.

The three of them leaned forward in their seats, clearly awaiting her answer. Logan was obviously the most interested because she looked everywhere but at Jillian, and Jillian's heart clenched. She did owe Logan an explanation of what had happened in her life the last few months, she thought. Not because of the undeniable, sizzling attraction between them, but because deep down, there was a bond of friendship and mutual respect. They could not sit here and be polite strangers, pretending indifference. Not after what they'd been through together last year.

She addressed her answer to Logan and tried to sound casual. "No, I haven't. I guess I haven't gotten used to the whole being-single-again thing yet." She smiled helplessly, as though they would all understand. "I don't think it's ever as easy as movies and books make it seem. Especially when you're a parent, too." Maddie sucked crumbs from her fingers, completely oblivious to the topic.

"I guess some women are scared off by kids, huh?" Lisa was trying to sound sympathetic, but in truth, Jillian had no idea if women were scared of dating her because she had a child. She hadn't gotten that far with anyone yet, nor had she any real desire to.

Jillian was noncommittal. "I'm sure the right kind of woman isn't."

Dorothy tipped her coffee mug at Jillian. "Here's to the right kind of woman who is not scared off by kids. They are out there, you know."

"Thanks, but it doesn't really matter to me at the moment."

Logan flashed her an empathetic look, and Jillian immediately understood that Logan was one of those women who was not afraid to get involved with a single mom. She was good with kids. No, *great* with kids. She was as down-to-earth as they came. Unbidden came images of Logan playing with Maddie—teaching her how to ride a bike, reading a story to her, playing catch with her. She gasped a little, just to herself, because thinking of Logan as part of Maddie's life felt more real than abstract, more like a memory or maybe a premonition than just a nice fantasy.

"Mommy, it's time to dance," Maddie announced to everyone.

"That's something we do at home, honey, not when we're at someone else's house."

"Why?" Maddie wasn't exactly whining, but she was close to it.

Jillian looked an apology to her hosts. "It's just something we do every night after dinner. We dance for a song or two."

Dorothy leapt up, pure delight on her face. She clapped her hands enthusiastically. "Oh, yes, let's put some music on."

Lisa laughed and went along with the idea, but Logan looked horrified. It made Jillian smile. Yes, it would be just like her to be afraid of having Jillian see her do something as primal and carefree as dance. Jillian's smile turned into a low chuckle. *This just might be worth the price of admission.*

"Can we, Mommy?"

"All right, honey, as long as it's okay with Dorothy and Lisa."

"Oh, it's more than okay," said Dorothy before dashing to the iPod docking station in the next room.

In moments she called for them to join her. Maddie was nearly bouncing off the ceiling in anticipation. Logan slunk into the room last, like a dog with its ears down, dreading what was next. Her resistance was comical, especially when Dorothy cranked Natalie Cole's "This Will Be (An Everlasting Love)." Logan tried melting into the wall as the rest of them began to move unabashedly to the disco beat. Maddie always came out of her shell to music. She lost herself in whatever crazy beat was going on in her head, which never matched the song. But that was more than okay with Jillian, who loved to watch the bliss on her daughter's face and the jerky, totally spontaneous movements.

Lisa and Dorothy were having a good time together, twirling each other, laughing like teenagers as they were transported into their own little world. Logan drifted closer, and Lisa grabbed her by the hand and brought her into the circle. By the time The Temptations' "Ain't Too Proud To Beg" came on, Logan was laughing with her head back and moving as adeptly and joyously as the rest of them. Jillian moved next to her, and they began dancing together. They were subtle about it, but their bodies found an immediate synchronicity. It was like they were both part of the same instrument, one's movement filling in and guiding the other's, like a sail responding to a gust of wind. They didn't touch, but Jillian found herself wanting to, even if it was just their hands or the brushing of their hips. Something, anything, to feel the heat and electricity from Logan's body.

The song ended and Maddie moaned with disappointment, wanting more.

"No, honey, it's time for us to go. It will be late by the time we get home, okay?"

Maddie protested again but did not defy her mother. Jillian thanked her hosts. She had mixed feelings about leaving. It was for the best, even though she couldn't deny that she wanted more time with Logan.

As if reading her mind, Logan offered to escort her and Maddie to her car. So, they would have a moment alone. Or sort of alone, if she didn't count Maddie.

Jillian buckled her daughter into her car seat, then stood beside her own open door, waiting for Logan to say something or waiting for an epiphany that would provide her with something brilliant to say and just the right way to say it—anything that would give them a chance to maybe see each other again without any pressure, without it seeming like a date. Jillian did want to see Logan again, but as she watched Logan grow more uncomfortable by the second, she felt her prospects dim.

"Are you upset with your sister for not telling you I was going to be here?" Jillian ventured.

Logan laughed, more to herself. "I was a little at first."

"And now?"

Logan blew out a nervous breath, taking time to gather her thoughts. Jillian liked that about Logan. She rarely blurted things out. Her words were measured, well reasoned, honest though just a little aloof sometimes. *We will work on that, Logan Sharp.*

"Now I'm glad."

"Just...glad?"

"Yeah. Glad." Logan leaned against the open driver's door as Jillian climbed in and sat down.

"I'm glad, too." Actually, Jillian was relieved. Thrilled. Scared. Seeing Logan did all of those things to her and more. She closed her eyes for a moment, the way a swimmer might before diving into a pool. "Logan?"

"Yes?"

Jillian swiftly swallowed her fear before she succumbed to it. "Would you like to come to my place for dinner next weekend? It would just be us. Maddie will be with Steph."

Logan's eyes scanned the horizon, now darkening with the progression of sunset. The waiting was killing Jillian, and it was at least a minute before Logan looked at her again. The smallest smile curved her lips, and there was a rare cockiness in her expression.

"I would love to. Am I wrong to think of it as a date?"

Jillian's mouth had gone dry. *A date.* It was going to be a date. Of course it was, just the two of them, dinner at her place. What else was Logan to think? And she deserved an honest answer.

"Yes," Jillian said with finality. "A date."

CHAPTER NINE

It was just as she'd always imagined: Jillian's house was on a street with wide boulevards and lined with perfectly spaced maple trees. The house was a brick bungalow. Pragmatic, cozy, nice, unpretentious. Logan parked her Corvette in front of it and sat for a moment. She was nervous. Tonight was a date, and it both thrilled and scared the crap out of her. She hadn't been on a real date in…She couldn't remember when. She didn't even know what was expected of her. Would she kiss Jillian at the end? God, she hoped so! And what kind of kiss should it be? A kiss on the cheek? A quick kiss on the lips, or the way she'd kissed her in Kandahar?

Oh, Jesus, Logan, get over yourself!

Logan laughed and shook her head at herself and her adolescent musings. She could drive herself crazy with the possibilities, or she could just let whatever was going to happen, happen, and not worry about it.

Jillian greeted her on the porch, not with a smile but a frown.

Of course, it was the most adorable frown Logan had ever seen.

Logan nearly let go of the bottle of wine in her suddenly moist hand as Jillian's displeasure intensified. *Shit.* "What's wrong, Jillian?"

Jillian smiled, but it wasn't a cheerful one. "I'm so sorry, Logan. My oven just broke. I was all set to put the chicken parmesan in, and it just quit working. I can't believe it. Of all the times for it to happen."

Logan followed her into the kitchen and set the wine on the counter.

"Thank you for bringing that, Logan. You didn't have to do that." She leaned forward on her toes and gave Logan a quick kiss on the cheek. "Sorry for the lousy greeting earlier."

Logan swept her eyes over Jillian's form-fitting, short-sleeved blouse and designer slacks. Damn, it was going to be hard to behave herself, but the last thing she wanted to do was pressure Jillian by throwing herself at her. *Oh, yes, I would love to throw myself at her feet right about now!* There were any number of things she could do to Jillian while on her knees, Logan thought, immediately feeling a blush work its way up her neck. She cleared her throat and forcibly expunged her naughty little fantasy.

"It's nice to see you, Jillian, even if your stove isn't working." She expelled a nervous breath. "Why don't I have a look and see what's going on with it?"

Jillian let out a long overdue laugh. *God.* She was every bit as nervous as Logan was, and the thought was reassuring. "Don't tell me you have a second job fixing appliances or something."

"Nope. Just an unnatural preoccupation with how things work."

Logan opened the oven door and noticed immediately that the bottom element had burned out. She pointed it out to Jillian, who wore her disappointment in the cutest frown Logan had ever seen.

"Damn, I wanted to cook you something nice, Logan. This really sucks. I'm so sorry about this."

Logan engaged Jillian with a smile. She really wanted to tilt her chin up with her index finger and give her a kiss on the lips, but she was not brave enough for that level of intimacy yet. Hell, she didn't even know where any of this was going. For all she knew, it could be their first and last date, though she sure as hell hoped not.

"I would love to take you out to dinner," Logan said, then worried she might have insulted Jillian, who was still wearing an adorable little apron around her waist. "I mean, I would love your cooking, but we could take a rain check on that and go out for dinner tonight."

Jillian shook her head, but she was smiling. "Honest, I wasn't trying to get you to take me out to dinner, you know."

Now Logan really wanted to kiss her. The sudden urge surprised her. She'd never had a desire to kiss a woman on the first date the way she wanted to kiss Jillian right now. She could almost picture herself closing the distance between them, pressing Jillian against the counter, her hands on either side of her on the granite surface, her body hard and aroused against Jillian, her lips brushing Jillian's softly at first, then much more demandingly. Oh, hell yes, she would love to...

"There's a great little Italian place just a few blocks away."

"Huh?" Logan had to wrest her mind back to what Jillian was saying.

"A restaurant. An Italian one that's very good."

"Right, right. Sounds great to me."

The tablecloths were checkered and candles flickered on each surface. Dean Martin, Frank Sinatra and Mel Torme crooned from the hidden speakers. It was a small place, a dozen or so intimate tables, and only half of them were filled.

"This is wonderful," Logan said, taking in their surroundings. She hadn't been to a nice restaurant in awhile, and Italian was her favorite. She inhaled deeply, closed her eyes against the wonderful smells of basil, garlic and sharp cheese. Being in a restaurant with Jillian was not something she would have imagined a couple of weeks ago. So much could change in such a short span of time. She'd certainly learned that lesson serving in Afghanistan.

Running into Jillian again two weeks ago at the hospital, and then at her sister's, and now on a date. It was an unexpected, if totally delightful, turn of events.

"Wait until you taste the food." Jillian winked, and with that, a flash of wetness surged between Logan's legs, sending her momentarily reeling. Memories of Jillian in her white bikini flooded her mind with sudden ferocity, causing Logan to clamp her legs together. Jillian was hot. Far hotter even than Logan remembered from their time in Kandahar. She was sure Jillian had been just as hot then. Logan probably just hadn't allowed herself to fully appreciate it. It was different now. They weren't confined by any sort of protocol or the close quarters of the base. More than that, Jillian was single now.

Oh, God, I need to get a grip. She'd not had sex in a couple of years, not since a one-night stand while on leave one weekend near her base in Petawawa, Ontario. It had been a far from satisfying experience and one she had not been anxious to repeat. Since then, she'd found that her left hand did the trick just as nicely and without the complications. Now, though, she wanted sex. Sex with Jillian. Lovemaking with Jillian. The need to touch Jillian and be touched by Jillian burned in her like a fire that couldn't be extinguished.

Jillian was talking about her favorite restaurants in the city. Logan had to force her attention away from sex and tried to concentrate on what she was saying. It was just...Jillian tapped into this place of such raw feeling inside her. She couldn't help but think of all the wonderful things she would like to do to her—all the ways she wanted to love her.

Logan nearly choked on the water she had begun drinking, the word "love" reverberating in her mind and flustering her in a way she couldn't ever remember being flustered. *Goddamn, what is happening to me!* And now Jillian was looking at her funny, as though reading her mind. The goddess must have been looking out for her, though, because the waitress, an older, heavyset woman with a thick Italian accent, chose that moment to bring her overbearing personality to their table.

It was exactly what Logan needed to focus her attention again—five minutes of the chatty, demonstrative woman and her nearly unintelligible rundown of the menu, not to mention the short, laughable serenade she gave them. It was all Logan and Jillian could do to smother their laughter and order their meals, but the minute she disappeared, they both laughed long and hard.

"God," Jillian said, her eyes still sparkling from tears of laughter. "It's so good to laugh with you, Logan. It's good to laugh, period."

"You haven't had much of that lately, I presume."

"No." Jillian sighed deeply, but her face remained impassive. "I haven't."

Logan needed to know what had happened between Jillian and her partner. Every detail. Now. She asked as gently as she could, "What happened to you and Steph? Will you tell me?"

It was a long time before Jillian answered. So long that Logan thought she wouldn't.

"Nothing was the same for me when I came back from Afghanistan. I just...I don't know. I didn't look at anything the same again, you know? I remember sitting in a restaurant with Steph shortly after. It was weird, but I noticed things like I'd never seen them before. The reflections in a man's glasses, the wrinkle in a woman's dress at the next table, the way Steph held her knife and fork. It was like I'd been in some fog before, and all of a sudden I was not only noticing the most common and mundane things, but I was finding them fascinating. Was it like that for you, Logan? Was it like coming out of a dark room into the light?"

The obtrusive waitress arrived with a bottle of Tuscany Chianti and made a big show of pouring them each a glass while she prattled on about it being a very good year. Logan had never wanted to put a muzzle on anyone the way she wanted to on this woman. Or maybe she could just do a little surgery on her larynx, yeah. That would silence her for good.

Jillian smiled across the table at her, probably thinking of her own ways to get rid of the obnoxious waitress. They waited her out, not engaging in conversation with her until she finally took the hint and left.

"Sorry, Logan. She must be new here. I wouldn't have brought you–"

"It's fine, honest." Logan reached across the table and touched Jillian's hand for just a few seconds—seconds that she wished were minutes.

"So," Jillian said softly. "What I was saying before. Did you feel different after you left Afghanistan?"

Feeling different didn't even begin to describe things. She still felt like a stranger in a room full of people who all knew each other—disjointed, a little outside herself, a little alien. It was like being the last person in the room to get a joke or the only person to show up in street clothes to a black-tie event. She knew she would never be the same again, that she bore invisible scars. Yet at the same time she felt terribly exposed. "Yes, of course," Logan understated. "How could you not?"

"But I didn't even see five percent of what you saw over there."

"Doesn't matter. You saw enough to know that life is cheap in some places, that horror and tragedy can visit anyone, anytime. That life is to be cherished, always."

"I think Steph just thought I was totally fucked up from being there and that I should just get over it and get back to our life. She couldn't see how things had changed for me."

"How were they different? I mean, besides noticing things you hadn't noticed before?"

"Oh, God." Jillian thought for a moment, her forehead an adorable roadmap of concentration. Logan wanted to kiss the lines smooth again. "I could barely even look at her anymore. It was like something shifted in me, like I just wasn't the same person anymore, you know? And when I looked at her, and me, and us as a couple, I felt like an imposter."

"An imposter?"

Jillian took a long sip of her wine. "Yeah. Like I was living this life of domesticity but that it wasn't really me. It was someone else, because I sure as hell didn't feel happy with Steph. It just didn't feel like *my* life anymore, you know? I mean, how could I sit at home folding laundry a week after nearly getting blown up?"

Their food arrived. The waitress barely said two words to them, which nearly shocked Logan out of her chair.

"Miracles never cease." Logan winked across the table and watched as Jillian erupted into laughter.

"Oh," Logan moaned after taking her first bite of the four-mushroom penne in a gorgonzola cream sauce. "This is wonderful."

"The food is great if you can put up with the waitress."

"For this, I would put up with anything." Logan saluted Jillian with her wine glass and took a sip. For this food, wine and the woman sitting across from her, Logan would do just about anything, even kiss the annoying waitress's shoes!

They ate in silence for a few minutes until Logan broached the subject of Jillian and Steph again. She had to know if Jillian was finished with that part of her life, because she could never just be friends with this woman again, not the way they'd been in Kandahar. "So you realized after being in Afghanistan that you weren't happy with Steph?"

"Yes. God, it sounds like some kind of a B-grade movie, doesn't it? Woman has a life-altering, traumatic experience and decides she can't go back to the life she was living." Jillian stared into her wine glass for a long moment, then turned large, moist eyes up at Logan. "I never thought I'd be a cliché, that I would wake up one day and feel totally unhappy with her."

Logan had never had that experience. Her only serious relationship, Nic, had ended in surprise and not of her choosing. But she did know what it felt like to have the rug pulled out from under her. She knew what it was like to feel like the relationship had been a lie. "Do you think you were always unhappy with her or just all of a sudden?" She remembered Mark's words, how Jillian and Steph had never been right for each other, but it was up to Jillian to tell her that.

"I thought I was happy, early on. And she always let me take off around the world for my photo assignments, which I thought was great. Then I began to realize in letting me go, she always played the martyr, always made me feel guilty about how generous she was being in letting me go. We'd both begun to resent each other without admitting it." A tear slithered down Jillian's cheek, and Logan almost regretted pushing her on the subject. "I lost myself with her. A little bit at a time so that I didn't even really notice I'd changed. But it was like I didn't even recognize myself anymore. Coming back from Afghanistan, I just realized I needed to live my life for me, to look after my own happiness for a change, because life is too damn short, you know?"

Logan nodded. She knew that all too well. Lisa had talked to her about the same thing after she'd returned from her second tour. She'd asked Logan point-blank when she was going to start living life for herself, to find what truly made her happy. Logan had decided not to renew her contract with the army, but had brushed Lisa off, not wanting to think that deeply about things like personal happiness. Now she couldn't help it. Jillian had found the courage to do it, and Logan had so much respect and admiration for her that it nearly took her breath away. "Was it hard?"

Jillian laughed, but it wasn't out of joy. "Oh my god, Logan. It was the hardest thing I've ever had to do. Maddie is what made it so hard, changing the only way of life she'd ever known." Jillian wiped a final tear from her cheek. "Someday she'll understand why I had to do it. I hope she does, anyway. I want her to know that you have to live your life for yourself first. That you have to be true to yourself."

God. What she wouldn't do for a little of Jillian's courage. Sure, Logan had been brave in the face of war and brave in battling everyday medical traumas. But the brand of bravery Jill had...no, that was something Logan didn't have. To her own ears her voice sounded rough, emotional. "Does Maddie split her time between the two of you?"

"Yes. I have sole legal custody, but generally Steph gets her every other weekend. Under Michigan law, Steph was never allowed to adopt Maddie, but she wants a relationship with Maddie, and I would never deprive Maddie of that."

Logan raised her eyebrow. It was shocking how far behind this neighboring state was with respect to gay rights. In Logan's country, gays had been allowed to legally marry since 2003 and allowed to legally adopt children since well before that. "Is Maddie adapting okay?"

"She is now. It was really hard the first few months."

"And you? How are you adapting?" Logan practically had to sit on her hand to keep it from reaching across the table and holding tightly onto Jillian's.

"I'm doing okay." Jillian's smile lit up Logan's heart. "I'm doing much better now."

Now as in lately or now because we're on a date? Logan was dying to ask. She gave Jillian an innocuous smile instead. "I'm glad."

They finished their meal in companionable silence, until Logan, after deliberating for a few moments, asked, "Did you ever think about getting in touch with me the last few months?"

Jillian, in spite of her perpetually tanned skin, blushed a little. "Yes. Many times, Logan. But I didn't want to confuse my issues. I needed to do what I was doing for the right reasons. It was something I needed to do on my own, by myself, without any distractions."

Logan didn't want to push the issue any further. She was afraid to. "Shall we go?"

"Yes, but only if you come in for coffee at my place."

Logan nodded eagerly. She would like nothing better.

Jillian couldn't remember ever being so nervous on a date. *That's because it's not a date with just any woman. It's a date with Logan Sharp. The woman you felt something so deep for and tried so hard to pretend it wasn't happening. A woman who made you finally notice how much you'd lost of yourself.*

Realization nearly sucked Jillian's breath away. She had

deliberately not given much thought or credit to Logan's influence on her since she'd left Kandahar. She hadn't wanted to admit how much her time with Logan had forced her to look at her life and seek changes. Just being able to talk with Logan the way she had, to express feelings she had so expertly choked off in recent years—it had made her realize that she needed to reclaim herself. It may have been at a subconscious level at KAF, but she knew now that with Logan she could not only truly be herself but also be appreciated for being herself.

Jillian gave Logan a long searching look as she sat at the other end of the couch, contemplatively sipping her coffee. It was hard to fathom what was going on in her head so much of the time. Logan liked to keep her thoughts and feelings close—too close sometimes—and that left Jillian playing a guessing game.

"What are you thinking right now?" Jillian bravely ventured.

Logan looked so serious, her mouth set, her eyes darker than usual, and for an instant, it seemed perhaps that the date was a bad idea. But Logan's voice came out soft and gentle, and Jillian knew it had been the right thing to ask.

"You said leaving Steph and going out on your own was the hardest thing you've ever done. How do you feel now?"

Logan was so sweet with her concern, so sincere, it made Jillian want to confess everything. "I feel better, like I'm returning to the person I am and was meant to be. Like I'm learning to love myself again. God, though, I felt like such a failure for awhile. Still do, to some degree."

"Why?"

"Leaving a relationship, especially with a young child, just made me feel, I don't know, like I'd made bad decisions all along and everyone would judge me on it. Like I'd screwed up and was still screwing up."

"Did your parents or friends give you that kind of grief?"

"No, they haven't. I've been fortunate that way. My parents have really been supportive, and Mark is always there for me, no matter what. I guess it was more how I viewed myself, that's

164

all. I mean, when you think about my success from a career perspective…to not be able to copy that in my personal life made me feel like a failure."

"But you know that's not true now, don't you?"

"Yes." Jillian rolled her eyes. "Mostly." She would probably never feel guilt-free about all the choices she'd made, but the important thing was to accept the past and move forward. "My life with Steph just was what it was. I can't change it."

Point-blank, Logan asked, "Do you feel ready to move on?"

She had moved on by leaving Steph, hadn't she? And yet that didn't seem to be what Logan was asking. For sure she had moved *away* from Steph, but she had not truly moved *forward* yet. She was keeping busy doing local freelance photography, but mostly she was just going through her days until they stacked up like poker chips. "I would really like to try. That's all I can do."

Logan set her coffee cup on the table in front of them, her motions very deliberate. She turned to Jillian, moving closer, and as she did so, something changed in her eyes. They were dancing suddenly. There was joy in them. And something a little mysterious.

Jillian's heart fluttered, and the feelings kindled by the soft tender kiss they had shared on her tiny cot at the air base rushed back. It felt again as though her insides were scalding lava, hot and fluid and unpredictable. Only this time, she allowed herself to absorb the thrill of it, to accept it as appropriate and deserving. She wanted it with every molecule in her body.

Kiss me, Logan. Please kiss me.

Logan moved even closer and rested a warm hand on Jillian's knee, their faces just inches apart. But she didn't kiss her. Instead, lips just a breath away from Jillian's ear, she whispered, "I would really like to kiss you, Jillian. Would that be okay?"

Jillian's heart lurched in anticipation. It was a miracle that she found her voice. "It would be more than okay."

Logan's mouth was butterfly soft on hers. The sensations it sparked coursed through Jillian in tiny shockwaves, causing her eyes to flutter shut and leaving every nerve ending prickling sweetly. Logan's lips explored hers, tenderly and then more firmly, and Jillian pressed back, signaling her desire. The kiss was pure delight. It was better than the one in Kandahar, if that were possible, because Jillian not only wanted it, but fully accepted it and craved it. There was no guilt, no shame. Just wanting.

Logan moved her mouth, so soft and warm, to the underside of Jillian's jaw, her lips caressing her skin with the tiniest of kisses. *Oh my god*, Jillian thought, her insides melting. Another woman's kisses had never made her feel this way. Never. This was both sweet and electrifyingly delicious, turning her body into a quivering, barely-controlled mass of need. She needed this woman's touch. She'd needed it all her life. She pressed into Logan, needing more of that strong, beautiful body against hers.

"Oh," Jillian moaned softly. She turned her head into Logan, trapping her mouth for a long, scorching kiss. As much as she didn't want it to end, it was...too much. She pulled away abruptly, needing a moment to collect herself. "Will you dance a song with me?" she asked.

"Yes. I would love to."

Jillian found the jazz playlist on her iPod, which was ready to go on her Bose docking station. She hit the play button. Joss Stone and Al Green sang the first bars of "How Can You Mend a Broken Heart?"

Yes, that's perfect. Jillian began to sway to the music. She crooked her finger, inviting Logan to join her.

Logan's smile was evident even in the dim light of the living room. She took both of Jillian's hands in hers and began swaying with her. Their eyes remained locked on one another. Time was suspended. Nothing else mattered but this moment, the music and the wonder of their bodies, moving in rhythm, just inches apart.

Jillian stepped into Logan's embrace. Their bodies molding naturally to one another, they moved in perfect slow sync. Jillian closed her eyes and nestled into Logan's shoulder, letting the music and Logan's strong body guide hers. She couldn't remember ever feeling happier. She'd known somewhere deep inside that it would be like this dancing with Logan so intimately, but at the same time, it was mind-blowingly better than she could have imagined. It was as if they'd done this all their lives, and yet there was the magic and wonder of discovery.

Jillian tilted her head up, begging suddenly to be kissed again, needing Logan's lips once more. She was like a flower opening and reaching out for the sun's kisses, for the ruffle of a warm breeze. Wordlessly, Logan complied. The result was every bit as sizzling as the ones on the couch had been. They stopped moving to the music. The kiss deepened. Tongues began to explore lips, then to dart provocatively inside. Jillian's desire for Logan swelled even more. Sweat began to prickle on her forehead. The butterflies in her stomach intensified, and the wetness between her legs flashed hot. *Oh, God, I want you, Logan Sharp.*

She wasn't sure what to do with her want. Didn't want to think about sex right now, because she honestly didn't know if she was ready for that. *Don't think, Jillian,* her traitorous body commanded. *Just feel.*

Logan's hands had dropped, cupping her hips. Jillian could feel their warmth through her slacks. She continued to kiss her, silently welcoming the small, caressing circles Logan's fingers were tracing. Jillian felt her nipples harden. She tightened the arms she had wrapped around Logan's neck and thrust forward, aching for some sort of relief. As if by command, Logan's hands snaked up Jillian's sides, smooth against her silky blouse, gliding toward her need. Logan's lips moved to her throat, sending hot surges of desire through her. She moaned softly. She wanted Logan's touch so badly...

"Jillian, you are so beautiful," Logan whispered. "You're the most beautiful woman I've ever set eyes on."

Jillian bubbled over with happiness. She'd never felt as desirable as she did tonight. "Thank you, Logan," she said breathily once she found her voice. "You make me feel beautiful."

Logan moved her blouse aside just far enough that her lips could kiss Jillian's shoulder blades. She shivered with each exquisite caress. When finally Logan slid a hand over her breast, softly brushing her nipple, Jillian nearly exploded. She was close, so very close. It was all she could do to not rip her blouse off and thrust her bare breast against Logan's palm. She heard herself moan from somewhere deep in her throat.

"Logan, I–"

Logan stiffened against her. She pulled back just a fraction, then another. "Jillian, wait."

"No."

"Yes," Logan said, her breath hitching in her throat. She dropped her hands to Jillian's waist, instantly dampening the intimacy between them.

"What?" Jillian asked shakily.

Logan looked nervous, as if she might bolt. "I'm not sure I can do this with you right now."

What the hell? Jillian swallowed hard, her pride painfully bruised. Wasn't she sexy enough? Was she damaged goods in Logan's mind? Was Logan resentful because Jillian had not contacted her after leaving Afghanistan? Or was it because she was a single mother?

Logan softly pressed her finger to Jillian's lips. "It's not you, Jill. You have done nothing wrong, and I enjoyed every minute of tonight." She turned and walked to the door.

Jillian felt her eyes widen in bewilderment. There would be no further explanation, she knew. This was the way Logan was hard-wired. She would keep her thoughts to herself until the time was right, until she was ready.

Damn it, Logan Sharp! You are an infuriating woman sometimes!

Logan gave her a last, apologetic look.

"Will I see you again?" Jillian demanded, frightened of the answer.

It seemed like hours before Logan answered. "We'll see each other again, Jillian."

She closed the door quietly behind her.

CHAPTER TEN

Logan picked at her bagel and cream cheese in the hospital cafeteria. Her appetite was almost nonexistent, but not her self-flagellation, which was annoyingly abundant. She shouldn't have just left Jillian standing there the other night, looking so bewildered and crestfallen. *If she was even half as turned on as I was...God, she must be ready to kill me. Or write me off as certifiable. I was such a fool, rebuffing her.*

Lisa nodded severely between voracious bites of her breakfast burrito as Logan recounted what had happened. Nothing got between Lisa and her appetite.

"You couldn't do *it* with her? What exactly do you mean by it?"

Logan shrugged. "Sleep with her, I suppose."

"And why not? You two are ridiculously attracted to one another. My god, Logan. At our house two weeks ago, I could practically *taste* how badly the two of you wanted to jump each other." She leveled an accusatory eyebrow at Logan. "You're not worried there isn't enough lust between you, are you?"

"No. There's definitely lust there."

Lisa dug her fork in for another bite. "Good. For a minute there I thought maybe you'd lost your mind. Or your lesbian membership card."

Logan rolled her eyes. "Don't worry, I'm still a sane, card-carrying member." *Well, mostly sane.*

"Good. I'm sure there's a couple of dozen women in this hospital alone who would be glad to hear that. Not that you ever pay them any attention."

"Earth to Lisa. We're talking about Jillian here and not these imaginary women you always claim are making eyes at me."

"There you go again, having no clue how many women find you attractive. However." Lisa waved her fork in the air. "You're off the hook because Jillian Knight seems like such a great catch. *And* she's mad about you."

Logan's spirits dropped another notch. "More like mad *at* me than about me." She explained how she abruptly left Jillian after a hot makeout session. *Crap. She probably thinks I'm not interested in her as anything more than a friend, and I can't exactly blame her.*

"So why did you just leave? Why didn't you haul her into the nearest bedroom and do her the way you know you want to?"

If only life were as simple as Lisa made it out to be. "It's too fast, Lisa. I mean, it was the first date!"

"Too fast?" Lisa's mouth hung open. "Jesus, Logan, it's 2009! Most lesbians do have sex on the first date or at least some pretty significant foreplay. It's not like a first date, anyway. You've known each other off and on for almost a year and a half, and besides, you're not asking her to marry you, for God's sake."

Logan sighed. "I've hardly seen her in that year and a half, and of course I'm not asking her to marry me. Jesus, Lisa!"

"Whatever. The point is, you two are crazy about each other and you're attracted to one another and you're both single. So what the hell are you waiting for?"

"I don't know." Logan had to admit she really didn't have a clue when it came to women. Not since the breakup with Nic.

Whatever skill or nugget of knowledge she'd ever learned about relationships and dating had evaporated after that, and that was just fine with her. Until now. Now she did want to have a clue, because she didn't want to ruin things with Jillian. She just didn't know how *not* to.

"Look, Logan." Lisa rested a hand on her arm in sisterly companionship. "Don't lose this woman over your pride or your fears or whatever it is, okay? Talk to her. Or at least talk to me about what you're feeling. And then talk to her."

Logan paused for a few minutes. She was not like Lisa, or Jillian for that matter. They seemed to be able to tap into their feelings as easily as pulling a book off a shelf. "I don't want to rush her, Lisa. She's just coming out of a long-term relationship."

"Maybe you should let her be the judge of that." Lisa's eyes bore into her, the way they did when she was about to give Logan holy hell for something. "I think you don't want to rush *yourself*, for whatever reason."

Trust Lisa to give me three cents' worth. She's never been content to stop at just two cents' worth. Right now, though, Logan just wanted to go away and brood, to figure out if Lisa was right. It took her awhile sometimes to delve into that deep cauldron of feelings roiling around inside her and sort them out. She wasn't afraid of much. She wasn't afraid of blood and gore, trauma, people's misery, war zones, authority figures. Relationships scared the hell out of her, however. She didn't want to blow it with Jillian, but she didn't want to get hurt either. Not the way she had been hurt by Nic.

Logan stood abruptly. "I've got to get back to work." She glanced at her watch. It was eight thirty. "It'll be crazy soon, if it isn't already. I'll talk to you later."

Lisa stood, too, and touched the sleeve of Logan's scrub shirt. "Are you going to at least call Jillian soon? I mean, she must be wondering what the hell is going on with you."

"Yeah, I'll call her," Logan muttered. She just wasn't sure when.

Monday mornings in the ER were one of the busiest times of the week in Logan's experience. Busloads of sick people would start piling in around nine. The neighborhood folks who'd just woken up after a long hard weekend of drinking or doing drugs and were feeling like crap. The ones with the pesky colds who would come in before work because the colds weren't going away and what the hell, it got them off work for a couple of hours. There were those who didn't have a family doctor and who could come in any time of the day or night, but just liked to start their week off with a visit to the ER. It was mundane but it was work, and right now work was a good thing. It kept her mind off Jillian, kept her mind off Afghanistan and the daily tribulations that were surely going on in her absence. There was much to be said for not having to worry about getting a bullet in her ass or her head taken off by an RPG. Logan smiled as she surveyed the harmless carnage around her.

Her routine started out smoothly enough. Logan and the other two ER doctors were moving patients in and out as though they were on an assembly line. Soon, though, complicated cases that required much more than a prescription and a lecture began clogging things up, and people began to get cranky. Logan overheard them ambling up to the desk and asking in a whiney voice how much longer it would be. If the line stretched around the world, you would be in Siberia, she thought sarcastically. As chairs became scarce, people began standing against the wall, and restless kids started to run around. Hospital security was called to deal with a drunk who was getting out of control. A nurse was miming and slowly sounding out words for someone who couldn't speak English. Frequent Flyer Floyd walked in the door just then. One of the regulars, he had probably run out of his pain meds.

Oh, God, Logan thought. *War zones are more efficient than this.*

An ambulance crew ran by with a ninety-six-year-old they'd intubated. *Yeah, sure, let's see if we can get another two years for the poor old woman.* Bipolar Ben was being dropped off by his parents, who were asking not-so-quietly if they could just leave him and come back in a day or two. It was like a hurricane, blowing hard with no sign of a letup. She took a few deep breaths and plunged back into her work.

It was early afternoon when a thirteen-year-old girl came in with her parents. She was showing classic signs of a urinary tract infection, or at least that was what Logan thought at first. But a seed of doubt nagged at her. The girl, Malina, said she was having trouble urinating instead of the more common burning sensation. She'd been to a different ER in the city three days ago and been diagnosed with a urinary infection, but she was not improving with antibiotics. In fact, things were getting worse.

Malina was tired and weak, barely urinating at all anymore, the girl's mother explained. When Logan asked the girl to give a urine sample for analysis, she could hardly produce more than a few drops. The infection could have spread to her kidneys, thought Logan, which would explain the girl's malaise. She directed a nurse to catheterize Malina, thinking the procedure might help things as well as produce a sample for them.

Twenty minutes later, the nurse searched out Logan and told her there was more than a liter of urine in the girl's bladder.

"Wow," Logan muttered just under her breath. She set down the chart she'd been looking at. That much urine was rare, a volume usually reserved for old men with gigantic prostates who were in severe distress. But this girl did not look in distress at all. "All right, I'll take another look at her."

So much for a simple UTI, Logan thought, her worry growing. She examined the girl again and noted that she could barely stand, let alone walk, though her upper body was normal. She had no reflexes in her knees or ankles and little feeling in her legs.

The girl's parents were clearly worried as well, and Logan tried to reassure them that she would get to the bottom of it. Could it be a herniated disc or something else compressing her nerves? Whatever it was, she decided, she couldn't diagnose it on her own. Sending the girl upstairs for an MRI, she called Lisa to help guide the case. Her twin loved getting a crack at interesting cases, and this one certainly qualified.

It was near dinner time and the tail end of Logan's shift when she was called to view Malina's MRI results. She was surprised to see a mass in the middle lumbar area of her spinal cord.

"Okay." Logan breathed out steadily. At least they had a clue now. "Probably benign at her age," she said to Lisa.

Lisa's mouth twisted in worry. "I'll write her up for more tests and call surgery for a look. They may want to biopsy."

"I can arrange it. Why don't you go on home to Dorothy?"

"You're almost done, too, Logan. You could go on home and give that girlfriend of yours a call."

Logan frowned at her sister. "Nice try. Seriously, go home and I'll get things started here."

Lisa gave her a cynical smile. "I know it's an avoidance tactic, but okay. Don't stay late, all right? They'll admit Malina and start the tests tomorrow. There's no point in you staying here half the night."

Logan got Malina settled, convinced her parents to go home, and ordered tests and a surgery consult. There was little more she could do, and it was frustrating as hell. At the base hospital at KAF, diagnoses and surgeries happened very quickly, and what they couldn't handle got sent out right away to Germany. She was used to quick action, to the immediacy of war, and not the snail's pace of civilian medicine. She drove her Vette home through the slowly darkening streets, cranked some Kanye West and tried to shake work and her worry about the girl from her mind. It was wrong to compare this brand of medicine with her time at KAF. She knew that, but she couldn't help it. As much as she hated to admit it to herself, part of her was still over there, like a ghost, fighting that damned war.

Her thoughts drifted naturally to Jillian, who was forever connected to her time in Afghanistan. At least Jillian understood a little of what it was like over there, of what they all went through day in and day out. Lisa was right. She should call Jillian. She just had no idea what to say.

"Hi, Jillian. Sorry I didn't stay and make love to you or at least make out with you longer. I really was turned on, honest. I know it was a funny way to show it."

Or how about, "Hey, Jillian, sorry I'm such a schmuck, walking out on you like that and not calling you sooner. I really have no excuse."

Or, she could just try the truth.

"I'm sorry, Jillian. I'm scared and confused, okay? I don't want to hurt you, and I don't want to hurt me either, and I just don't know how to go about this."

Logan considered the possibilities, growing more pessimistic with each mile. No matter what she told Jillian, her actions had spoken louder than any words could. Jillian probably thought she was some wack job or at least someone with a lot of emotional baggage. Too much for a woman in Jillian's situation to want to deal with right now.

At home, Logan fixed herself a vodka and orange juice and sat in the dark until she was too tired to even sit up straight. In less than twenty-four hours she had to be back at work for another twelve-hour shift. She could think later.

When Lisa tracked her down at work the next evening, Logan could tell immediately that she had bad news.

"Malina, the case from yesterday?" Lisa prompted.

"Like I could forget," Logan mumbled. Challenging cases like Malina's didn't come along every day. She enjoyed a good mystery and wanted to see this one solved. Malina wasn't just a mathematical problem or a scientific experiment, however. She was a kid with her whole life ahead of her. Logan tried never to forget the people behind the cases. "What's up?"

"It's not good."

Logan switched off her emotions. She could do that when she needed to, which was often in her line of work. She had to in order to be able to function. The cold hard facts, that's what she needed now.

"Martinez took over the case," Lisa continued. *The oncologist. Damn!* "He thinks it's Glioblastoma Multiforme of the spinal cord. And I concur."

"What?" Logan squeezed her eyes shut against the news, trying to stay calm though her stomach was roiling. It was the worst brain tumor there was and one that was usually deadly within months. "Goddammit, Lisa." It came out barely audible.

"I know."

"Christ, I didn't even know it could occur in the spinal cord. And at her age?"

"It's very rare in the spinal cord and very rare for her age, too. It usually happens to people in their fifties and more to men than women."

"The family knows?"

Lisa nodded solemnly. Logan was glad she'd not had to break the news. It would have been almost more than she could bear. "Martinez and I talked to them a couple of hours ago. They took it pretty hard, as you can imagine."

No, Logan really couldn't imagine. She remembered the fear and worry on Jillian's face when she'd brought Maddie to the hospital. She'd seen it and felt it enough, but she didn't actually know what it was like to fear for the well-being of a child. To want to make everything all right, to know the feeling of having failed to protect them. *How on earth do you find the strength to take care of a dying child? How in hell's name do you learn to live with your own futility and failure?*

For the rest of the night, Logan just went through the motions, working on autopilot. She wasn't devoting one hundred percent to the job, she knew that. *Tough.* Some shifts she just didn't have it to give. Not often, but every now and again, she had to hold something back for herself. This was one of those times. She needed to distance herself, to retreat within, to just not feel anything for a few hours or even a whole day. Keeping things at bay this way kept her functioning, kept her good at her job, made her fit to come back and do it all again the next day.

Jillian would probably tell her, just as Lisa always had, that she was hurting herself every time she shut down like this, when she walled herself off. *No.* They were wrong. She was protecting herself, plain and simple. It was what worked for her. It had enabled her to function at KAF for two bloody tours and even before that. It would continue to do so. It would have to.

Jillian and Mark stood on the sidelines, watching Maddie and a dozen other toddlers run around on the soccer field. It was comical, as they ran around with little regard for the ball. It was really just exercise and socialization, mostly games of tag and keep away.

"I can't wait until she's old enough to play hockey," Mark enthused, beaming proudly at his biological daughter. He'd long ago signed away any legal rights, but Jillian had given him her word that she wanted him to always be a part of Maddie's life. Someday, when Maddie was older, she would be told he was her sperm donor. For now though, Mark was the fun, adoring uncle.

"I have no problem with her playing hockey, as long as you're the one sitting in cold arenas for hours, listening to the other parents bitch about the coaches not giving their kid enough ice time or enough attention."

"How do you know I won't be one of those parents?"

Jillian gave Mark a cool once-over. "You do and I'll kick you where it counts."

"Ouch." Mark grimaced and clamped his legs shut. "No need to be nasty!"

"No need to be one of those dickhead sports parents, either."

"I would be on my best behavior, I promise. Hell, maybe I'll even coach the little munchkins someday."

Mark had pleasantly surprised Jillian with his patience around Maddie, though she wasn't surprised by his playfulness with her since he was a big kid himself.

"Maddie would love it if you coached her."

Mark stretched his legs out in front of him. They sat on a bench on the sidelines, waving and calling out encouragement to the kids, then enjoying a few minutes of companionable silence.

"What?" Jillian noticed the smirk on Mark's face. He was up to something.

He shrugged evasively.

"Don't give me that, you're thinking about something."

The smile was a little evil, even for him. "So who's the mystery woman?"

Jillian's heart skipped a beat. "What mystery woman?"

Mark looked at her like he held the secret combination to a treasure chest. "Last Saturday night."

Crap, how does he know about that? Jillian's mouth went dry. She hadn't wanted to tell anyone about the date beforehand, and she certainly didn't want to talk about it now. Not only had it ended so abruptly and without explanation, but Logan had failed to call, making it so much worse. Jillian was confused, hurt and more pissed by the day. Was it too much to ask for Logan to just talk to her and explain her feelings? If they were moving too fast for Logan, there was an easier solution than just walking out.

She tried to play dumb. "Do you want to tell me what you're talking about or am I supposed to guess?"

"Your *date* last Saturday night! Don't tell me you've forgotten about it already. Jeez, mystery woman must not have been much of a catch, huh?" He nudged her playfully, but Jillian was in no mood to joke about it.

"What makes you think I went on a date last Saturday night?"

Mark continued to look smug. "My friend Jake and his wife were at Azzura's for dinner and saw you there."

Shit. Busted. "All right, so I was on a date. Big deal."

"It is a big deal!" Mark looked hurt suddenly. "Your first date since Steph, and you weren't going to tell me?"

Jillian shrugged and turned her eyes back to the soccer field. Mark was right, it *was* a big deal. She hadn't been on a date with anyone since her breakup with Steph. She wasn't the type to casually date, and Mark knew it, too. "All right, I'm sorry." She meant it. She should have told him because he was her best friend.

"It didn't go well? Is that why you didn't want to tell me?"

Jillian looked at Mark again. Disappointment sagged her

shoulders and flattened her voice. She had never been good at hiding her feelings. "It went fine."

"Then how come you don't look happier about it?"

"It just didn't end the way I wanted it to."

"Does that mean you didn't get lucky?"

"Shut up."

"All right, all right. Are you going to see this woman again or what?"

Jillian took a deep breath and plunged on. *What the hell, he might as well know the whole truth.* "I was with Logan Sharp, Mark."

Mark nearly fell off the bench. He was actually speechless for a moment. *First time for everything!*

"Logan Sharp? How—Never mind." He studied her for a long moment, slowly shaking his head and looking puzzled. "Why didn't you tell me she was back in your life?"

"You and she weren't exactly best friends in Kandahar. I figured you'd just try to talk me out of seeing her."

"Well, you're wrong, Jill. I like Logan. A lot."

"You do?" It was Jillian's turn to be surprised. Relations had certainly thawed a little between the two of them by the time they'd left the base last year, but she would never have expected Mark to be an advocate of Logan's.

"She's a good woman, Jill. You could do a lot worse, you know."

"Like Steph?"

Mark's jaw stiffened predictably. It was no secret that he'd never been a big fan of her partner, but they'd never really discussed it before. "Okay. I never much cared for Steph. Since we're being honest."

"I know that. I figured you wouldn't care for whoever it was I chose."

"Why, because I'm some kind of jealous lunatic or something? Please. Give me more credit than that."

"Okay. Then tell me why you never liked her."

Mark looked away. It wasn't like him to consider his words

before he spoke, but he did now. "I never thought she was good enough for you."

Jillian felt her mood get darker, if that were possible. "You could have just talked to me honestly about her all these years instead of saying all the snipey little backhanded things about her instead."

"You're right. I was a bastard, okay? I didn't want to lose your friendship by telling you the truth."

Jillian let out an exasperated breath. "You could have given *me* more credit than that, you know."

"Maybe. But usually the buddy loses if he steps in between a couple."

Jillian considered this. "You're right, I suppose. I wouldn't have listened to you about Steph. But now you're telling me you approve of Logan?"

Mark grinned at her, his answer more than evident on his face. "I saw how you were together, Jill. I think she could be the best thing that's happened to you. Next to Maddie and me, that is."

Jillian smiled, her mood lifting like a kite taking flight. Mark surprised her sometimes with his insight and sensitivity. She leaned over and kissed his cheek.

"What's that for?"

"For being a good guy."

"Okay, I'll take it. Just remember what you said the next time you get pissed off at me."

Jillian frowned. "Which will probably be by tomorrow."

"So, aren't you going to ask her on another date?"

"I asked her the first time. The next one is up to her."

Mark laughed. "Okay, got it, doing the equality thing, huh? You might want to tell her about this fifty-fifty rule, though, in case she's waiting for you to call."

Jillian's eyes dropped to the ground. She wouldn't call Logan. Logan was the one who left, the one who said she couldn't do it with her, whatever *it* was. *No.* She'd done all the work up until now. It was up to Logan to step up to the plate, tell her what it was she wanted or didn't want.

Logan tossed and turned, her body clammy from sweat. The sheets were tangled around her legs. Her T-shirt was damp from sweat. So was her hair.

Fuck. She said the word over and over to herself, silently, then out loud. The dream was so vivid, it was as though she were back in Afghanistan again. Back at the base hospital.

It took her a moment to determine whether it had been a memory or a fabrication. Casualties had been pouring in. So many that they couldn't handle them all. They were coming in by the dozens, these mangled bodies, some barely alive, others smashed and burned beyond recognition as human forms. Meg was there, as were a few other doctors and nurses she'd worked with. They were trying their hardest to do what they could. They were frantic, yelling out orders, calling out responses. Logan stuck a chest tube in one patient, ran to another to perform an emergency tracheotomy. Palpated the heart of another. *Christ!* It was never-ending, this mountain of battered soldiers to save, and she was losing them. Losing them all because there were too many of them and not enough medical staff.

It was frustrating and futile, and on finally awakening, Logan let the frustration course through her veins and pound in every beat of her heart. Sometimes, it just wasn't enough. No matter what she did, no matter how much knowledge and experience she had, no matter who was helping her, it just wasn't enough. She couldn't save everyone she touched. She knew that. It had happened to her enough times for the message to more than sink in, but it never got easy. It never got comfortable to live with.

Logan stared up at the ceiling, barely discernible in the dark but for the faint glow of the streetlight.

"You can't save them all." It was one of the first things her med school professors had taught their eager young charges. Logan had filed the information away, not knowing then, of course, what it would be like to live with that knowledge.

Malina, the kid with the spinal cord tumor, was one of those she couldn't save. Knowing it and feeling it were two totally different and incompatible things. And now, Logan admitted, the knowledge was getting harder and harder to live with. Maybe because the farther along in her own journey she traveled, the more she realized how much there was in life to lose. And how little say one had in it.

Logan swung her legs to the side of the bed and sat up. She was trembling. She was scared. She wanted to cry but wouldn't allow herself.

She needed shelter. Needed loving arms around her, soothing words to tell her everything was going to be all right. She'd lived much of her life without those things, and she was tired of it. So tired.

She looked at the clock. Five fifteen. Much too early to call Jillian. She lay back down, calming her breathing as she did so. *Yes*. She would call Jillian in a few hours. She needed to call Jillian. There was no denying it any longer. She needed Jillian Knight in her life, because if there was any chance of her feeling whole again and soothed and loved, she was sure it would be with Jillian.

CHAPTER ELEVEN

Jillian let her GPS guide her to the parking lot of Logan's condominium. She felt her smile deepen as she spotted Logan standing beside her Corvette, leaning back against it, watching for her. To the casual observer, Logan looked completely relaxed, as if she hadn't a care in the world. But Jillian observed the slight rigidity in her shoulders, the way her eyes were busy scanning the approaching cars even though her head hardly moved. Logan didn't miss much. She was always on her guard. Undoubtedly the two tours in Afghanistan had shaped this part of her personality, because it was a matter of survival there.

Jillian pulled in beside her and got out, unsure how they would greet one another. She really didn't know what to expect. Logan's phone call this morning asking to see her again had been awkward, given the abrupt way their first and only date had ended. Jillian didn't quite know what to make of it all, but she was ecstatic that Logan had called and she had done a crappy job of hiding it. She should have been a little more aloof, letting Logan know she was pissed off at her. *But, hell.* Life was too short for dumb-ass games. Logan had finally called and they were seeing each other again, and that was all that really mattered. The rest would work itself out.

"Hi," Logan said, beaming.

Jillian couldn't stop herself from grinning back. "Hi, yourself."

Logan leaned down and kissed her on the cheek. "You look great. Thank you for coming."

"Thank you for asking me." They would need to talk about their date last week and what had gone wrong, but not just this minute. Jillian wanted to enjoy this warm, sunny summer day, and for the moment at least, she didn't want any complications. Maddie was with Steph, and Jillian had no other responsibilities for the day.

"Care to get in?" Logan gestured toward the passenger seat.

"Sure. Where are we going?"

"To one of my favorite places around here. Do you mind if we do a picnic dinner?"

Jillian peeked in and saw a picnic basket in the back of the Vette. She hadn't known Logan was a romantic, but then, she'd never had the opportunity to show that side of herself. "Nice. But aren't you going to give me a hint?"

"Nope." Logan walked around the car and opened the passenger door for Jillian. "Impatient, are you?"

Jillian climbed in, laughing. "Never."

Logan, smiling, hopped into the driver's seat and started the car, the powerful engine loud and intimidating. Jillian had pegged Logan as a careful, methodical driver, and she wasn't wrong. Logan maneuvered the car expertly through the city, shifting smoothly, turning onto a highway that took them southwest and out into the countryside.

They made small talk as Alicia Keys and then Annie Lennox belted out tunes on the stereo. There would be time for a heart-to-heart later. For now, Jillian was happy just being with Logan in this low-slung car. It was like a cockpit inside, and with the split roof off, the warm wind ruffled their hair.

"She's not much for curves."

Jillian's mind took a detour at the mention of curves. Did Logan like her curves? She remembered Logan's fingers brushing the outside of her breasts when they danced, and the way her hand had rested on the gentle swell of her hip. But those weren't the curves Logan was likely referring to. "Sorry?"

Logan patted the steering wheel. "This baby. She likes the straightaways best."

It was obvious how much Logan loved her Corvette, to the point of nearly producing a twinge of jealousy in Jillian. "How long have you had her?"

"I bought her in March."

"Did you always want a car like this?"

Logan shrugged, but there was joy in her voice when she spoke about the car. "I always loved the old Vettes. I love just about anything from the seventies, I guess."

Jillian laughed as Stevie Wonder came on the radio, singing "Signed, Sealed Delivered, I'm Yours." *How apropos.* "I can see that."

"Sorry."

"Don't be. I love the music of the seventies, too. Even the cars. Well, okay, not the Gremlins and Pacers. Or those ones that blew up if they got rammed from behind."

Logan laughed long and hard. "Good point. Not everything that came out of the seventies was good."

"The decade produced us, didn't it? That was pretty darned good."

Logan glanced at her, her eyes shimmering with something that made Jillian's heart lurch with nervous excitement. "Yeah, that was pretty darned good."

Logan pulled into a Tim Hortons coffee shop and into the drive-through lane.

"Ah, iced cappuccinos," Jillian announced, remembering the creamy iced coffee drink at KAF.

"I do recall you liking them." Logan gave her a wink that

nearly melted her, then ordered two of the drinks.

The memory of them drinking the iced cappuccinos back at the base came flooding back to Jillian as she sipped on her straw. Logan obviously remembered, too, judging by the look on her face. It had been the first time they'd begun to feel comfortable alone together. The first time they'd talked alone, the first time Jillian began to see the real Logan Sharp behind the doctor/soldier mask.

"What?" Logan looked over at her, smiling.

"Just thinking about the time we were drinking these on the boardwalk at KAF."

"Me, too. I was trying so hard to figure you out then."

"You were?" That was a surprise. Logan was so serious when they talked about the mission, less so when they talked about growing up just a few dozen miles apart. But she'd had no idea Logan was trying to figure her out. "In what way?"

Logan turned the Vette onto a narrow, heavily shaded street. They were heading toward water, the Detroit River. "Trying to figure out if you were married, because of the ring on your finger. Trying to figure out if you were the vulture kind of journalist or critical of the mission or a friendly. Just...trying to figure out how such a beautiful woman could be sitting there in that ugly place. With me."

"Well, I guess you found the answers to your questions, huh?"

"Some of them," Logan answered evasively.

"So there are more?"

"Oh, lots more." She said it with a smile that penetrated to the roots of Jillian's hair. When Logan looked at her like that, like she was the only person in the world who mattered, it was as though everything stopped for one brief, dazzling moment.

"Good," Jillian answered after steadying her voice. "Because I have a few myself."

They pulled into a parking lot that announced they were at Fort Malden.

"What's this place, Logan? I mean, besides the obvious."

"The British built it around the turn of the nineteenth century. It was one of the focal points in the War of 1812. A lot of action happened right here."

"Ah, right, the only time our two countries fought."

Logan retrieved the picnic basket, and Jillian fell into step beside her, wanting to hold her hand but resisting. Logan had been skittish on their first date, and Jillian didn't want to scare her now. Knowing Logan, it had probably taken a lot for her to call this morning.

"Well," Jillian said lightly. "I'm glad our countries kissed and made up, so to speak."

"Yes. I don't think we could kick your asses again."

Jillian guffawed loudly. "I beg your pardon! It was officially a draw!"

"All right," Logan conceded with a mock sigh that was meant to tease. "It was. We both had our victories and our losses."

They walked along the curved pathway, the river to their right, the grassy slopes of the earthworks to their left, cannons perched above and pointing toward the river and imaginary foes. They sat down on a bench, the picnic basket unopened at their feet.

"You've done some reading on the war?" Jillian asked.

"I love history, especially military history. Did you know this fort was pretty much destroyed in the fall of eighteen thirteen when the Americans chased the British out? The British burned it down just before they deserted. They rebuilt it after the war."

"It's very peaceful here." Jillian's gaze settled on the river, calm as though it were early morning and not late afternoon. A freighter slowly ambled past while gulls in the distance swooped down toward the water, calling out, making the only sound.

"Amazing, isn't it? To think that cannons once boomed from here, and battleships, right here in front of us, went at each other."

"Yes. Amazing that peace can come from such brutality. Do you think Afghanistan will ever be peaceful?"

Logan shook her head sadly. "I don't know, Jillian. I honestly don't know."

Jillian knew she'd strayed into potentially dangerous territory with Logan. She just hoped like hell she wasn't going to step on a land mine. "Do you feel like you made a difference over there, Logan?"

It was a long time before Logan answered, and when she looked at Jillian, her eyes were hard and desolate. "Sometimes I think so, other times not."

Jillian snaked her hand into Logan's and held it softly. "You saved lives, Logan. You helped people. How could that not make a difference?"

Logan shrugged. "All I know is the war is still going on over there, with no sign of it ending. It feels like the work there will never be done."

Jillian took a deep breath, convincing herself to ask the question she wanted to ask. She was afraid of the answer, but she needed to hear it. "Do you wish you were still there?"

Logan looked at her thoughtfully. "I did what I could. I think I'm beyond thinking that my being there could make any real difference anymore."

Okay, Jillian thought. *You didn't really answer the question, but I don't think I could bear it if you wanted to go back to that place.* "Can I ask you something else?"

"Of course. Within reason, I mean." Logan smiled nervously.

"Don't worry. I'm not going to ask you to reveal your bank card numbers or anything."

"Whew! For a minute there I was worried you were after my money."

"Okay, I'm going to remember that comment. You only think you got away with it."

Logan's eyes lightened considerably, and her smile was mischievous. "I can't wait for my punishment."

Jillian dropped her mouth in surprise. "I think I'm going to ignore that one, Logan Sharp."

"Oh, I must really be in trouble for you to use my full name!"

Jillian shook her head, loving Logan's sense of humor. She watched Logan open the picnic basket and look around quickly to make sure they were truly alone before taking out two plastic wineglasses and a bottle of Chablis with a handy screw top. She poured them both a glass, handing one to Jillian. Logan, a stickler for rules, was undoubtedly worried about getting caught with open liquor in public.

"So," Logan said after a moment. "You had a question for me."

Jillian sipped her wine patiently. Another answer she was almost afraid of. "Why did you suddenly call me this morning, after more than a week of not hearing from you?"

"I'm sorry about that, Jill."

"I wasn't looking for an apology, but thank you. I was more interested in the explanation." *Interested* was an understatement. She *deserved* an explanation.

Logan looked suitably chastened, which made Jillian feel instantly better. "I was scared, Jillian."

"Of me?" *Okay, I wasn't expecting that.*

"Yes, but more scared of me."

"Was I giving you mixed signals or something? Because I didn't think—"

"No, no. You weren't. I just...I wasn't sure what was supposed to happen next and what you wanted."

Jillian's annoyance slowly rose in her like the inching in of high tide. "We could have talked about it, Logan. Running out the way you did doesn't solve anything."

"I know that. It's just hard for me sometimes to talk about what's going on inside me."

Oh boy, that's certainly true. It took a moment of gazing at the calm water for Jillian to harness her emotions. "Okay, so what exactly *is* going on with you, Logan?"

Logan bought herself more time, fiddling with the picnic basket and coming up with two cellophane-wrapped sandwiches. "Sorry, my culinary skills aren't the greatest. Chicken sandwich okay with you?"

Jillian took hers, content to let Logan take her time. "Yes, thank you." It actually looked homemade, with mustard and lettuce and Swiss cheese and mayo. Tasted good, too, and the fact that Logan had made them with her own hands made Jillian a little giggly.

Logan finally answered once their sandwiches were mostly gone. "I was afraid my wanting you would scare you. That I was moving too fast for you."

"You know, you could let me decide whether it was scaring me or if I thought you were moving too fast."

"I know. God, I know I need to be more trusting. To let go and not control everything."

"It's hard, isn't it?"

Logan looked like she was blinking back tears. "I don't know if I know how to do it."

Jillian tossed the last of her sandwich toward a hovering gull and clutched Logan's hand with both of hers. "You can try. With me."

Logan didn't answer for a long time. It was as though she hadn't even heard that last part. *Goddamn.* This was one tough woman to get inside, so thick were the walls she'd built around herself. But somehow, Jillian knew the effort would be worth it. She would not give up on Logan Sharp.

"Logan," Jillian prodded gently. "Will you tell me who has broken your heart?"

The sun was setting, pink and gold ribbons dancing on the water. Their gazes fixed on the mesmerizing sight, the women sat quietly, loosely holding hands, neither in a hurry for anything. Jillian knew Logan would tell her about her past when she was ready. She was not a woman to be rushed into sharing the things she guarded so tightly. Forcing her to do so would only push her away. Jillian had always been able to sense the hurt in Logan; knew it lurked quietly but potently just beneath the surface of her calmness and control. It was a haunting sort of hurt, one that Jillian wanted to see expunged forever from Logan's heart.

"Her name was Nicole." Logan spoke so quietly that Jillian

had to strain to listen. "It was a long time ago." She gave Jillian an apologetic look. "Really. It doesn't mean anything anymore."

That couldn't be true. It may have been a long time ago, but there were still invisible shackles there, keeping Logan from letting love into her heart again, preventing her from taking a chance with a woman again. And it was a damned shame. "Go ahead. I'd like you to tell me anyway."

"Jillian, it was just—"

"No, Logan. Stop apologizing for your feelings, for what she did to you, and just tell me, okay?"

Logan let out a long, ragged breath. "We met while we were still both in school. She was a graduate student. I was in med school. It was pretty much love at first sight, my first meaningful relationship. I was crazy about her."

"Was she crazy about you, too?"

"Yes. I could lie and say I have no idea. But it's true, we were crazy about each other. We moved in together after a few months."

"What was your relationship like?"

"Good at first. Great, I mean. We were young, totally in love. We could talk about anything and everything, you know? I thought we were meant for each other."

Jillian did know, because she'd felt that way with Steph at first, before the tiny misgivings niggling at her began to grow, finally exploding after Afghanistan. Sometimes that was just the way it was, the doubts so tiny and infrequent that they were easy to ignore, until finally one day they suddenly loomed big enough to swallow you whole. "When did things go wrong?"

"I didn't know they had, really. It was about three years later. We were both busy in our lives, doing our things. I was doing a residency, she was on contract to teach at the university, hoping to get tenure." Logan's eyes drifted toward the river again, and when she spoke, her voice was rough with emotion. "I never saw the signs, you know? I had no clue she was having an affair with a fellow professor. Christ, and it wasn't even with a woman."

Jillian heard herself gasp. "I'm so sorry, Logan."

"She blamed me, of course."

"What, for making her straight all of a sudden?"

Logan laughed bitterly. "No. For pushing her into someone else's arms because I wasn't around much."

"But she wasn't around much either, right?"

Logan shrugged. "It doesn't matter now. At some point she gave up on me, obviously. She didn't even have the decency to tell me. She just let me walk in and find her in bed with this guy."

"Oh, God." Jillian couldn't imagine what a punch in the gut that must have been for Logan. She could picture Logan walking in, oblivious to being about to have her heart broken. It nearly made Jillian sick. "You don't really blame yourself, do you?" If Logan had been carrying that albatross around her neck all these years, it was a damn shame. And a waste.

Logan shook her head. "No. I guess I bought into it for awhile, but no. My being busy with my residency was an excuse for her to hang the affair on, to avoid dealing with the fact that she didn't love me anymore. It hurt, though, because I was still in love with her. I thought everything was fine, you know?"

Jillian squeezed Logan's hand. "Is Nicole the reason you haven't fallen in love with anyone else? Because, I mean…" Jillian held her breath for a moment before taking the plunge. "That's really what you're afraid of, isn't it? Falling in love?"

Logan looked so fragile, so vulnerable that Jillian wanted to take her in her arms and hold her, soothe away all the past hurts. But Logan was a big girl now. She had to stand on her own feet, own up to her fears. "Sounds pathetic, doesn't it?"

"What, being afraid of getting hurt again?"

"Yes, that's part of it." Logan stared at the quickly darkening water. The lights of boats twinkled in the distance. "The hard part is not wanting to fail again. I failed, Jillian."

Ah, that made sense. Logan was a perfectionist. Her relationship with Nicole had been a failure in her mind. A failure she could not forgive herself for. Jillian knew something about that. "Oh, Logan. *You* didn't fail. *It* failed. The relationship failed for probably a hundred reasons. God. Don't you think I've been struggling with the same thing for the last few months?"

Logan squeezed Jillian's hand in return. "You're right, I'm sorry. I'm so busy talking about myself, I didn't think about what you've been going through."

"No, Logan. Don't. We're talking about you right now. I just want you to know that I understand, okay? We're both driven, accomplished women who don't like it when things don't work out. I just think we have to find a way to get past that if we want to be truly free to move on in our lives, you know?"

"Yeah. I do know. It's just hard."

"I know it is. Believe me, I know. There's no secret formula, that's for sure."

"It's getting dark. Any darker and we won't be able to see our way back to the car." Logan stood, protectively clutching Jillian's hand. "You okay if we pack up and head back?"

Jillian stood on her toes and gave Logan a quick kiss on her cheek. "Yeah. Let's go." She didn't want the evening to end, but they couldn't stay out there in the dark all night.

Logan pulled the headlight lever and watched the Corvette's headlights pop up out of the hood. She always breathed a sigh of relief when the mechanism worked. Parts for the thirty-one-year-old car were a pain in the butt to find.

The ride back to the city was quiet, Jillian's words still resonating in Logan's mind. *We have to find a way to get past that if we want to be truly free to move on in our lives.* It was true, she was long ago done blaming herself over Nic, but failure left such a bad taste in her mouth. That was why it nearly killed her inside whenever she lost a patient. All those losses felt like failures.

You can't save them all. It was a great motto, a terrific piece of advice, especially in her profession. She was not God, she could not save everyone, but sometimes it was just so damn hard to move on to the next one. Her job demanded it, though. There were always more sick and injured people who needed her services. She never forgot the ones she couldn't save, however. And never quite forgave herself for not being perfect or able to do the impossible. It was her nature and she supposed she wouldn't change now, but Jillian had a good point. Blaming yourself kept you stuck, prevented you from really moving on.

Logan rested her right hand lightly on the gearshift. She wanted so badly to sneak it onto Jillian's thigh or to simply hold her hand. Holding hands on the bench at the fort had given her a peace she hadn't known in such a long time. Jillian did that to her. Made her feel somehow whole, undamaged, almost perfect. She wanted to give Jillian those things, too. *God.* How she wanted to give Jillian things she'd never fully given to another woman. Not even to Nic.

Jesus, Logan. Don't start comparing. But she couldn't help it. The two were nothing alike. In hindsight, she could see that Nicole had been selfish, self-absorbed. Had cared about things Logan didn't, like attending the right parties, having the finest clothes, being seen with certain people. They were all part of what Nic claimed was necessary to get tenure, to get the approval she needed, but Logan disagreed. The quality of your work was what mattered, not that other superficial crap. Jillian let the quality of her work speak for itself. And Jillian genuinely cared about others and cared about doing the right thing. Respect really was an important ingredient in a relationship, she decided, and she respected Jillian in ways she'd never respected Nicole.

Logan trembled inside just a little. Is that what this was with Jillian, a relationship? New fears began to worm their way in, subtle and painless but toxic just the same. Did Jillian even want a relationship? Did Logan want one, with all its responsibilities and unfamiliarity?

Logan glanced at Jillian, her head back, her eyes closed, the smallest hint of a smile on her lips. She cared for this woman. She desired this woman. She wanted to talk to her, touch her, look into her eyes, just be next to her. She didn't want to let her go again, of that she was certain.

Jillian's eyes popped open as soon as Logan pulled into her parking lot.

"Tired?" Logan asked.

Jillian shook her head lightly. "Nope. You?"

"Not at all. Um…" Logan swallowed her hesitation. "Would you like to come in for a drink?"

Jillian's eyes gave away nothing as she probed Logan's. Then she smiled broadly, and Logan's heart melted. *Yes. Please say yes.*

"I'd love to," Jillian answered.

Logan was infinitely pleased when Jillian took her arm and allowed Logan to lead her into the thirty-story building. Logan's two-bedroom unit was on the nineteenth floor—high enough to offer a great view of the river and the Detroit skyline, which looked spectacular at night.

The place wasn't particularly homey, something Logan was acutely aware of as Jillian took in her surroundings. There were a couple of framed photos of her family on the mantle of the gas fireplace, and books and medical journals filled a bookcase against the wall. The furniture was leather and generic, the coffee table and end tables were contemporary and also lacking in personality. She'd meant to stay just a few months and then start looking for a place to buy, but time was getting away from her. She had yet to look seriously at a house.

Jillian moved to the floor-to-ceiling windows, her back to Logan. "Wow, Logan. This is an awesome view!"

The lights of the Renaissance Center, the Cadillac Tower and the other skyscrapers provided a dazzling light show. It was easy to get mesmerized by the lights, and Logan had spent plenty of nights just watching them in the dark while nursing a glass of wine or a soft drink.

"I could sit here all night and look at this view," Jillian enthused.

"Feel free to. I can bring you out a blanket and pillow." Logan wasn't entirely kidding. "Seriously, if you're too tired to drive back tonight, you're welcome to stay."

Jillian turned to look at her, perhaps gauging whether her offer held any hidden agendas. "I'll be fine. It's still early."

"Can I get you a glass of wine or something else?"

"A glass of wine would be great. Just one, though, if I'm going to make that drive back." She winked. "I don't want the border guards detaining me."

"Coming up." Logan didn't want Jillian to leave. She would love to wake up and find Jillian still in her apartment. Hell, who was she kidding? She would love to wake up and find Jillian lying next to her. *Just stop it, Logan. You're moving way too fast, for both her sake and yours.*

Logan brought two glasses of wine out and set them on the coffee table, her hands trembling a little. Jillian joined her on the sofa, looking far more relaxed than Logan felt. *God, I have got to relax.* She took a quick sip of her wine.

"Do you know I've never had a woman up here before," Logan said by way of excusing her nervousness.

"Glad I'm the first." Jillian sipped her wine, contemplating Logan over her glass. "Does it make you nervous to have a woman here?"

"You're not just any woman, Jillian." Logan made herself scoot closer. If she let her nerves take over, she would end up like a schoolgirl, all fumbly and stuttery and feeling more and more foolish by the minute. Far better to try and be brave. "I'm glad you're here."

"So am I. And you still haven't answered me. What made you call me this morning?"

Logan had to hand it to Jillian. She wasn't going to let her get away with anything. It was daunting, revealing herself like this. Lisa knew most, but not all, of her vulnerable areas. Her friend Meg back at KAF had seen some of them, too, but Jillian—her sharp eyes seemed to see them all. There was no hiding. And Logan wasn't even sure she wanted to hide, which was remarkable in itself.

"I had a bad time of it at work the other day. Bad news about a patient."

Jillian sipped her wine. "Go on."

"A fatal tumor for a young girl. It was shocking because it was so rare and unexpected. Her family is devastated, of course. I just…Sometimes the outcome of these things is hard to live with."

"You've had a lot of that in your life, haven't you?"

"Yes." Logan took a sip of wine, enjoying the cool taste of it. It surprised her how easy it was to talk to Jillian like this. "I know I'm only human, I know I can only do so much. Believe me, I know. But it's still damn frustrating sometimes and just plain sad. And I realized when I woke up this morning that I just really needed to talk to you. To be with you."

Jillian reached over and stroked her hand, and Logan felt it all the way into her belly and down her legs. It was like tiny electrical shocks on her skin and a very pleasurable tickle deep down inside. She loved the way she felt when Jillian touched her. And she wanted more, much more.

"I'm here for you, Logan. Any time you need me."

Logan couldn't bear the distance separating them any more. She put her arms around Jillian and buried her face in her shoulder. She closed her eyes and smelled Jillian's unique scent—her skin, soap and shampoo, sweat. She needed this woman like she had never needed anyone before. Not even close. Jillian made her want to tend to all those old wounds, restore herself and then take on the world again.

"Oh, Logan." Jillian was slightly breathless, her chest heaving a little from the intimate contact. Her arms enclosed Logan tightly.

Oh, yes, this is what it's like to be held by the woman you love. Based on past practice, Logan knew, she should be cowering in fear at this point—or running away from feelings this overpowering. Instead she only wanted to embrace them, to explore them deeper. She was safe with Jillian. She was loved by Jillian. And right now, that meant everything.

The words came out before she even thought them. "I need you, Jillian."

"Oh, honey," Jillian whispered, moving her lips lightly along Logan's temple. "I'm right here."

Logan nuzzled Jillian's neck, enjoying the kisses, wanting more. She kissed Jillian's neck, the underside of her jaw. She wanted her kisses to tell Jillian exactly how much she wanted and needed her, because words certainly weren't sufficient to the task. Her lips found Jillian's, softly, almost haltingly. It was enough for now, for the moment. Or it was until Jillian began to kiss her back, her lips firmly pressing against Logan's, then separating, then sucking on Logan's bottom lip. *Oh, God*. This was almost too much, it was so damned good. Logan's clit was hard and on fire, every muscle in her body was tense and ready to be touched. She wanted this woman on her, under her, inside her.

Logan moaned from deep in her throat. Her tongue explored Jillian's lips and mouth, pushed its way inside, engaged in a teasing dance with Jillian's tongue. Her right hand moved up Jillian's side, caressing tiny, insistent circles. She could not stop touching Jillian now, could not stop doing the things she'd wanted to do to her on their first date, when they danced close together. Yes, she'd wanted to touch Jillian then and in all the ways two women attracted to one another need to touch.

She cupped Jillian's breast, and it was only a moment before her thumb found Jillian's nipple, stiff and erect. She brushed it softly until Jillian cried out against her mouth. Breathing heavily, she exposed her neck to Logan, who took the hint and began sucking on the soft skin there.

"Oh, God, Logan. I can't…believe…what you…do to me."

Yes, I can, because you do the same thing to me. Logan's mouth moved lower, to the exposed V of Jillian's chest, where she planted more kisses. She cupped Jillian's breasts with both hands, feeling their heft, gauging their softness. They were a little more than a handful. They were round and perfect.

"I need to touch you," Logan urged, breathless herself now. "I need to feel your skin."

Jillian reached up with her finger, tilting Logan's chin up so she could look at her. "When the time comes for you to touch me like that, Logan, there is no going back. It means something to me. It means everything."

"To me, too, Jillian. You are so special to me. I want you so much." So much, it hurt.

"I want you, too, Logan, but you were right earlier when you were worried about moving too fast. I don't…" Jillian's eyes grew moist, and she glanced away for a moment. "I need to trust you. That you're not going to be scared of failing and bail on me. If you become a part of my life and Maddie's and…" Jillian looked frightened, a little sad, too. "I can't have you be around one day and then not the next."

Logan swallowed hard. "I understand that, Jillian." She needed to collect herself, to figure out exactly what it was that Jillian was asking of her. As much as she cared for Jillian, loved her even, desired her, she was not ready to make the sort of commitment Jillian might be asking for. "You're right, we shouldn't move too fast."

She would take her time, she promised herself. She would prove to Jillian that she was a keeper, prove to herself that she could do this relationship thing. Jillian was right. It would take some time.

Jillian sat up straighter and gently pushed Logan back a few inches. "So." A slow grin spread across her face. "Rules of engagement. Don't you think we should set them out?"

Logan's jaw went slack. Then she smiled, knowing she could enjoy this little game. "Okay. You want rules, do you?"

Doubt was in Jillian's eyes. But it was too late. She had trapped herself, and Logan wanted to see her squirm.

"Sure," Jillian said lightly, having to clear her throat. She was trying to act cool about it, but it was clearly an act. "Rules are good, just so we don't go too far."

"All right. Kissing is definitely allowed, right?"

"Of course."

"Some touching, too, because I can't *not* touch you when I kiss you, Jillian." Goddamn, this was going to be hard.

"Yes. Touching is most definitely allowed. Over the clothes, though."

Damn. Disappointment clamped down on her. Under the clothes would have been heaven. But that was fine. She would get Jillian begging for more eventually. Begging for those rules to be thrown out the window. *Oh yeah!* "So kissing and all the touching we want so long as it's over the clothes."

Jillian paused for a moment, and Logan was afraid she would want to further define the touching rule—confine her to just above the waist or something. *Because that sure as hell isn't going to work.* Logan needed to touch Jillian all over, even if it was through a cloth barrier.

"All right," Jillian agreed, not looking so sure now.

"Good, then where were we?"

It was an hour later before Jillian painfully disengaged from Logan's arms, insisting that it was late and she needed to get home.

Crap. It was much harder, these stupid damn rules, than she thought it was going to be. It was divine being in Logan's strong arms, kissing her, being kissed by her, having Logan's mouth and hands travel to her breasts, working them, loving them, giving her a taste of what could be. Jillian's nipples, painfully tight with desire, had screamed out for mercy. She'd nearly passed out with dizziness when Logan's finger traced an invisible line up the seam of her pants, stopping just an inch or so from her dripping hot center. For minutes that felt like hours, Logan had caressed the inside of her thighs, until Jillian thought for sure she would explode. She was so wet, so hard, so throbbing with desire that she'd nearly pushed herself into Logan's hand and demanded that she make her come. Logan had looked surprised, shocked even, when Jillian suddenly pushed her away and stood up, insisting it was time to go.

Jillian gave her a teasing grin. "Thought you'd break me, huh?"

Logan's whole body sagged as she stood, but she managed a weary smile. "Next time."

Jillian threw herself into Logan's arms for a long hug. "Thank you for a wonderful date, Logan. I enjoyed every minute. Even the torture session on the couch."

Logan laughed. "You're welcome, I think." Her eyes roamed over Jillian, a question in them. "You're not going to take a page out of my book and not call me for a week, are you?"

Jillian narrowed her eyes playfully. "I probably should, but no. Do you have a free night later in the week when you could join Maddie and me for dinner?"

"I'd love to. I'm off Thursday night."

"Good, it's a date." She kissed Logan on the lips—a soft, slow, tantalizing kiss. "Now you don't have to worry about whether I'll be calling you for a date. It's all set."

Logan came back at her for another searing kiss. "I'll be there."

Jillian could still feel the wetness in her underwear on the drive home. She was still tight and turned on, remembering every touch, every caress, every kiss. There was so much promise in Logan's touch and in her kisses. So much love. But Jillian wasn't sure whether she could trust what was there. She needed time. Needed to learn how to go about this. Needed to see if Logan was ready for this, too.

The orange wall lights of the Detroit-Windsor tunnel flashed past her as she drove, the traffic fairly light. She remembered going through the tunnel as a kid, and the scary yet intriguing fantasy she used to have then of water gushing in from sudden cracks in the walls. Her fears had never come true.

Please don't let them come true with Logan.

CHAPTER TWELVE

The peacefulness that flooded over Jillian shocked her. She knew Maddie would take to Logan. She'd known that back in Afghanistan, and so she shouldn't have been so surprised. But to see it happening so naturally made her feel so happy, so complete.

They'd eaten a spaghetti dinner together—Maddie doing her usual fine job of making a supreme mess of her face and plate—and now, in a bid to outrace twilight, Logan was teaching Maddie how to fly a kite. They had the neighborhood park to themselves, and Maddie screeched in delight every time the kite took flight, as though it were magic.

Jillian laughed when Logan handed the ball of string to Maddie and told her to run as fast as she could. Her little legs pumped comically, but try as she might, she could not get up enough speed to make the kite soar. Maddie frowned deeply, near tears, until Logan put her arm around her and promised that she would get the kite flying high, and that once it was, Maddie could hold onto the string. That did the trick. Maddie laughed and clapped her hands together as Logan ran until the kite took flight. She ran fast and hard, letting out string until the kite was well on its way.

Assured that it was stable, Logan trotted up to Maddie and Jillian. She carefully handed the ball of string to Maddie, who took it dutifully and promised not to let it go. It was cute how seriously she took her task. Jillian smiled and blinked her thanks to Logan. It was only their third date and it really wasn't necessary for Logan to ingratiate herself with her daughter, but Jillian knew Logan wasn't trying to impress her or follow some script. She was doing what came naturally, and she was a natural with kids.

"You're quite the expert at this," Jillian observed.

"Jeez. I haven't flown a kite since I was a teenager. It was a great idea you had."

"Maddie's been asking me since the spring to take her kite flying. She saw it on a commercial, and she's been talking about it nonstop."

Logan flashed her a look that was so tender, Jillian felt her breath leave her in a rush. The three of them together like this felt more like a family to her than she'd felt in a long time with Steph. In Maddie's first year they were busy just looking after her needs, and by her second year they were both so busy with their jobs that they really didn't make the time or effort to do fun things together. Yes, thought Jillian, this is what it's like to be a family.

"You doing okay?" Jillian whispered to Logan.

"Couldn't be better."

"You sure?"

"Jillian, doing this makes me feel like a kid again. Thank you, it's wonderful." She leaned down and kissed Jillian's cheek, then whispered in her ear, "Seeing you like this kind of turns me on."

"What do you mean, seeing me like this?"

Logan's grin was lopsided and sexy as hell. Lust darkened her eyes. "As a M.I.L.F."

"A what?"

"You know." Logan grew adorably sheepish. "From that stupid *American Pie* movie." She glanced quickly at Maddie, making sure she was still occupied with the kite before leaning close to Jillian's ear. "It means 'Mother I'd Like to Fuck.'"

Jillian nearly tripped. She stared openmouthed at Logan, and then started to laugh from deep in her belly. The phrase was something she would have expected to come out of Mark's mouth, not Logan's. "Why, Logan Sharp, I didn't know you had it in you!"

"What, to be a perv?" Logan giggled and snuck a kiss. "You do bring certain things out in me."

Jillian smiled back, but inside she churned with uncertainty. She was attracted to Logan. She desired her in a way she hadn't desired another woman in years. She wanted to jump Logan's bones, and she was pretty sure Logan would happily surrender. She had no idea what would happen later, once Maddie was put to bed. She had been trying not to think about it all evening, but it was always there in the back of her mind, like the almost imperceptible hum of the streetlights. Now she couldn't seem to stop thinking about being in Logan's arms later, about kissing the way they'd kissed at Logan's condo, about Logan's hands cupping and stroking her breasts. *Oh, God.* She pulsed with a yearning so strong, it seemed it just might consume her in the next breath. She was wet, too. Very wet.

Logan was looking slightly mortified. "Are you okay? I didn't offend you, did I?"

"No, Logan, you didn't." She took deep, calming breaths. "Quite the opposite, actually." She turned her attention to Maddie. "You're doing great, honey. Are you having fun?"

"Look how high it is, Mommy!" With that, Maddie tried to point at the kite, and predictably the ball of string popped out of her hands. Logan sprinted off, miraculously closing the distance between herself and the runaway kite in just a few strides. Maddie began to whimper, tears just seconds away, and Jillian silently cheered Logan on.

"Ah, always the hero," Jillian said fondly as Logan returned triumphantly with the kite in hand.

Logan bowed and handed the kite to Maddie. "Your kite, madam."

Maddie giggled and took the kite, which was almost bigger than she was.

"It's okay, I can hold it for you," Logan offered.

They walked back to the house with Maddie between them, holding her mother's hand. It wasn't long before her free hand sought out Logan's. Back at the house, Maddie resisted brushing her teeth and getting ready for bed. A little bribery finally did the trick. She would hurry if Logan promised to read her a bedtime story.

"Do you mind?" Jillian asked. "Sorry, she's been learning the fine art of manipulation and negotiation lately."

"I don't mind at all."

"Good. I'll put some tea on. And keep it short, okay?"

Logan winked at her, knowing full well that Jillian was anxious for some alone time together. "Don't worry, I have no intention of reading her *War and Peace*!"

The tea was still warm by the time Logan returned to the living room.

"Thank you for doing that, Logan."

Logan sat down on the sofa next to Jillian and took the cup offered to her. "She's a great kid, Jillian. You've done a great job with her."

"Thank you, Logan. She's not too much for you?"

"No way. Are you kidding me?"

"But this is all so new to you."

Logan set her cup down and took both of Jillian's hands in hers. "Jillian, I love spending time with you. I know you and Maddie are a package deal, and I want you to know that is more than okay with me. I'm just honored that you're giving me this chance."

Jillian leaned in and kissed Logan on the mouth. There was not another person on this earth she wanted to give this chance to. She wanted Logan to be a part of her life and Maddie's. A big part. Still, she couldn't help but worry about how an instant family would feel to Logan—whether she would wake up one morning and want back her single, uncomplicated life. *Christ, Jill, you're getting way ahead of yourself.* As life with Maddie constantly reminded her, it was crucial to just live one day at a time. That is what Jillian needed to do now.

Logan was intensifying the kiss, her tongue parting Jillian's lips before darting purposefully inside. Her hands softly stroked the sides of Jillian's ribbed, short-sleeved top, and Jillian felt her insides slowly turning to liquid. Fingertips edged toward her breasts, and her mind skydived into a joyful abyss. She was determined to just feel and not think.

Jillian pulled away from Logan's mouth and groaned into Logan's neck. Her body was on fire, wanting so much more. *Those goddamned rules.* It would be funny if it wasn't so painful right now. She wanted Logan's hands on her skin, her mouth, too. She wanted Logan's body fully against hers, pushing into her, grinding against her.

"Do you want me as much as I want you?" Logan whispered urgently. Her fingers brushed over Jillian's breasts. Her lips planted tiny kisses along Jillian's throat.

"Oh, God," Jillian murmured, her voice strangled. "Yes."

Logan's mouth found hers again, and they kissed with an urgency that bordered on desperation. Their hands were on each other, all over one another. Jillian pulled Logan down on top of her.

"Those damned rules of yours," Logan said between breaths.

"I know. Kiss me again, Logan."

Logan's mouth was hot against hers, and so was her body. Jillian ran her hands over the firm muscles of Logan's back and down toward her ass. *God!* Logan felt so good beneath her fingers. So strong. So capable. As Logan shifted and placed her thigh between Jillian's legs, Jillian had to bite her tongue to keep from crying out. Logan rocked against her, slowly and gently, and Jillian felt her clit stiffen and throb in time to the thrusts. If they didn't stop any second, there would be no going back. There would be no flipping a switch and turning off all that desire.

Logan's hands slipped beneath her shirt and danced over her naked stomach, drawing tiny fiery circles. *Okay, that is definitely against the rules!* But Jillian could no more protest than she could get up off the sofa and walk away. Besides, she didn't give a flying fig about those rules right now. *Whose stupid idea were they anyway?*

Logan's lips moved down Jillian's throat. She nibbled and sucked, her thigh still softly grinding into Jillian's center. Jillian was afraid she might explode right then and there into the sweetest, deepest orgasm she'd ever had. She could, too, with just a little more pressure. But when Logan did make her come, she wanted them both to be naked, their hot skin melding. They were not teenagers playing around, trying to get to second or third base.

"Logan, wait."

Logan halted and looked sharply at Jillian, probably expecting the worst.

"This is killing me," Jillian said breathlessly, frustration knotting her gut.

Logan broke into a slow, mischievous smile. Her eyes twinkled with victory. "You want to amend the rules?"

"Christ, no. I want to throw them out!"

Logan laughed so hard her body shook.

"Okay, you don't have to enjoy it so much."

Logan touched her face, tears of laughter still in her eyes. "Oh, sweetheart, I'm sorry. But you did kind of ask for it."

Jillian rolled her eyes. She was woman enough to admit defeat. "I know I did, but that was before I knew you were so good at this."

Logan kissed her quickly. Her thigh still rested between Jillian's. "Honey, I would make love to you right now in a heartbeat."

Jillian heard the smile in her own voice. "You would?"

"Quicker than a heartbeat. But I want you to be sure what it is you want." Her finger traced the outline of Jillian's lips. "I am ready to go to the next step when you are."

Jillian sucked in her breath. Her stomach fluttered at the possibilities. Her body wanted Logan, there was no question of that. Her heart wanted her, too. She loved Logan, even if she was too afraid to utter the words right now. It was not what she had expected, not so soon after Steph. None of this had been on her radar when she went to Afghanistan. It was like a storm had blown in overnight and turned her life upside down, wiping out everything she had known, but the sun was shining in its wake and there was a pristine surface on which to start over.

Jillian studied Logan's eyes for a long moment. She saw love reflected there—her own and Logan's, too. "Yes, Logan. I'm ready."

Logan raised herself up from the sofa and held out her hand. She gave Jillian a rakish grin, and her eyes glinted. "Will you lead me to your boudoir, my love?"

As hard as it was for her to be patient, Logan took her sweet time with Jillian, wanting to savor every touch of her body. Ravishing her the way she wanted could wait. For now, she trailed a finger over Jillian's stomach, exulting when she felt it tighten in response. They had shed their clothing moments ago—an act that came surprisingly easy, particularly since it was something Logan hadn't done with another woman in quite some time. Not this way anyway. She'd had a lifetime of seeing naked women in locker rooms and dorm rooms, but none of it compared to the exquisite intimacy of this.

"You're beautiful, Jillian. Just like I knew you would be." And she was. Her body was strong and toned, her skin soft, her curves sexy as hell. Her breasts were the most perfect Logan had ever seen—firm, round, baby soft. Her nipples stood rigid, and Logan could no longer resist them. She firmly planted her mouth on one, swirling her tongue around its hardness while her hand cupped the fleshy underside of Jillian's breast. Jillian squirmed in delight.

"Oh, Logan. My God, I love the way you touch me." Jillian squeezed her eyes shut and threw her head back into the pillow, her body completely open to Logan.

Logan alternately sucked and licked, slowing and quickening her pace, knowing and loving that she was driving Jillian to the brink. She moved more fully onto Jillian, whose body was taut with desire. Her hips undulated against Logan, begging for more. *Oh, yes. She wants me as much as I want her.* Logan moaned. She pushed her thigh between Jillian's legs, moved against her slowly but firmly, and felt Jillian's wetness on her own skin. She was drenched herself, but it was Jillian's wetness that nearly drove her insane. She needed to feel her there, with her fingers and with her tongue.

She slid her mouth over Jillian's abdomen, stopping for some teasing nips and flicks of her tongue. Moving down slowly but steadily, Logan lingered over Jillian's center and submersed her senses in the beauty and desire that was Jillian. She breathed in Jillian's scent before bringing her mouth to her hot, slick softness. Her tongue slid languorously over Jillian's clit and down to her opening. Jillian groaned and shifted her hips, tilting herself up to draw Logan's mouth in tighter. Logan complied. Her tongue toyed with Jillian's opening, swirling just inside, their wetness melding deliciously. Jillian began grinding into her mouth, faintly and then more forcefully, her body begging for so much more of Logan's tongue. Logan obliged. With one quick motion she rammed her tongue into Jillian as far as she could. She pumped furiously and was greeted with a muffled cry of joy—Jillian was covering her mouth with her arm to keep herself quiet. *Damn, that's right. We don't want to wake up Maddie.*

Logan didn't want to stop. She could have stayed forever in that soft, wet flesh, but she didn't want Jillian coming yet. There was so much more she wanted to discover. So much more she wanted to share. She withdrew her tongue and inserted a finger.

"Oh, God, Logan," Jillian whispered urgently. Her breathing was short and shallow. When Logan's tongue found her clit and began stroking it firmly, Jillian caught her breath loudly. "Oh, yes, I'm going to come!"

Logan broke away. "I don't want you coming too fast."

Jillian was thrashing her head around. "I can't help it. Don't make me wait, Logan. I need you so badly."

Logan happily resumed her oral ministrations, finding just the right synchronization for her tongue and finger. She worked Jillian's clit, thrust a second finger inside and felt something intangible shift deep inside Jillian. It was like thunder rumbling in the distance, then drawing closer and closer. Jillian's orgasm approached with growing force, the shaking beginning in her legs and surging through her body, like an earthquake rippling outward. Logan felt the contractions as Jillian squeezed and spasmed against her fingers.

Jillian cried out as she gave a final, violent thrust, then quieted into tiny tremors. Logan slowly withdrew and crawled up Jillian, wrapping her arms around her. She held on tightly as Jillian rocked against her. *God!* She wanted to hold Jillian like this every night. The intensity of the urge jolted her. Who was this person she became in Jillian's presence? She'd never wanted to hold someone and be held the way she did now. Not even with Nic. Making love with Nic had been like a sport, each session an exercise in climbing higher, going faster, coming harder just to prove they could. It was not tender and full of wonder like this.

"Oh, honey," Logan soothed, caressing Jillian's head. "You felt so wonderful. You *are* so wonderful."

Jillian shook softly against her. Logan pulled away to look at her and saw the tears sliding down her cheeks. She kissed each one and thumbed away the tears. "Are you okay? Did I upset you in some way?"

Jillian shook her head against Logan's shoulder, burrowing in deeper. "I'm good," she finally muttered. "I'm better than good."

"Are you sure?"

"Yes, I'm sure. You just…make me feel things I've never felt before. You make me feel so loved and desired."

Logan froze. They hadn't mentioned the "L" word before,

but it was exactly the way she felt about Jillian. She did love and desire her and had for a long time, she realized. "That's because you are." She said it softly. She didn't trust herself to look into Jillian's eyes, knowing she would probably lose it if she did.

Jillian's hand was on her thigh, tracing an invisible pattern, sending tiny currents of electricity surging through her body. She was wet. She was burning up with desire. She wanted that hand to move up, to touch her, to take her.

Logan squeezed her eyes shut. "Oh, Jillian. I need..."

"Yes?" Jillian's eyes told Logan she was willing to give her anything.

Oh, God. She needed so much from Jillian. Love. Tenderness. Comfort. She also needed it fast and hard right now. And deep. *Oh, yes, I need you deep inside me.*

"I need...I need you to make love to me." She swallowed hard against her tightening throat. "And I don't want you to be gentle."

Wordlessly, Jillian moved on top of her and began sucking hard on her breasts. Logan's nipples responded, almost painfully. Oh, yes, she needed this from Jillian. Needed to feel their desire for one another deep in every muscle and tissue. She could never get enough of Jillian like this. Only if their bodies could climb inside one another's would it ever be enough.

Logan moaned quietly and squirmed a little beneath Jillian. "Oh, yes, Jillian. You are so beautiful. You make me want to come just like this."

"No," Jillian whispered. "Not yet."

She moved her hand down and squeezed Logan's clit between two fingers. Logan moved her hips in a circular motion to the rhythm as Jillian began palming her. She was so wet and she throbbed inside. Only having Jillian's fingers in there would quench her desire. As if on cue, Jillian thrust a finger inside. The sensation sucked Logan's breath away. Feeling Jillian there, where she needed her most, was overpowering. It was like a coming home of sorts, a train coming into the station after a long journey. It was a union that was so much more than just sex.

When Jillian thrust a second finger inside and began pumping hard, Logan let out a muffled cry. Her mind emptied as her body absorbed the sensation of Jillian on her and in her. She bucked her hips in time to Jillian's powerful thrusts, their timing in perfect sync as if they'd done this hundreds of times before. When Jillian's thumb found her clit and pressed on it, Logan could no longer hold back. She threw her head back as her body stiffened with orgasm. It started in the center and shot outward, curling her toes and fingers into fists. She let the powerful convulsions rock her body, riding the waves as colors flashed behind her eyelids.

Jillian held her tightly as the last ripples of orgasm ebbed. Logan buried her face in Jillian's hair, shocked by tears that rose suddenly and bubbled just below the surface. She had never cried before during sex, but she was ready to now. She was spent but so incredibly satiated too…mind, body and soul. She held Jillian closer, needing her tight like this, the length of her body. I need you, she almost mumbled but didn't.

Jillian kissed her on the lips. "You were wonderful, Logan. Are you okay?"

A smile cleared away Logan's unspent tears. "I feel great. I feel like I just reached out and touched the sun."

"Oh, honey." Jillian kissed the tip of her nose, then her eyelids. "I didn't know you were a poet! My, you are multitalented, aren't you?"

Logan laughed. "I have many more talents to show you, didn't you know that?"

"Good, because I look forward to each and every one!"

Logan rolled Jillian over, pinning her with her much stronger body. "I could show you more of them right now."

Jillian's eyes widened with pleasure. "You won't get any argument from me."

Logan nipped her neck, enjoying the little shivers it gave Jillian. It wasn't long before she felt Jillian undulating against her again, demanding, pushing into her. She slipped her hand between them, smiled at Jillian's wetness and dipped a finger inside.

"Oh, yes, Logan," Jillian whispered urgently. "I need you to take me like that."

Logan slipped another finger in. She positioned her thigh behind her hand and began to grind into Jillian. Hips, pelvis and fingers rose and fell together to a fast beat. The candle on the night table flickered, its orange light dancing on the walls as Jillian came against her, spurting her wetness onto Logan's hand.

"God, I love it when you come, baby," Logan uttered softly. She could do this to Jillian all night long.

"Oh, Logan. You make me feel so safe, so loved."

Logan kissed her gently, as Jillian went limp in her arms. "Can I hold you while you fall asleep? You look like you're about to drop off."

Jillian's eyelids fluttered open. "Not until I make love to you again."

"Oh, no. There's lots of time for that later, sweetheart. Right now you need to sleep."

Jillian snuggled in tighter, her head on Logan's shoulder. "Okay. Just for awhile."

Logan drifted off moments after she felt Jillian breathing rhythmically against her chest. She dreamed she and Jillian were walking along a beach somewhere, their pants rolled up to their knees, the water lapping against their ankles, the sand squishing between their toes. She didn't know how long she'd been asleep when she felt Jillian extract herself from her embrace and get out of bed.

Years of being a doctor and a soldier woke Logan sharply. Instantly she was alert. "What's wrong?"

"I hear Maddie awake. I need to go check on her."

It was a quarter to three. "Do you want me to come, too? Do you think she's sick?"

"No, I'm sure she's fine. She does this sometimes, probably bad dreams."

Jillian disappeared, and Logan settled back in bed with her hands behind her head. She almost couldn't believe that she was in

213

Jillian's bed. Jillian, who would always be a mother first. This was new territory for Logan, and yet it pleased her no end that Jillian was a mom. And a good one at that. She was patient, deliberate, kind and loving. All qualities so indisputably on display with her daughter. It made Logan fall for her even more. She loved that Jillian gave of herself so easily and so unselfishly.

Logan drifted back to sleep, resuming her dream of the two of them on the mystery beach. She didn't know when Jillian had climbed back into bed, only that she had. Her body, like a magnet, drifted to Jillian's and snuggled into her. They spooned, their body warmth mingling. A sigh of contentment escaped Logan. She could lie just like this forever, forgetting there were sick and dying people out there, forgetting there was a war going on in a distant, godforsaken place. This was a sanctuary where nothing could touch them.

CHAPTER THIRTEEN

Logan stared for a long time at the envelope, dreading opening it. It was from the Department of National Defense—the armed forces. She was done with them, her contract having expired months ago. She'd done her four years, plus a few months to help train other doctors heading out on a tour. She was free to go, thanked for her services with a medal for serving two tours in Afghanistan. She was back in civilian life and happy to be there. Wasn't she?

When she could no longer stand the suspense, she tore open the envelope. She needed to know what they wanted with her. She scanned it quickly, then read it again more slowly. They were lean on doctors—as always—and wanted her to rejoin the Regular Forces for a six-month tour, to be done again at KAF. They would give her a nice bonus if she did so and possibly another promotion. Logan carefully folded the letter and set it down on her desk. She would ignore it. That's what she'd do. They'd get the hint when they didn't hear back from her. Or they'd keep bugging her, knowing them, in which case she would flat out tell them no.

Logan got ready for work—another night shift—and let her mind drift to Jillian. Only two more nights and they would be together again, this time at Logan's place because it would be Maddie's weekend away. Logan liked numbers. It was exactly thirteen days since she and Jillian had first made love, not that she was counting or anything. She couldn't wait until she saw Jillian again, which at this rate was about every five days. They were both busy, and while it wasn't enough, it would have to do for now.

Logan had just finished putting on her scrubs in the doctor's lounge when her cell phone rang. The number came up unknown, but she picked up anyway, in case it was Jillian.

"Sharp here."

"Hey, Logan. It's Meg! How are you?"

"Jesus, Atwood, is that you?" Logan reeled in surprise. It'd been months since she'd heard from Meg, and that had been an e-mail, not a phone call.

Meg chuckled on the other end. "Yeah, it's me. Did I catch you at a bad time?"

Logan glanced at her watch. "I start my shift in four minutes."

"All right, I'll make it snappy, Major."

"Just plain old Logan now."

"I know, I know. Listen, I'm going to be in town tomorrow. Meet me for a drink?"

"Sure, I'd love to, but what the hell are you doing in Windsor?"

"I have to be in Sarnia in a couple of days to do some recruiting PR crap. Thought I'd divert down to Windsor for a night and see you. Are you off tomorrow night by chance?"

"Fortunately, yes. How about dinner and a drink?"

"Perfect. Just tell me where."

Logan gave her the name of a restaurant on Riverside Drive and promised to meet her at six thirty.

"Will I recognize you out of uniform or out of your scrubs?" Logan teased.

"Yeah, I'll be the one in stilettos and the revealing dress."

"*That* I would pay to see!" Meg dressing that way was about as unlikely as Logan doing so, but the vision did give her a few minutes of entertainment.

Meg gave her a long, exuberant hug at the restaurant.

"God, it's good to see you, Logan. Did you miss me?"

Logan beamed at her friend, who, she was happy to note, was not wearing stilettos and a revealing dress. Just khaki pants and a blue polo shirt. The world was not ready for Meg to be all girled up. "Yeah, I did. It's great to see you. You look good, Meg." She looked happy, fit. Like she hadn't a care in the world, which was so typical of Meg.

"My God, Logan, you look for once like you don't have the weight of the world on your shoulders. Something—or someone—is treating you right." She winked for effect, but Logan ignored the bait.

They took their seats beside floor-to-ceiling windows that looked across the river and the Detroit skyline. The scene was so familiar to Logan that she barely noticed now.

"Great view," Meg enthused.

"Haven't you been to Windsor before?"

"Once or twice when I was a kid, that's all."

"Looking forward to your recruiting duties tomorrow?"

Meg rolled her eyes. "Not exactly, but it beats sitting at my base treating colds or torn MCLs all day long."

Logan knew what that was like. At home, base life was pretty boring, and at least this road trip was getting Meg off the base, doing something different, meeting people. With her outgoing personality, Logan was sure Meg excelled at recruiting, even though it was reportedly getting easier the last few years. Perversely, the war was helping, along with a sour economy. Potential recruits were attracted not only by a sense of duty and accomplishment, but also by the prospect of action, the thrill of war.

Dread crept into Logan's stomach. Surely Meg wasn't here to recruit *her! Was she?* It wasn't like Meg to be disingenuous, but the timing was certainly suspect. "You wouldn't know anything about the DND contacting me, would you?"

Meg looked genuinely perplexed, and Logan let herself relax a little. Meg was her friend first, a member of the armed forces second, as far as Logan was concerned.

"They contacted you?"

"Got a letter yesterday. They're looking for another six-month tour."

Meg ordered herself a double whisky. Logan ordered a Bud Light. They were in no hurry to order dinner.

"Jesus, Logan." Meg let out a low whistle. "I knew they were hard up for docs, but you've barely even had a break yet."

Logan hadn't entirely left the military yet. At least not mentally. She'd stuck her uniform in a box and hadn't looked at it since her return, but civilian life still seemed a little unfamiliar to her. It was like visiting a place you'd once lived. You knew all the landmarks, knew your way around, but it didn't feel like *home*. Logan had gotten accustomed to the routine, liked being busy at work, enjoyed seeing her sister regularly. And Jillian...*Well!* Jillian was the light in her life. But a part of her was just going through the motions, not yet fully here. Like one foot was still back in Afghanistan.

"I'm getting used to it," Logan replied, purposely evasive. Meg couldn't truly understand what it was like. Meg was a career soldier and military nurse, someone who once said the only way she was leaving the army was in a box.

Their drinks arrived, and Meg took a long swig of hers. That was the one thing about the army Logan didn't like, the culture of drinking. She understood the reasons. The alcohol provided instant numbness, an antidote against the nightmares and the flashbacks, a way of living every day like it might be your last. And while she understood it, she'd always avoided going down that road. It was just too damned tempting to get sucked down that rabbit hole. Potentially destructive, too.

"Do you miss it?" Meg asked.

Logan shrugged. "Sometimes. I miss the camaraderie, that feeling of being part of an instant family, you know?" Meg nodded at her response. "I miss working toward a common goal all the time, like everyone's part of the same job. I miss the work."

"But you get all the action you need at work here, right? I mean, of course it's not the same, but…"

"It's not the same at all. Here I don't have to worry that the kid I just had a coffee with is going to come in with his intestines hanging out of his body cavity two hours later."

"Jesus, I know." Meg's eyes drifted toward the river outside. She was lost in her own thoughts, her own terrible memories.

"Have you changed your mind about leaving the army some day, Meg?"

A nervous smile edged onto Meg's face. "Funny, I was just going to ask you if you'd ever go back in."

Logan hesitated, and even as she did so, she knew her hesitation spoke volumes to Meg. "It's not easy adjusting. I mean, it's harder than I thought."

"But it must help having your sister here. Plus the fact that you grew up here."

Logan took a sip of beer. "It helps. It's certainly easier than if I'd tried to settle somewhere else." Logan shrugged. *Christ.* How could she distill her feelings into a few sentences? Explain this feeling of not quite being fully there? How the only time she truly felt in the now these days was with Jillian and occasionally at work. "Sometimes I feel like the only time I was really ever living in the moment was over there." She said it so quietly she wasn't sure Meg had heard her, except Meg began nodding slowly behind her glass.

"That's because we have to over there. You can't afford to not be totally one hundred percent there. People can die if you're not. *We* can die."

"It's almost like a drug, isn't it?"

Meg smiled. "Yup. And I'm addicted."

That was the part that turned Logan off. She didn't want to

219

be addicted to that lifestyle. She didn't want to be addicted to anything—to give up that much control. "Then maybe it's like I'm in withdrawal or something."

"Are you having any flashbacks or nightmares?"

Logan couldn't remember a time when she and Meg had talked so freely and openly before. They'd been close buddies, but this was a whole new level to their friendship. She liked it. "Yeah, I have some." That was an understatement, but she didn't feel like going into a lot of detail with Meg. She was only seeing her for a few hours. She didn't want to talk about how the tours had fucked them both up.

Meg finished her drink and signaled for another. "I get them too sometimes. They'll fade. This helps." She pointed to her empty glass.

"I think I'll let them fade on their own."

"Yeah, well, you always were the pure one." Meg's eyes were tracking a gorgeous woman who was gracefully taking a seat at the bar.

Logan laughed. "I see you haven't changed."

"Hell, no. A good woman's always the cure for whatever ails you, believe me."

"All right, you do have a point."

It took a minute for the comment to register with Meg. When it did, her eyes widened and she let out a whoop. "Well, holy shit! Don't tell me you've finally met someone!"

Logan felt a blush work its way up her cheeks. *Dammit.* She hated when that happened. She knew it was written all over her face that she'd fallen for someone. *Not just someone. Jillian.* Logan tried to be evasive, cool, even though she knew Meg wouldn't let her off the hook. "I might have, yes."

"Oh my God!" Meg held her freshened glass up in salute and took a belt. "Logan, I don't believe it. Finally! God, how did you even manage? Do you even know how to ask a woman out?"

"Okay, Atwood, now you're just being obnoxious." She was smiling even as she spoke. She couldn't *not* smile when she thought of Jillian.

"Sorry, couldn't resist." Meg's eyes shone with mischief. "Does this mean you've lost your virginity to her?"

"Shut up." Logan glared, then broke into a grin. "Maybe I have."

"God, Logan, it's about time. So who is this wonder woman, 'cause I gotta meet her."

Logan drew a nervous breath. It was hard to tell Meg this next part, that it was Jillian. For one thing, she didn't want Meg to think they had something going on back at KAF when they hadn't. For another, Meg was going to tease her that she knew it all along. *Argh!* "It's someone you already know," she said, stalling for time.

"Hmm. Don't tell me. The cute little X-ray technician who shipped back around the same time as you?" Meg waggled her eyebrows. "I wouldn't have minded a round with her myself."

"Like you did in the supply room with that private I caught you with?"

It wasn't in Meg to blush or look chastened. She was predictably smug instead. She'd never been apologetic for being a player. As she'd said many times, she'd been there and done the long-term relationship thing. "Something like that." She sighed for effect. "Some of them are much harder to get than others."

"Well, you always gave it the ol' college try, didn't you?"

Meg narrowed her eyes at Logan. "We're talking about your love life, not mine. So tell me my little lamb, who is it?"

Logan squared her shoulders and looked Meg square in the eye. "Jillian Knight."

"Oh my God! That gorgeous photographer?"

Logan nodded. She could no more keep the smile from her lips than she could stop breathing. "Yeah. That's the one." Even her voice had softened at the mere mention of Jillian. *God.* Jillian did that to her. Turned her into instant mush.

Meg's mouth dropped open. "You're kidding me."

"Do I look like I'm kidding?"

"You're right, what am I thinking? You would never kid about something like that. Jesus." Meg began grinning like the know-it-all she was. "Okay, I always knew there was something hot between the two of you. Not to mention that I could tell you were crazy about her."

"Did you really know all along?"

"Hell, yes. You were a complete basket case when you thought she'd been hurt."

An avalanche of emotions rocked Logan. Even then, she hadn't known what she'd do if something happened to Jillian. Now...*Christ*. Now she would be absolutely devastated. Just considering the possibility made her feel sick to her stomach.

"Jesus, Logan. I'm sorry. You look green all of a sudden."

Logan pulled herself together. "I'm fine. Sorry. Not a good memory, that's all."

"I know. So how did you hook up with her again?"

Logan told her the story of Maddie getting hurt and Lisa inviting Jillian and Maddie to her house for dinner without telling Logan.

"And?" Meg prompted, that gleam there in her eyes again, and it wasn't from the whisky.

"And what?" Meg would have to work for it if she wanted more out of Logan.

"Did you start dating right away? Are you sleeping with her? And...wait. Shit. I thought she had a partner or something."

Logan laughed. It was so typical of Meg to let her mouth get ahead of her thoughts. "Yes to all three, but she and her partner broke up a few months ago."

Meg nodded slowly, taking it all in. Processing. Gone was the smart-ass attitude of a few moments ago as realization dawned. "You're totally in love with her, aren't you?"

Logan bought a few minutes time by taking a long sip of her now lukewarm beer. They would need to order food soon or Meg would be well on her way to getting drunk. "Shall we order dinner?"

"Yes, but not until you answer my question."

Logan sighed and gave in to the inevitability of Meg's persistence. "I think I am in love with her." It was an understatement, but she would not declare her love for Jillian to others when she had not yet said the words to Jillian.

Meg settled back in her chair, appraising Logan with a sloppy grin on her face. She was quiet for a long minute. "Logan, I didn't know you had it in you. My God, do you know how great I think that is?"

"You do? You're not going to give me your Meg pep talk on how many fish there are in the sea just waiting to get hooked?"

Meg shook her head slowly. She could not seem to wipe the silly smile from her face. "No matter how much I've teased you about your celibacy and how crazy I thought that was, I know you're not the type to go out there and sleep around. You're just not wired that way, Logan Sharp."

"You're right about that. I'm almost thirty-six years old. If I haven't sown my wild oats by now, I'm not going to."

"Is she the one, Logan?"

"The one?"

Meg looked at her slyly. "Yeah. As in the one you've been waiting for?"

Logan was leery. She still half expected Meg to start teasing her or chastising her for passing up all the other opportunities out there. Opportunities Logan had zero interest in. Logan stared straight into Meg's eyes. "What if I told you I do think she is the one?"

Meg held her gaze for a long time, until her eyes began to grow moist. "I would say you are one hell of a lucky woman. I might not be cut out for that kind of life right now, but for you, my friend? I could not be happier."

"Really?"

"Absolutely."

Logan knew and appreciated that Meg was so candid and genuine. "Thank you."

"So." Meg winked at her. "Tell me all about her. And her daughter, too."

Over dinner, Logan talked nonstop about Jillian and Maddie. She even told Meg about their visit to the old fort. Best of all, she talked about how Jillian made her feel—loved, desired, supported. Like she really mattered. Happy. Whole.

"Looks like you hit the jackpot, my friend. It shows on your face. Hell, on your whole body."

Logan smiled sheepishly. "You won't see me disagreeing with that."

"Guess that means you're going to rip up that letter from the DND, huh?"

"What do you mean?"

"Being in love and all, it's not exactly conducive to running off to Afghanistan."

Logan shrugged. "Lots of people over there are married or have significant others back here."

"You think Jillian would be okay with it?"

Logan instinctively knew it would not be okay with Jillian. Just as it wouldn't be okay for Jillian to wander off to Afghanistan or Iraq on another photo assignment. It would be different if Logan was there to keep an eye on her, to help keep her safe. But to go over there alone? Logan would never let that happen. "I don't think she would like it, no. And I don't blame her."

"So?"

"It's a nonissue. Who said I wanted to go back there for another tour?"

"You didn't, but you were at least thinking about it, weren't you?"

Crap. Okay. It was just a kernel of a thought, but Meg was right. She hadn't dismissed the option out of hand. "I'm not seriously considering it, okay?"

"All right, whatever you say. But you need to talk to Jillian about it. Even if you're not thinking seriously about it, okay? Talk to her."

"How do you know so much about girlfriends, Miss Girl-in-Every-Port?"

Meg threw her head back and laughed. "I've always been a good listener, and women love to talk to me."

Logan guffawed loudly. "You have time for conversation in

the sack?"

"How do you think I get them in the sack?"

Logan shook her head. "You really are something, my friend."

"That's right, and don't you forget it."

CHAPTER FOURTEEN

Logan's ravenous appetite hid her nervousness. They'd brought in take-out, and now they were sipping wine in front of the large windows of Logan's condo, enjoying the Detroit skyline again. The sun was setting behind the skyscrapers, leaving them in shadow, their blunt angles looking somehow softer.

They'd had a nice little make-out session before dinner. Logan hoped it was just the warmup for what would come later. She was dying to get Jillian into bed. She forced thoughts of sex from her mind, images of sucking on Jillian's breasts, of touching her in the places that made Jillian cry out for more. There would be time for that later. Right now they needed to talk. They needed to talk about the letter. They needed to talk about what was pushing and pulling Logan, about what both repulsed her and attracted her about the army's offer. And they needed to talk about the two of them.

They snuggled together on the sofa, their legs up on the coffee table in front of them. Logan's arm was draped loosely over Jillian's shoulders, and Jillian's head rested against Logan. The skyline loomed before them, lights twinkling on. Logan almost didn't want to break the companionable silence. It was nice like this. It was perfect, actually. Just being together with no distractions, no interruptions, no agendas. Other than getting to bed, of course.

"Something's on your mind," Jillian ventured softly, her prescience jarring Logan. It shouldn't have surprised her because, face to face, it was hard to keep anything from Jillian. They were too connected for that to happen anymore.

"I'm not denying it, but what makes you think so?"

"I can feel it in your heartbeat."

"You can?"

Jillian nodded against her. "Is it something serious?"

"Sort of."

They both straightened, both tense. Jillian looked her in the eye, kindness in her expression but worry, too. She forced a smile. "Whatever you need to say to me, Logan, I want you to know that it doesn't change how much I respect and adore you."

Logan's heart leaped into her throat. She hadn't expected that. *Christ, she must think I'm breaking up with her or something.* Sure enough, Jillian had paled a little. Logan instinctively reached for Jillian's hand and gave it a squeeze. "I got a letter the other day from the Department of National Defense."

Jillian swallowed visibly. "And?"

"They asked me to go back to Afghanistan for a six-month tour."

Jillian slumped a little. Her eyes closed, then flickered open. Her mouth was a straight line of worry. "I was afraid of this."

"I can't say I'm surprised either."

Jillian grew very still. "What are you going to do?"

"I…I don't want to go."

"That's not answering the question, Logan." Jillian jumped up and began pacing. "Christ, I can't have you go off there. Not when I just found you again. Not when you've become such an important part of Maddie's and my life." Her voice caught, and Logan's heart melted. She hated that she was putting Jillian through this angst, but it was angst she was going through herself. She couldn't not share it.

"Okay, hold on, Jill. You're jumping to conclusions."

Jillian spun around. "Am I?"

"Yes. I never said I was going."

"You never said you weren't."

Logan took a deep, steadying breath. She wasn't one to escape in alcohol, but she could use a drink about now. "You're making me a little nervous pacing around like that."

Logan patted the sofa, and Jillian complied. "Sorry. I don't mean to, but you're scaring the shit out of me."

"Sorry. I just…" Logan drifted off into her own space, trying to figure out the best way to express herself. She was new at this stuff, new at including someone else in her thoughts and plans and actions. She liked manuals, could devour them quickly, and right now it would be heavenly to have one on how to communicate with your girlfriend. Divine inspiration was not about to strike, however, and she could stall no longer.

"I don't know that I can make any more of a difference over there than I've already made. I've done my part. I've done a one-year tour and a six-month one before that…"

"And yet it feels like unfinished business?"

"Yes." That's exactly how it felt, and yet this was the kind of business that would probably never be finished, no matter how many bodies, or resources, or money the world threw at the war.

"Is it unfinished business for *you*, Logan? Because that's what matters here."

"It's not up to me to save the world. I know that. I believe that. I can't make a difference in the outcome of the war. But I can make a difference in some people's lives."

"You're making a difference in people's lives right here, Logan, and not only in your work. You're making a huge difference in my life and in my daughter's life."

Jillian's words resonated with Logan, took root in her gut.

Yes, Jillian was right. It wasn't just about Logan and the damned war and the soldiers over there, nor the people here she helped heal on a daily basis. There was Jillian and Maddie to think about. Family. They could be a family together. Logan knew instinctively her world, her destiny, was sitting right beside her. This was about building a future together, about being loved and giving love. For the rest of her life.

Logan pulled Jillian in for a fierce hug. She was sure she would be safe in Afghanistan, that she could get through it just fine, at least physically. But at what cost? Could she really expect Jillian to wait around for her? To place their fledgling relationship on hold and then pick it up again as if nothing had happened? Would they even be the same people in six months? Would she come back with memories and nightmares even more devastating than the ones she had now?

Tears burst from her with surprising force. Jillian held her close while sobs racked her body, rocking her gently. Logan had never cried like this in front of anyone before. The shock of it appalled her for an instant, but she allowed the emotions to spill out until they were spent. She allowed Jillian to absorb all her hurt, confusion, fears. She was safe with Jillian. She was loved with Jillian.

"Logan, listen to me," Jillian whispered finally, taking Logan's face gently in her hands. "I'm not going to throw my fears and needs at you right now, okay? I just want to say this to you. It's your life, Logan. *Your* life. What do you want to do with it? What makes you happy?"

"You make me happy," Logan said, her voice cracking.

"And you make me happy. Happier than I've ever been. But you need to decide what fulfills you as a doctor and as a person."

Logan slowly pulled away from Jillian's arms and sat back in the sofa. She closed her eyes, thought about the little girl with the rare form of cancer. There were lots of people she couldn't save, lots of people she could barely help, or who she could only help for a few minutes or a few hours or a few days.

And then there were the ones whose lives she did make a

real difference in. She'd gotten a nice letter from a soldier a few months ago, thanking her for working on him, for saving his life. He was learning to walk again, but he was alive, and he was grateful for that. And just a month ago at work, a mom had sent a basket of fruit to the hospital, thanking Logan for treating her son's broken leg and for making him feel calm and cared for.

It wasn't about gratitude, though. It was about doing the best job she could, and that meant not just caring *for* people but caring *about* people. Logan couldn't do that kind of work just anywhere. Only where Jillian was. Without the everyday presence of Jillian's love, her work would feel empty.

"You," Logan said, opening her eyes and looking pointedly at Jillian. "That's what fulfills me. With you I'm the person I really am inside. The person I've always wanted to be—and a better doctor. Gentle, loving, compassionate, competent, patient."

"You're all of those things, Logan. Even without me. Those were the qualities that attracted me to you in the first place."

"But with you, it's safe to be all of those things, Jill. With you I want to be the best person I can be. With you, I can be everything and do everything I could ever want to do."

"Oh, Logan." Jillian kissed her softly. "I only want you to be happy."

Logan *was* happy. Happier than she'd ever been or expected to be. Because now, this very moment, was the culmination of everything she'd ever done, everywhere she'd ever been, all that she was. It was all right here. There was nothing else to seek. There was work to be done right here, and differences to make—or not. She didn't need to travel to the other side of the world, to go back to places she'd already been and things she'd already done, in order to search for her future. Her future was here. Right now.

A tear slipped down Logan's cheek, just a solitary one this time. She returned Jillian's kiss with an intensity that came from the deepest part of her soul. "I am happy. So happy, because I love you, Jillian Knight. And I am so deeply in love with you."

Jillian's eyes widened for just a second. She smiled and joyful tears welled in her eyes. "Oh, God, Logan. I love you, too. And I am just as deeply in love with you."

Logan kissed her again, then laughed. "Care to show me, my love?"

"Yes! Care to show *me*, my love?" Jillian teased back.

"Now that is a challenge I am more than happy to take."

Their lovemaking was the most intense yet. They took their time, exploring one another's bodies with fingers and mouths. There were kisses and touches that were fast and slow, light and rough. Friction that was alternately feather-like and intense. They took joy from each other and gave it back. They let their bodies express their feelings, convey their love and desire, communicate their need.

Jillian's second orgasm of the evening made her cry tears of joy and relief. No one had ever reached inside her like this before and touched that sacred part of her, the part that was full of wonder and beauty. But Logan had. Logan owned that place now. Being with her was like coming home. *Yes, I am home with her. She is my home.*

Logan was still inside her. Not moving anymore, but just there, as Jillian's orgasm ebbed. It was a moment Jillian wished could last forever. Just like this. She kissed Logan on the nose and told her that if she died this minute, her life would be complete.

"Wow." Logan grinned. "I've never had a woman say that to me after making love before."

"Don't you know by now I'm not just any woman?"

Logan slowly removed her finger and held Jillian to her. "You're right about that, sweetheart. You are *my* woman. Forever."

"Oh, do I like the sound of that!"

They lay quietly in each other's arms. Candles burned on the two nightstands. A distant siren sliced through the night, a portent of grief or tragedy or hardship in someone's life, but not in theirs. Nothing could touch them here. The siren had long ago faded when Jillian finally said, timidly, "So I take it you're

231

not going back into the army?" *Please, please, not after all this, don't tell me you're going.*

"Sweetheart, everything I could ever want is right here. With you and Maddie. My sister and Dorothy. My work."

"No regrets?"

"No. I need to leave my past right where it is."

Logan slipped out of bed and went to her closet. She retrieved a box from the top shelf. Jillian sat up, watching as Logan pulled out her dress uniform. She held it up, not to Jillian, but to herself. The brass buttons and medals gleamed even in the flickering candlelight.

"I haven't taken it out of this box since I returned," Logan said quietly, her voice impassive.

"Why not?"

"I was afraid, I guess. Afraid it would bring back too many memories, both good and bad."

"But memories are there, and they come out whether you want them to or not."

"I know that now." Logan carefully laid the uniform back in the box, smoothing it, flicking a piece of lint off it. "I was worried, too, that seeing it would draw me back somehow."

Jillian held her breath. "Does it?"

Logan slid the box back into its spot in the closet, then turned to face Jillian. It was too dark to see the expression on her face, and Jillian was scared of the answer. "No." Logan's tone was definitive. Jillian felt the air rush back into her lungs. *Thank God.*

Logan knelt beside the bed. "I've made my decision. You don't ever have to worry, okay? I love you, and I plan to spend the rest of my life with you."

Jillian let the joy from Logan's words wash over her. It was like a warm caress. "I love you, too, Logan. And I am so happy you feel you have everything you want right here. Because I do, too."

Logan leaned in for a kiss, and Jillian happily complied.

"Can I ask you something Logan?"

Logan nodded as she sat on the bed beside Jillian.

"Do you have flashbacks or nightmares?"

Logan shrugged lightly. "Sometimes."

"Seriously, how bad are they?" This was not the time to be evasive. If Logan was suffering, Jillian wanted to help her.

"Not so bad anymore. I have a nightmare every couple of weeks. Flashbacks, almost never now. Except sometimes if there's a loud, unexpected noise, like a car backfiring or something. Scares the crap out of me when that happens."

"Yet you were so calm and cool in Afghanistan when we were under that rocket attack on my first day at the base."

"I know, but all that stoicism wears on a person."

"I know it does, honey." Jillian stroked Logan's arm. "Have you seen anyone about it?"

"No, but I've read a lot."

"You know, there's a support group that gets together just outside of Detroit every week. It's for anyone who's worked in a war zone. Soldiers, health professionals like yourself, journalists, civilian workers. I went to a few sessions and I found it very helpful. Would you come with me sometime?"

Logan was silent for a long moment. "All right."

"Wow, that was easy."

"Just don't tell anyone I'm such a pushover where you're concerned."

"Okay, I won't. But why don't you crawl back into this bed with me? I think we have some unfinished business," Jillian purred.

Logan dove onto the bed beside her. "This is exactly the kind of business I hope never gets finished."

Jillian laughed. "Not in this lifetime, it won't be."

Epilogue
Three months later

It was the kind of late September day that could fool you into thinking summer was just about to reach its zenith, instead of being in decline. It was hot but without the signature mugginess so common to the area.

Dorothy was playing with Maddie in the pool just a few feet away. Lisa was barbecuing. Jillian sat in Logan's lap on the cedar Adirondack chair on the pool's deck, watching her daughter splash around. It was the kind of moment Logan wished she could take a snapshot of and just hold it in her heart and mind forever. This was her family, and she didn't want a single thing to change. Ever. *Well, maybe one thing.*

"You know," Lisa said, pointing her burger flipper. "The old McKenzie home around the corner just went up for sale."

Jillian perked up. "Is that the beautiful three-story Victorian with the great stained glass double front door?"

"That's the one."

Logan looked at her lover. "You've been studying the houses around here or something?"

"Oh my God, Logan, that house is gorgeous. I've always wanted a house like that."

"And I've always wanted a woman like you."

They kissed until Dorothy and Lisa began making derisive noises.

"Who says you can't have it all," Jillian teased.

"Exactly," Logan added. "So, Jillian. My sweet."

"Yes, Logan, my darling."

"What do you say we buy that house."

Jillian's eyes lit up. "Seriously?"

"Seriously."

"And live in it together?"

"Well, yeah, that is kinda the idea."

Jillian threw her head back and laughed, and Logan wanted to nibble on the smooth skin of her exposed neck. "It's a wonderful idea, Logan. But we can also find beautiful Victorian houses to live in across the river, too."

"Yeah," Dorothy piped up. "But they won't be in *our* neighborhood."

"True."

"There is another really good reason for living on this side of the border, sweetheart."

Jillian gave Logan a skeptical look. "Universal health care?"

It was Logan's turn to laugh. "Among other things, yes."

"What other things did you have in mind?"

Logan carefully extricated herself from beneath Jillian. None of this was planned, not a single second of it. In fact, it was so un-Logan-like, it blew her mind for an instant. But only for an instant, because then she was too busy worrying about Jillian's reaction.

Oh, what the hell, she told herself. It was too late now, she was already on bended knee, and Jillian had the strangest look on her face—bemusement, confusion, curiosity, concern. Logan felt everyone's eyes on her, knew they were all wondering if she'd just lost her mind. Well, they were about to find out.

"Jillian Knight, honey." Logan swallowed back her sudden nervousness, but managed to hold Jillian's gaze. "Will you marry me?"

There was not a sound, not a movement, just her own heartbeat in her ears. She'd begun to wonder if it hadn't been a huge mistake, when a wide grin split Jillian's face. Logan's heart danced as Jillian threw her arms around her, laughing wildly, covering her face with rough kisses. Lisa and Dorothy were clapping and whooping, and even Maddie was squealing from the excitement.

"Is that a yes?" Logan ventured, half-kidding, half-serious.

"Oh my God. Yes!" Jillian rested her forehead against Logan's. "Yes, Logan Sharp, I will marry you. And yes, let's buy the house around the corner, you sly devil."

Logan laughed and happily hopped up from the ground. "Hey, that house being for sale was pure coincidence."

Jillian cast a look of doubt at Lisa, who simply shrugged.

"I had no clue my sister was about to pop the question, but if you want to give me some of the credit, I'll happily take it."

Jillian shook her head. "I have a feeling you Sharp sisters make a pretty potent duo when you put your heads together."

"Oh, God," Dorothy called out. "Jillian honey, you and I are both going to be in trouble with you guys just living around the corner."

They all laughed, but the prospect of living so close to Lisa and Dorothy, in her old family neighborhood no less, pleased Logan no end.

"Will it be difficult, I mean legally, for Maddie and I to move here?"

Logan confidently shook her head. She'd already done the research during a slow night at work recently. "You'll get permanent resident status as soon as you marry me."

"What about Maddie?"

Logan grew nervous again. "She will too if I legally adopt her."

Jillian looked at her for a long moment, expressionless. Logan figured she'd just blown it when Jillian suddenly broke into a smile. Her eyes were dancing. "I'd love that and I think Maddie would, too."

Relief swept through Logan, so powerfully that she reeled for a moment. "What about Steph, will she cause any problems?"

Jillian shook her head firmly. "Steph has no legal rights with Maddie, thanks to our archaic laws. Still, she is a big part of Maddie's life, and for as long as Steph wants to, I'd like her to have visitation rights."

Logan didn't particularly like it, but there was no getting around the fact that Steph would be part of their lives for a long time. "All right. We'll work it out, honey. Now, let's call that real estate agent, shall we?"

"Whoa," Lisa countered. "It's Sunday. I think you might have to wait until tomorrow."

"Not on your life," Logan said. "I'm not giving Jillian another minute to change her mind about any of this."

Jillian threw her arms around Logan's neck. "That, my dear, you don't ever have to worry about."

Publications from
Bella Books, Inc.
The best in contemporary lesbian fiction

P.O. Box 10543, Tallahassee, FL 32302
Phone: 800-729-4992
www.bellabooks.com

WALTZING AT MIDNIGHT by Robbi McCoy. First crush, first passion, first love. Everybody else knows Jean Harris has a major crush on Rosie Monroe, except Jean. It's just not something Jean, with two kids in college, thought would ever happen to her $13.95

NO STRINGS by Gerri Hill. Reese Daniels is only in town for a year's assignment. MZ Morgan doesn't need a relationship. Their "no strings" arrangement seemed like a really good plan. $13.95

THE COLOR OF DUST by Claire Rooney. Who wouldn't want to inherit a mysterious mansion full of history under the layers of dust? Carrie Bowden is thrilled, especially when the local antique dealer seems equally interested in her. But sometimes secrets don't want to be disturbed. $13.95

THE DAWNING by Karin Kallmaker. Would you give up your future to right the past? Romantic, science fiction story that will linger long after the last page. $13.95

OCTOBER'S PROMISE by Marianne Garver. You'll never forget Turtle Cove, the people who live there, and the mysterious cupid determined to make true love happen for Libby and Quinn. $13.95

SIDE ORDER OF LOVE by Tracey Richardson. Television foodie star Grace Wellwood is not going to be golf phenom Torrie Cannon's side order of romance for the summer tour. No, she's not. Absolutely not. $13.95

WORTH EVERY STEP by KG MacGregor. Climbing Africa's highest peak isn't nearly so hard as coming back down to earth. Join two women who risk their futures and hearts on the journey of their lives. $13.95

WHACKED by Josie Gordon. Death by family values. Lonnie Squires knows that if they'd warned her about this possibility in seminary, she'd remember. $13.95

BECKA'S SONG by Frankie J. Jones. Mysterious, beautiful women with secrets are to be avoided. Leanne Dresher knows it with her head, but her heart has other plans. Becka James is simply unavoidable. 13.95

GETTING THERE by Lyn Denison. Kat knows her life needs fixing. She just doesn't want to go to the one place where she can do that: home. $13.95

PARTNERS by Gerri Hill. Detective Casey O'Connor has had difficult cases, but what she needs most from fellow detective Tori Hunter is help understanding her new partner, Leslie Tucker. 13.95

AS FAR AS FAR ENOUGH by Claire Rooney. Two very different women from two very different worlds meet by accident—literally. Collier and Meri find their love threatened on all sides. There's only one way to survive: together. $13.95